Welcome to Prima New Beginnings

Prima New Beginnings is all about women facing up to the glorious unpredictability of life – warm and compelling stories that are relevant for every woman who has ever sought to open a new chapter or wondered "What's next?".

Because every life has more than one chapter.

In *Prima Magazine* there is something for everyone – advice on how to look and feel your best, time- and money-saving solutions, quick-and-easy food, beautiful homes and gardens and, above all, everything you need to make your life simple.

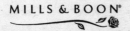
MILLS & BOON®

Marie Ferrarella wrote her very first story at age eleven on an old manual Remington typewriter her mother bought for her for seventeen dollars at a pawn shop. The keys stuck and she had to pound on them in order to produce anything. The instruments of production have changed, but she's been pounding on keys ever since. To date, she's written over one hundred and fifty novels and there appears to be no end in sight. As long as there are keyboards and readers, she intends to go on writing until the day she meets the Big Editor in the Sky.

prima
new
beginnings

STARTING FROM SCRATCH

Marie Ferrarella

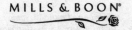
MILLS & BOON®

All the characters in this book have no existence outside the
imagination of the author, and have no relation whatsoever to anyone
bearing the same name or names. They are not even distantly inspired
by any individual known or unknown to the author, and all the
incidents are pure invention.

First published in Great Britain 2007
by Harlequin Mills & Boon Limited, Eton House,
18-24 Paradise Road,
Richmond, Surrey TW9 1SR

© Marie Rydzynski-Ferrarella 2005

ISBN: 978 0 263 85863 1

39-0607

Printed and bound in Spain
by Litografia Rosés S.A., Barcelona

From the Author

Dear Reader,

Thank you for joining me on my newest adventure, which is a woman's journey into awareness. By the time most people enter their fifth decade of life, they usually think that "This is it." Their lives, for better or worse, are set. At forty-six, Elisha Reed knew there was no Prince Charming riding into her life, no children to raise. She was a high-powered editor working for a well-respected publishing house and felt her life was good.

And then her world gets turned upside down. Her brother dies and leaves her with his two daughters to raise. Suddenly, it's a whole new world, with new choices to make and new insecurities to face. Nothing is set in stone. As she struggles to find her way along this new path, Elisha discovers help and support from an unexpected quarter. She also finds that love takes on many shapes and wears many faces. And it's never too late to fall into it.

The main lesson here, for Elisha, for you and for me is that life isn't over until the very last breath is taken.

Thank you for being there and, as always, I wish you love.

Marie Ferrarella

To Tara Hughes Gavin,
for letting me explore new worlds. Thank you.

CHAPTER 1

By her own inner clock, she was running late.

By everyone else's method of timekeeping, she was ahead of schedule. But Elisha Jane Reed had gotten to her present position of senior editor in the exclusive publishing firm of Randolph & Sons by following, to a good extent, Henry David Thoreau's advice about marching to a different drummer. She marched to that drummer, in double time, so that she could elude his other equally famous phrase, the one about most men leading lives of quiet desperation.

Because the line applied equally, perhaps even more truthfully, to women, as well.

Desperation, as contemplated by the late nonconformist, came to her only in the wee hours of the night, when everything bad was magnified by the shadows in the room and everything good was obscured behind the dust motes. It was then that she took stock of her life, measuring it by the old-fashioned standards that refused to die even in this day and age. The standards that had been laid down for all women since Eve had opted for a more extensive wardrobe than just her long hair and a random fig leaf. Namely, a husband and tiny miniature copies or combinations of herself and the man who had won her hand and her heart.

In that column, as far as her life went, was a very large zero. No children, no husband, not even an ex-husband buried beneath disparaging rhetoric. As far as she was concerned, marriage was the name of a mythical realm into which she had never traveled, never even been invited to tour.

Desperation of the more common garden variety existed for her by the truckload within the halls of Randolph & Sons. This more familiar desperation, coupled with exasperation, involved deadlines, temperamental and at times overpaid authors, not to mention the constant, daunting influx of market statistics, which, even when good, were never as good as Hayden Randolph, the seventy-five-year-old retired, but never-quite-out-of-sight, head of the publishing company, desired them to be.

The old man, as she secretly called the publishing magnate, was going to be there tonight, Elisha thought as she searched in vain for the mate to the diamond stud earring she'd wanted to wear to the party. He made it a point, despite the retirement party he'd authorized to be thrown for him last year, to have his finger in every pie that came out of the Randolph & Sons oven. He didn't seem to trust his own son to preside over the festivities despite his twenty-four years in the business. Tomorrow, Sinclair Jones's latest thriller, *Murder By Moonlight*, hit the bookstores. Tonight was the book's coming-out party.

"Come out, come out wherever you are," Elisha coaxed in an impatient, singsong voice. No diamond stud appeared in reply.

The diamond studs were her lucky earrings and although she wasn't superstitious by nature, the one time she hadn't worn them to one of these affairs, the author's book had sold abysmally. She would take no chances. Someone had once told her that as an editor, you were only as good as your author's current book.

Carole Chambers would really love for her not to find her earrings, Elisha thought, taking the wide, rectangular jewelry box and dumping the contents out on the top of her bureau. Carole Chambers was the assistant that Hayden's son, Rockefeller, had saddled her with about six months ago. She remembered the day well. She thought of it as Black Monday.

"I want you to train her, Elisha. Make her a junior version of you. Not that I expect anyone to ever be as good as you," he'd said to her in that light tenor voice. "But Dad wants this to happen. So it's either have you train Carole or we kidnap you in the dead of night, whisk you off to some mad scientist's laboratory and have them create several dozen clones in hopes that at least one will be enough like you to satisfy him."

Smiling at the scenario he'd created, Rockefeller Randolph, Rocky to the select few who numbered among his friends, had raised and lowered his eyebrows and rubbed his hands together like the imaginary mad scientist's slightly madder assistant. She'd said yes because what choice did she have?

Elisha sighed in disgust and reached for one of the twelve pairs of reading glasses—all with slightly varying prescriptions— that she kept scattered throughout her penthouse apartment. She hated needing glasses. But where once she could have made out every single detail of every single piece of jewelry spread out on the honey-colored bureau, now entire pieces melded in a semicolorful glob. Colors were no longer as intense as they once were and letters had become black specks on a surface.

Getting older was the pits, she thought, putting the glasses on. She began sorting through the pieces.

Rocky would be at the party tonight, too. Probably sitting off in some corner of the room, communing with glass after glass of whatever wine they were going to be serving. Elisha shook her head. He always seemed to shrink to half his lanky size whenever he was in the same room as his father. Rocky was a very talented, sweet man, but he was considerably short on self-confidence, especially whenever his larger-than-life father was anywhere in the vicinity.

"Too bad the man can't stay retired," Elisha murmured. A necklace had formed a threesome with a pair of her dangling ear-rings. She gave a halfhearted attempt at separating the pieces, then moved them aside. The tangled ensemble joined the realm of "projects to do" when she got half an hour of downtime. Which by her calculations should come into being around the next millennium.

Rocky had been the one who'd hired her twenty-four years ago. She'd begun as a proofreader for the company and later found out that hiring her had been Rocky's first official act for the company.

Because he enjoyed making his son jump through hoops, Hayden Randolph had almost unhired her the very next day in a fit of temper that had nothing to do with her and everything to do with his wife's discovery of his latest mistress's existence. Rocky had mustered up his courage, intervened on her behalf and she was back on the payroll before she was ever actually re-moved. She remembered feeling as if she'd been standing up in the first car of a roller coaster as it took its first hill.

The memory came back to her in large, neon lights. She looked up into the oval mirror over the bureau. "God, was that really twenty-four years ago?" It didn't seem possible. "Almost a quarter of a century ago."

Saying the words out loud created a sudden shiver that slid down her Donna Karan–clad back. A quarter of a century made her sound ancient.

A quarter of a century. She doubted Carole Chambers was much older than that.

Without realizing it, Elisha frowned. Carole made her think of Anne Baxter in *All About Eve*. Except that in the movie, Anne Baxter hadn't initially come across as devious. One look into Carole's baby-blue eyes had been all she'd needed to know that leaving her back exposed to the younger woman would be a fatal mistake. In another life, Elisha had no doubt, Carole Chambers had gotten from place to place by slithering on her belly.

"Finally!"

Feeling every bit as triumphant as a big-game hunter who had bagged his prey, she held up the diamond stud she'd finally located. Somehow, it had gotten hidden beneath a chunky gold bracelet. Her mood brightened considerably. She pushed her glasses on top of her head. All in all, she'd spent only a little more than ten minutes searching for the second stud. Not really that much time in the grand scheme of things.

Angling her head and watching herself in the mirror, Elisha fastened the second stud into place. A whimsical smile played on her lips.

"If only the other kind of stud was as easy to find." She dropped her hands from her ear and stared at her image in the mirror. "I just said that out loud, didn't I?" She sighed, and shook her head. "God, I've got to get myself a pet so it at least I can pretend I'm talking to another life-form instead of just myself. They lock up people who talk to themselves constantly."

Crossing back to her king-size bed, she slipped on the black pumps that she'd left there, then picked up her wrap. It was black, just like her dress. The thought occurred to her that perhaps she should have put on something more festive, but black was slimming and she needed that right now. Somehow or other, five pounds she neither knew or wanted had decided to make themselves at home on her body. It wasn't the first time. When she was younger, dieting was a matter of closing her eyes and loudly declaring, "Be gone." That and a week of skipping lunches did the trick. Now, skipping food for a month wouldn't bring about the same results. Just acute hunger pangs that could only be dealt with with the massive influx of food.

She was going to have to exercise, Elisha thought. The notion did not make her feel all warm and fuzzy. She didn't like sweating. Besides, where would she find the time? She'd already used up her extra ten minutes for the month looking for her second stud.

Adjusting the wrap around her shoulders, Elisha slowly surveyed herself in the wardrobe mirror that ran from one end of the bedroom wall to the other. The wardrobe mirror gave the illusion that the bedroom was twice as large as it was. Luckily, it didn't have the same effect on her.

"Not bad," she decided. "Maybe even elegant."

The price tag that had been on the outfit was certainly elegant, but money had long since ceased to be an object. Her job paid very well, and her needs, other than a centrally located Manhattan apartment, were reasonable and few. She didn't even take long vacations to recharge anymore, the way she once had, because now it was work, not downtime, that recharged her batteries.

Besides, vacations somehow underscored the fact that there was no one in her life to share a sunset with since she and Garry had gone their separate ways. She to her work and he to the arms of some tight-skinned, nubile size four named Kelly. Kelly, it had turned out, was exactly the same chronological age as some of his ties.

Elisha picked up her clutch purse from the coffee table and took out her key. A bitter taste rose inside her mouth. It always did when she thought about Garry Smallwood.

There was a time, in the beginning, when she'd thought that she and Garry might wind up facing eternity together. But as time progressed, the fabric of that belief had begun to dissolve until it was completely gone. She'd given Garry seven of the best years of her life and he had given her a migraine headache—her first—that had lasted three days when he'd left.

That was six years ago.

"You're dwelling much too much in the past, 'Lise," she berated herself. She glanced again at her reflection in the mirror. A corner of her mouth rose slightly. "Maybe that's because in the past, you had less skin."

For a second, she was tempted, but then resisted. She wasn't going to get caught up in that, wasn't going to place her fingertips along her cheekbones and push up, ever so slightly, the way she'd once seen her mother do. Her mother had been contemplating a face-lift at the time. Her father had come up behind her, kissed the back of her neck and declared that she wasn't to change anything about the woman he loved.

Elisha sighed. They didn't make men like that anymore, men who loved you and your extra skin. And she had made her peace with that. She had a perfectly good life that a lot of people would kill for.

People like Carole Chambers.

If she didn't hurry, the little scheming witch would get there ahead of her, she thought.

Elisha quickly let herself out of her apartment. She left the light on.

CHAPTER 2

As she hurried into the ballroom that Randolph & Sons had reserved for the evening within New York's venerated Grand Hotel, the first thing Elisha saw was the huge cardboard likeness of her author, Sinclair Jones, standing beside a table of neatly piled, freshly minted copies of his new thriller. True to the man, the cardboard likeness looked like Santa Claus on a holiday. Right down to the trimmed, whiteish beard.

The second thing she saw was Rocky, standing beside the small bar that stood off to the side. Aside from a few people sent by the hotel to oversee the food and drink, there was no one else in the large room.

She made her way over to Hayden Randolph's only offspring. "Hi."

Tall, thin, with a complexion like peaches that had yet to ripen, Rockefeller Randolph raised his almost-empty glass to her in a silent toast then took a sip before saying, "Knew you'd be the first one here."

"I'm not," she pointed out as she joined him. "You are."

The laugh was self-deprecating and fueled by another sip of wine. "I don't count."

Elisha looked around, surprised not to see Carole lurking in some corner, ready to pounce on Sinclair or someone of equal importance. In one area, a server was fussing with several piles of tiny cocktail napkins imprinted with the name of the new thriller. "I take it your father's around."

Rocky sighed. After finishing his drink, he placed the glass on the counter and nodded at the bartender who was busy at the other end, filling glasses. "My father's always around, even when you don't see him." He laughed. The sound was a little like a mule, braying. "Especially when you don't see him."

Elisha eyed the man she considered her friend more than her boss. "How many glasses of wine have you had, Rocky?"

He twirled the stem of the glass with his long, thin fingers. It tottered a little and he placed it back down. "This is the only glass," he told her solemnly. "The bartender keeps pouring wine into it, but I've only been using the one."

She pretended to frown slightly. "You're playing with words."

Rocky looked back at her, the soul of innocence. "Isn't that what we in the publishing world are supposed to do? Play with words?"

A server with a tray full of crab cakes approached. Remembering the reason for her wearing a slimming black dress, Elisha shook her head. The server then turned to Rocky, who took two servings, his own and hers.

"The authors, yes," she said, enviously watching him consume both of the tiny cakes, "not the editors. Or the executive editors." Elisha gave him a penetrating look.

Rocky plucked up one of the tiny napkins and delicately wiped his mouth. "Executive, my ass."

He was running himself down again. It was a lifelong habit, learned at his father's knee. "If you want to be executive of your ass, that's your business, but I suggest you do it on your own time, away from your father's watchful eye."

He looked at her as if she should know better. "I could be dead and buried six feet under and I'd still be under his watchful eye."

Because no one else had arrived yet, the server lingered at her elbow. The aroma from the warm crab cakes was getting to her. "You're paranoid," she told Rocky.

"Just because you're paranoid doesn't mean they're not after you." Turning back to the bartender, he nodded for the man to top off his glass. The balding man obliged. Rocky lifted the glass in another silent toast before bringing it back to his lips.

"Your father's not after you, he just wants you to be the best that you can be," Elisha consoled him. It wasn't long after she was hired that she undertook the job of attempting to bolster Rocky's sagging ego. The fact that she couldn't was in no way because she didn't say the right things, but that his father had conducted a scorched-earth policy long before she ever arrived on the scene.

"No," Rocky contradicted her, "my father wants me to be *better* than him and we all know that's not humanly possible."

Catching his arm, Elisha gently redirected Rocky's elbow to make contact with the bar, causing the glass to fall short of making contact with his lips. "You're wrong there."

"About me being better than him?"

She grinned. No amount of talking would convince Rocky that in many ways, he was actually better than the dynamic, take-no-prisoners Hayden Randolph.

"No, about him wanting you to be better than him. I think if you were, it would completely crush your father. He's always wanted to be nothing short of the best." The goal applied to his publishing firm as well, which the man saw, more than his own flesh and blood, as an extension of himself.

"Crush him, huh?"

She smiled at Rocky affectionately. In a way, she almost thought of him as an older brother. But he was less self-assured than her own younger brother. "That wasn't the key thought there. Keep up, Rocky."

"With you? Not possible." He took another sip of his wine. "You do the work of ten and your heart is pure. If this were the Middle Ages, there'd be a balladeer singing about you on every corner of the kingdom." He laughed and shook his head. "The best thing I ever did was hire you." He looked up at her. "Tell me, how is it that you and I never married?"

"Because you're gay, Rocky." It was one of those things that was regarded as an open secret, a secret he neither broadcasted nor guarded zealously. She'd had suspicions for a while before he had confided in her in a scene that had unfolded much the way this evening was heading.

He put a finger to his lips and winked. "Shh, not too loud."

"I guess that means I should cancel my posting on the Internet," she remarked glibly. Succumbing to both hunger and the aroma drifting around from the crab cakes, she finally took one from the server's tray. The man smiled at her knowingly.

"The old man doesn't know," Rocky said before popping another crab cake into his mouth.

She saw the facts in a slightly different light. Hayden Randolph was too savvy to be ignorant. "The old man doesn't want to know," she corrected Rocky.

"Yeah, it would be like Ernest Hemingway suddenly admitting that he fathered Truman Capote."

That was a little harsh. Up until now, she'd thought that he was putting her on as to his condition. But now she was beginning to grow concerned. She didn't want the man to embarrass himself tonight. Aside from his father and the staff, there would be the usual gaggle of literary critics attending. "So how long have you been drinking?"

"Since tenth grade."

"Tonight, Rocky," she emphasized. "How long have you been drinking tonight?"

He thought a moment. "Before I got here. That's the beauty of having a limo bring you. New York's finest can't arrest you for drunk sitting."

More people began to arrive, which brought the party to life. But her attention was focused on Rocky. Turning her back to the entrance so that her body partially shielded Rocky from view, she glared at him. "Why do you let him get to you like that? You're very good at what you do."

He raised his brow before bringing the glass to his lips again. "Drink? None better."

"I mean being the executive editor." His father had insisted he work his way up through the ranks. Rocky had a flair for picking the gem in a tray full of semiprecious stones. He'd schooled her until she'd developed the same knack and she never forgot that. "And, let's not forget, you were the one who convinced Sinclair Jones to leave his publisher and come aboard here."

Narrow, bony shoulders moved up and down within his custom-fitted jacket. "The man felt sorry for me."

She hated when Rocky did this, when he did his father's work for him and ran himself down this way. "When it comes to money, people don't allow their emotions to get in the way. You gave him the better deal and you were the one who saw that he had better books in him."

There was pure affection in the look he gave her. "You are good for me, Elisha. Promise me you'll never leave."

This was her life, for better or for worse. Luckily, most of the time it was for better. "I'm not going anywhere, Rocky."

He took a deep breath, then paused. "Funny, but you seem to be swaying some now."

Very gently, she disengaged his fingers from the stem of his glass. "I suggest you slow down your intake."

"There you go, mothering me." But he made no effort to pick

up the glass again. "We're the same age, Elisha, you can't mother me."

She gave him a reproving look. For the most part, Rocky didn't let his drinking get out of hand. But it was touch-and-go sometimes. "I'm three years younger than you are."

He winced. "Not like you to throw age at me."

"I'm not, just making you check your facts." She grinned. "Besides, they say that you're only as old as you feel."

"Right now, I'm not feeling much of anything. Especially my feet." He looked down at them as if to make sure they were still there.

"Okay, that does it. You're on the wagon for the rest of the evening." She glanced at the bartender, drafting him in her battle to keep Rocky from embarrassing himself. "What have you got back there that looks like alcohol but isn't?"

"Ginger ale?" the man suggested, putting a bottle of same on the counter.

She nodded, pleased. "Perfect."

"Ginger ale?" Rocky echoed in dismay. "Elisha, how do you expect me to get drunk on ginger ale?"

"I don't."

He contemplated the bottle, then nodded. The bartender poured the contents into his glass. "Then you have to promise me that when the old man comes out, you won't leave my side."

They both knew she had obligations tonight. They entailed holding her author's hand. Sinclair was terrified of critics. "As long as Sinclair doesn't need me, I won't."

"He'll be too busy soaking up the attention." He took a sip of the ginger ale and made a face. "No kick," he lamented. "You like working with him?"

"Sinclair?" She nodded. "He reminds me a little of my grandfather. Except he's less secure."

"They say the publishing world is like that."

"The world is like that," she told him. "Insecurity is more or less a way of life for everyone. Some just hide it better than others."

Rocky knew better. "Except for you," he told her affectionately. "You have the confidence of ten because your heart is pure."

"That's the strength of ten," she corrected him.

"Strong, too." He leaned back, as if taking complete measure of her. "God, you're pretty much the perfect woman, Lise."

"If you say so, Rocky." She smiled at him. "Will you do the perfect woman a favor?"

"What?" he asked cautiously.

She indicated the glass on the counter. "Drink your ginger ale."

Instead of picking up the glass, Rocky turned toward the rear exit. "Right after I visit the little boys' room."

Elisha looked at him, a little concerned. Rocky looked pale, but then, Rocky always looked pale. "Are you feeling sick?"

He grinned at her. "You really do need a pet. Or a kid."

"At this stage of my life, Rocky," she told him, "a pet is all I can handle."

As he walked away, Elisha reached for another crab cake. It was her second, but then who was counting?

CHAPTER 3

At this stage of my life.

The words she'd just uttered echoed back in her head. Elisha frowned.

What did that even mean? Did it mean she was settling, resigning herself to something? That she felt she was drifting in her middle age and beyond and wasn't even going to put up a halfhearted fight to remain in the game of life? Was this her subconscious saying that her life was set in stone and there was no point in attempting to create something different?

God, what had they put into these crab cakes?

Taking stock of herself, Elisha dusted her fingers off, then passed the tiny cocktail napkin over them to get the last of the residue. She didn't usually get philosophical during the course of the day and certainly never at a party.

Fine, she was doing fine, she silently told herself with as much passion as silence could muster. As for "this stage of her life," well, life unfolded in stages. Lots of stages. This was just another one of them.

Hell, she'd fought hard to get to where she was now and by no means was she going to just sit back on the sidelines.

Like Carole Chambers wanted her to do.

Elisha's dark green eyes narrowed. Sinclair Jones had just entered the ballroom and from out of nowhere, the sexy, dark-haired woman who had been the overly attractive thorn in her side for the last six months materialized. Completely unfamiliar with the words *subdued* or *understated*, Carole wore a gauze-inspired red dress that brought new meaning to the word *vivid*. Elisha frowned. She'd seen tourniquets wrapped more loosely than Carole's dress.

Since when had cellophane become a fashion statement?

Time for action, Elisha thought. Carole was heading directly for the author like a torpedo targeting a cruise ship.

Elisha tossed aside her napkin. *Over my dead body, sweetie.*

She made it across the room in record time, reaching Sinclair only two beats after Carole had joined herself to him. Sinclair looked a little startled. The statuesque younger woman had slipped her arm through the author's and was looking up at him with the adoration of a true believer, as if he were single-handedly responsible for both finding the Rosetta stone and bringing the restored Ten Commandments down from Mount Sinai.

When it came to kissing up, the assistant editor she'd been plagued with had absolutely no equal.

Someone should drop a house on the woman, Elisha thought.

A tight smile on her lips, she nodded at Carole. But then the tight smile faded, replaced by a genuine one as she regarded the tall, portly man wearing gray slacks, navy jacket and a perpetual line of perspiration just beneath his graying hairline. The man whose hand she'd held through every bout of writer's block over the last ten years.

Warmth and affection washed over her as she asked, "How are you doing, Sinclair?"

"Sweating bullets," Sinclair confided in response to her question.

Taking out a perfectly folded white handkerchief, he passed it over his brow. Within seconds, another line of perspiration swiftly arrived to take its place. Giving up, he pocketed the handkerchief.

Still hermetically sealed to his arm, the assistant editor's eyes widened at Sinclair's comment.

"Oh, Mr. Jones, you?" Carole declared in a syrupy voice that would have made Scarlett O'Hara more than moderately proud. "Why would you be worried? You're one of the bestselling authors of all time. People just love your books."

Never missing a beat, Elisha disengaged Sinclair's arm from the sexy barracuda's death grip and slipped her arm through it to take its place. She glanced over her shoulder at the woman she'd just usurped.

"Carole, be a dear and tell that server we need more crab cakes." She nodded toward the handsome young man whose tray she was partly responsible for depleting.

It was an obvious dismissal.

Carole pressed her lips together, as if she was swallowing a response that had leapt there. A response that could easily be construed as less than congenial. She was a woman who was biding her time. Praying it would be short.

"Of course." With a gracious, slightly seductive and suggestive nod toward the author, Carole Chambers retreated from the scrimmage line over which she'd lost control.

Elisha felt she kept her smirk well under control. *Score one for the over-forty set.*

She turned her attention back to Sinclair.

"She's right, you know," Elisha said to the man who seemed momentarily diverted and amused by the exchange. "People really do love your books. There is no reason for this." To punctuate her statement, she lightly wiped her fingertips along his damp brow.

"People are fickle, Elisha. They profess their undying love one day, then the next, they go rushing off to worship at someone else's altar."

She didn't know about people, but that aptly described men. At least the last man in her life. And maybe the man before that, she amended. She forced a wide smile to her lips as she banked down further musing along the wrong path.

Tonight was all about Sinclair. His triumph and his future royalties.

"Which is why you should be enjoying all this now," she told him, not for the first time. "You've earned it, you deserve it, and tomorrow you'll come up with an even better, bigger altar."

With a laugh, Sinclair patted the hand that was resting on his arm. His own hand covered it like a paw. "Keep talking. It's helping."

She pretended to look at him in disbelief. "You mean to tell me that little Miss Skintight-Red-Dress didn't gush enough at you?"

The comment was catty, she knew, but just for tonight, she'd allow herself that luxury. Sinclair had dedicated his about-to-be-blockbuster to her, a fact that she knew irritated the hell out of Carole. She had no doubts it made the woman even more determined than ever to unseat her from her present position.

Bring it on, Carole. I've outlasted better editors than you.

"Oh, she gushed all right," Sinclair told her, "but I have this feeling that the young woman would gush at anyone she thought might be able to get her ahead in the game."

Elisha grinned fondly. "That's what I like about you, Sinclair, you're so astute."

And then she felt all five foot ten of him stiffen into an almost military stance of attention. He was no longer looking at her.

"Speaking of astute, or pretending to be, they're here." He nodded at several people who entered the ballroom.

She didn't bother to look. She didn't need to, or even to ask who "they" were. She knew. The tightness in his voice told her everything. Enter the critics, the keepers of every writer's self-esteem, no matter what was protested to the contrary.

Elisha placed one hand over the man's thick barrel chest, as if she could somehow regulate his intake of air with the simple pressure of her fingers.

"Deep breaths, Sinclair. Take deep breaths," she counseled, never taking her eyes off his face. "Don't hyperventilate on me now. I left my paper bag in my other purse."

It was a standing joke between them, born of the one time, early in their association, when, spiraling into the depths of fear and insecurity over the direction of a book, he actually began to hyperventilate. Before stopping at his split-level apartment, Elisha had gone to the store to pick up some groceries in order to replenish his naked pantry. With lightning moves, she'd swiftly dumped said groceries on the floor and all but shoved the gasping writer's head into the bag, ordering him to breathe.

He'd recovered in a matter of minutes, emerging from the bag and the ordeal with a damp forehead and a new, healthy respect for her quick thinking. They'd built the foundation of their solid relationship on the actions of that afternoon.

"They're only people," Elisha was telling him. "They put their pants on in the morning one leg at a time, same as you and me."

Coming into his own, Sinclair pretended to look at her aghast. "My God, woman, you work with writers all day, every day. Is that cliché the very best that you can come up with?"

She smiled back, undaunted. "Clichés are just that because they're based on the truth." Her voice grew a little more serious. "And you could buy and sell any of these critics, Sinclair. Remember that." A mischievous grin curved her mouth. "And here's another cliché for you. Those that can, do, those that can't, vivisect those that can."

He laughed, delighted. "I don't think I've ever really heard that one put quite that way before."

To which she merely nodded. "Feel free to use it anytime."

With a chuckle born of enjoyment and gratitude, Sinclair took her hand with both of his and said, "Marry me, Elisha."

She played along. "I have the second week in November free."

Sinclair sighed, releasing her hands. "I have a book tour."

She nodded sagely, as if she'd expected as much. "Maybe some other time."

He winked, melting away the sweet-Santa-Claus veneer. "Count on it."

Well, it was time for her to begin acting as his editor, she thought. And yet Sinclair was more than just a writer assigned to her. He was a friend. And friends did things for one another. Things they didn't always relish doing.

"I'd better go run interference for you," she told him as she began to put distance between them.

He blew her a kiss. "You're one in a million, Elisha."

"So they tell me."

Into the Valley of Death rode the six hundred. The lines from Alfred, Lord Tennyson's poem echoed in her head as Elisha went to meet the enclave of critics.

CHAPTER 4

Her feet hurt.

Elisha kicked off her shoes the moment she walked across the threshold and shut the door. She loved the way high heels made her legs look, hated the way they made her feet feel. Like she was in training to become an early-Christian martyr.

One hand propped up against the wall, she massaged the bottom of her right foot with the toes of her left. It helped. A little. A hot bath would help even more, but she was way too tired for that.

The limo ride from the hotel back to her Park Avenue apartment had been swift enough, given the hour and the lack of traffic, but it wasn't fast enough to suit her. Elisha was bone tired, and, as happened once every few years or so, completely talked out.

Not to mention that she was feeling fat. The food that had been served tonight had been particularly good. She'd lost count of how many tiny offerings had found their way from the various trays into her mouth.

She sighed, shaking her head. If she wasn't careful, she was going to have to go looking for another little black dress. One in the next size up. That would put her, where? In size ten? Twelve? She couldn't remember. What she did remember was, at one point, she'd been a size six. She had the clothes to prove it. They were all nestled together on one side of her walk-in closet, patiently waiting for the day she was going to return to the small body she'd once had.

The one she'd taken for granted until it wasn't there anymore, she thought with a self-deprecating smile.

She'd gotten to her present size one snack at a time an eternity of snacks ago.

Elisha looked down at her torso, irritated with her own lack of willpower. Well, irritated or not, she couldn't do anything about it tonight. Bending down, she picked up her shoes. Wound up and exhausted at the same time, she knew she needed to get to bed. Tomorrow was another workday.

"Today," she corrected herself. "Today is another workday."

It was a little after midnight. Cinderella hours, she mused. Almost the first to arrive, she had been one of the last to leave, packing off not only Sinclair into his limo, but Rocky into his, as well. It was her Girl Scout training coming to the fore again, she supposed. She'd always been a stickler for detail, and although the marketing department had been the ones who'd arranged for the party to herald Sinclair's latest thriller, she had still wanted to make sure everything went off without a hitch from start to finish.

Besides, she had a hunch that if she left anytime before Carole Chambers rode her broom into the sunset, the woman would manage to undermine her in some fashion or other. She knew it was what Carole hoped for—to stand on Elisha's twitching carcass.

Maybe someday she'd allow that to happen, when she was ready to take her final bow and slip away from the fast-paced world of publishing, but not anytime soon. Until then, she was going to have to keep one step ahead of the likes of Carole Chambers.

Maybe two and a half steps.

God knew she'd certainly hate to lose her standing at Randolph & Sons. This was who and what she was, an editor who loved books. An editor who loved her job—for the most part— every exhilarating, mind-numbing, exhausting moment of it.

She was lucky enough to like the authors she worked with. Some, like Sinclair Jones, needed a lot of care, but they were worth it. The man was like the grandfather she'd never known. Others, like Jack Lewis, all but went into hibernation, emerging out of their cave every eighteen months or so, holding a brand-new offering over their heads.

Everyone had their own style and she was flexible enough to bend and work with them all. She had six well-known, first-tier authors, not to mention about ten or so writers who turned up occasionally, bringing her ideas or manuscripts that worked only half the time and even then, needed help.

That was when she'd roll up her sleeves, burn the midnight oil and completely live up to every aspect of her title of editor. She guided, molded, cut, suggested and, at times, added. She had no set style of her own, but, like a comic impersonator, could mimic voices with aplomb. The written voice of an author. She could make things flow when they were choppy, make them flow with such dexterity that often the writer would comment that they hadn't known they were that good. One of Elisha's gifts was that she was so clever at what she did, she could make writers believe that the words had actually come from them and that they'd simply forgotten they had written the passage. It happened all the time.

And so it went. Her authors garnered accolades and she garnered a feeling of satisfaction, of a job shamelessly well done, not to mention collecting a very nice paycheck, which was deposited electronically into her checking account twice a month.

On her way to the bedroom, dragging her wrap behind her,

Elisha stopped for a moment by the large bay window, drawn by the view. She never tired of it. By day it was impressive. By night, awe-inspiring.

Her apartment was located on the twenty-second floor of the Avery Building and situated so that it had a breathtaking, almost panoramic view of the city. At night the lights below twinkled through the glass like so many diamonds scattered at her feet.

Elisha took in a deep breath and then released it again, slowly. She thought of each light as representing a family, or, at the very least, a life in progress. If some part of her felt just the slightest bit sad because there was no one at her side to share this with, to slip his arm around her shoulders and pull him close to her, she refused to acknowledge it.

She'd never been one to dwell on the negative.

The positive side was that she had this and it was hers to enjoy.

Her eyes were drawn to the red light.

The flashing light reflected in the window was almost hypnotic. She stared at it for a few seconds, watching it pulse, before she realized that the light was coming from behind her rather than from some dwelling below.

Turning, she saw that the red light on her answering machine was blinking rhythmically like the eye of an asymmetric cyclops.

The sight pulled her back into the real world.

The sigh escaped her lips before she was completely conscious that the sound had come from her. She really was very tired.

Dutifully, she went over to the telephone on the counter that separated the living room from the alcove that was her den. Elisha stared down at the answering machine for a long moment.

Ordinarily, she would press the button that enabled her to retrieve her messages. But it had been a very long day. She didn't want to make it even longer. So rather than play the messages that she was way too tired to attempt to listen to and digest, she repeatedly pressed a button on the center of the receiver. The action yielded the telephone numbers that her caller ID had registered. She knew that if there was a message from Sinclair or from one of a handful of other writers who were considered hot properties she was going to have to answer it.

Like it or not, panic or a minor crisis would be involved, both of which she would have to handle because that was her job.

Scanning the numbers, she breathed a sigh of relief. From the looks of it, a total of three calls had come in while she was attending the book party. Two were labeled "out of area," which, more than likely, meant they had either come from telemarketers or one of her credit-card companies, hoping to convince her that they were offering her a deal she couldn't refuse.

The one that came between the two "out of area" calls had an area code she was familiar with and a phone number she knew by heart.

Henry.

She knew for a fact that she had mentioned the book party tonight because she'd invited him to come along. Her younger brother must have forgotten. That was so like Henry. A thousand things on his mind and he could only keep track of nine hundred and fifty.

Henry and the girls were the only family she had, now that both her parents were gone. Her brother was undoubtedly calling to invite her over for dinner the way he did at least once a month. Ever since his wife, Rachel, had died. In the beginning, she'd invited Henry and the girls over to her apartment, but for her, cooking meant opening a frozen package and sticking it into the microwave. And Henry didn't particularly like eating in restaurants.

So they had begun taking meals at his place. Henry did the cooking. Henry did everything he set his mind to. He always had.

She was proud of the way he'd soldiered on these last five years, never missing a beat. Not that he had much choice in the matter, really. He had two daughters to raise, Andrea and Beth. Andrea was fifteen and Beth was ten. And both were a handful in their own way. Between seeing to their needs and his job, Henry was left with very little time to spend on self-pity.

Still, she knew other men might have folded under the stress. Not Henry. He overcame every obstacle. Her brother was one of the good ones and, although he was four years younger than she was, he was one of her heroes.

Not that she would ever tell him.

She looked at the urgent blinking light again and shook her head.

"Sorry, Henry, not tonight. I'm just too damn tired to listen."

Because if she listened, she might feel compelled to return the call and then who knew what time she'd finally make it to bed. And she had to attend an eight o'clock meeting with the Japanese publisher that handled their reprints. The man wouldn't take it very well if she fell asleep in the middle of one of her own sentences, or, worse yet, in the middle of one of his.

"I'll give you a call tomorrow, Henry, I promise." And then she paused, remembering. "Today, later today," she amended. "I'll give you a call then." Giving up all attempts at being lucid, she mumbled, "Whenever."

Elisha yawned and her throat began to cramp up. All that talking, she thought, quickly massaging the area. Stifling another yawn, Elisha left the living room and made her way to the master suite located at the rear of the apartment. There was another room, just as large, located at the top of the short flight of stairs. It could have just as easily served as a master suite, but she'd opted to use the room as her office and tonight, she was glad she'd made that particular choice. If she'd had to face the stairs tonight, she knew she would have wound up sleeping on the sofa.

Making it into the suite, Elisha let her shoes slip from her fingers and shed her dress. She left it where it fell. Completely disregarding her panty hose, she crawled onto the bed.

With her last ounce of energy, she started to wrap the comforter around herself. She was asleep before she finished.

CHAPTER 5

"Hi, Elisha, it's me, Henry. Didn't you get my message?"

Elisha pressed her lips together as her brother's voice on the other end of the line penetrated the wall of Monday-morning fog around her brain.

Stalling, she looked at her business phone as a multicolored ribbon of guilt dragged through her like the tail of a kite that refused to catch an updraft and soar. She'd finally gotten around to playing her brother's message the morning after the party, listening to it as she moved around the room, getting dressed and thinking about what needed to be done at work that day.

She'd forgotten ever hearing the message the second she'd stepped outside her apartment and locked the door.

That had been four days ago.

"Yes, I did." She quickly followed up her admission with, "Sorry, sorry, sorry," before Henry could upbraid her.

Not that he actually ever would. Henry was the sweetest, most easygoing human being to ever traverse the earth. She couldn't remember a single instance when he'd even raised his voice, much less lost his temper and gotten angry. That just wasn't Henry.

The most he did was level a slightly reproving look in her general direction. That was it, just a look and not even an annoyed one. Even so, because it came from Henry, the closest being she'd ever known to merit sainthood, she was ready to run off and purchase seven hair shirts, to be worn simultaneously in an attempt to atone for whatever transgression she'd committed.

But she didn't have time to purchase any hair shirts today. The workday was only a matter of three hours old and it was already one for the books. One of those days when she couldn't draw a deep breath, much less two in succession, quick or otherwise. Back-to-back meetings, with an errant author who was going to be a month late with his already once rescheduled book sprinkled in for good measure.

Henry always gave her space and waited for his sister to say something more before he spoke himself. When she didn't immediately follow up her apology with a tentative date or anything remotely close to a new date, he felt free to continue with the reason for his call.

"All right," he allowed patiently, "it's a little too late for you to come over for Sunday brunch, seeing how it's Monday. How about tomorrow?"

She glanced at her calendar and saw that it was buried beneath a three-ring binder stuffed to the gills with notes. But then, she really didn't need to look at the page. It was another day filled with meetings. "For brunch? I can't make it—"

"No, brunch would be a little hard for me, too. And the girls have school. I meant dinner."

Elisha smiled to herself. Her brother's voice was in direct contrast to hers. She always sounded as if she'd just finished running a marathon, while his voice sounded as if he felt confident that he had all the time in the world. Each word he uttered was given the respect of clear enunciation and recognizable cadence. She didn't know how he did it, or how they could be related for that matter. But she was glad they were.

She did want to see him. She always enjoyed their visits. Quickly, she began to assess the situation.

There were several assorted piles on her desk. Manuscripts cohabited with incoming mail, several catalogs she'd brought from home in the vain hope of glancing through them during one of her so-called breaks, and three books by Albert Mann that she'd picked up God only knew when. The thought behind the last was to see whether or not the author might be a good addition to their prestigious stable. She'd heard that Mann wasn't happy with his present publishing house and now might be the time to begin wooing. If he was worth the effort.

She sighed. All these things, and others, contributed to making up an almost insurmountable wall around her, cutting her off from the world at large and any pleasure that wasn't somehow, directly or indirectly, attached to work.

Which meant that she was going to have to turn her brother down, much as she hated to.

"Tomorrow? Henry, I'm sorry, but I'm swamped. I really can't."

"When do they let you come up for air?" There was no sarcasm in his voice. Henry wasn't capable of it. But he was protective and she knew he was only thinking of her when he asked the question.

"How does New Year's 2010 sound? You can be my date if you're not married again by then."

Instead of a comeback or teasing banter, there was a long pause on the other end.

Damn, was this a bad day? Had she trod on his feelings again? Since Rachel had died, Henry had devoted himself almost exclusively to the girls and to his job. And to her when she could squeeze him in. Dating just wasn't something that entered into the picture, even when one of his well-meaning neighbors tried to set him up with someone. He politely but firmly turned them down, thanking them for the trouble they might have gone to on his account. He wasn't interested in looking for someone to share his life and his bedroom with.

They had that in common, Elisha thought, except that they had arrived here by different routes. He'd had the near-perfect marriage to the near-perfect woman and didn't want anything to detract from that memory. She, on the other hand, had had relationships so far removed from perfect they had a completely different area code. She was out of the game because she was tired of looking.

Her brother was a different matter. She was hoping that, in time, because he had so much to offer, Henry would find someone. Lord knew he deserved to achieve some measure of happiness on that level again, even if it wasn't completely perfect this time. Henry always seemed to bring out the best in everyone. She had no doubt that her brother could have married the Wicked Witch of the West and in no time at all the woman would have voluntarily transformed so that her personality rivaled that of the Good Witch of the North.

"No," he told her quietly, "I can pretty much guarantee that I won't be married by then."

There was something odd in his voice. A note of sadness that she hadn't heard coming from him in over five years now. Except when he spoke of Rachel.

Was he going through a bad patch?

Her ribbon of guilt grew into a sash. Maybe she could just call in sick tomorrow. The next moment, she vetoed the idea. If she called in sick, like as not, Rocky would turn up at her door after hours with a container of homemade soup from the deli that he frequented. And then he'd be annoyed because she'd lied to him.

Mentally she brushed aside the scenario. "Is something wrong, Henry?"

This time there was no pause, only assurance. Assurance that came so quickly, it didn't reassure her at all. "No, nothing's wrong."

Something *was* wrong, she thought, concerned.

"Henry," Elisha began, determined to coax her younger brother out of whatever stoic realm he had selflessly slipped into.

As quiet as she was animated, Henry shouldered every problem in silence. He had ever since he had been a small boy. She was certain that couldn't be healthy for him. More than that, she was afraid that someday he would explode, or implode or whatever the term for it was when you kept everything inside until there was no room for anything else.

The upshot in either case was that he'd be ripped apart. Definitely not something she was willing to risk. More than anything else, even though he was younger, Henry was her rock. He always had been. Henry was the one constant she was sure of, no matter what else went on around her.

But today being what it was, with fire drills and fires going off all around her, Elisha got no further than saying his name before the buzzer on her desk squawked loudly like a goose in heat, demanding her attention. Just the way everything else on her desk demanded her attention, she thought darkly.

Exasperated, edgy, she dragged her free hand through her hair. She felt as if her brain was the center of a taffy pull and it was being yanked in every conceivable direction, keeping her from focusing, from making progress in any direction at all. There was just too much work and not enough her.

One thing at a time, Lise. One thing at a time. Do what you can, as you can.

It was a mantra she silently recited to herself when she felt utterly overwhelmed by all the things she had to do.

She hated cutting her conversation with Henry short, but she needed to get going. The buzzer was to remind her about the meeting in the conference room that she was supposed to be attending in less than ten minutes. "Henry, my life is stuck in the fast-forward mode at the moment and I can't even access 'play,' much less hit it, so I don't have time to be patient and try to get this out of you by subtle probing and questioning. I'm going to ask you one more time. Is anything wrong?"

This time, his voice sounded a little sunnier than it had a moment earlier. "Only that I don't get to see you as often as I'd like."

She laughed dryly. "Now, why can't I get a guy to say that to me?"

There was a certain amount of give-and-take between them. There had been since they were both too young to cross the street alone. For the sake of the game, he played along. "I'm not exactly chopped liver, Lise."

"You're not a guy," she deadpanned. "You're a brother. That doesn't count."

The laugh was short, but it brought a warm feeling around her heart. "Thanks a lot."

He sounded better now, she decided, relieved. Probably whatever she thought she'd heard in her brother's voice was just a product of her own exhausted imagination. Henry was fine. Henry was always fine. It was the first axiom of her life.

The buzzer squawked again, louder if possible, despite the fact that there was no volume control on it. She frowned at it as if it were a living entity, subject to hurt feelings.

"Look, I've really gotta go, Henry. I promise I'll see you soon—at least before the next millennium. Give my love to the girls."

And with that, she hung up. The buzzer was squawking for a third time. The rest of her life was calling.

It didn't occur to her until later that she hadn't made arrangements for dinner.

CHAPTER 6

"Here's Elisha," Elisha declared the second Henry opened the door to let her in. It was almost a week since he'd phoned her at the office, but the way she saw it, better late than never. "Doesn't have the same ring as 'Here's Johnny,' but the spirit is there," she told him, stepping over the threshold.

Warmth came rushing up to her, a direct contrast to the unseasonably brisk weather she'd left behind her outside. The beginning of April had brought snow with it, a rarity in New York, and although it was now almost all melted, the memory and the temperatures lingered on.

Her cheeks stung for a moment until she acclimated herself, absorbing the warmth that the house had to offer. Both varieties of warmth, the physical and, more important, the emotional.

No doubt about it, Henry's home had a peacefulness that went beyond the comfortable spread of the twenty-four-hundred-square-foot layout, beyond the bricks and the concrete of the pleasant two-story building. There had been, and still was, love in this house, a great deal of love. She could feel it in every room.

Henry and Rachel had been the happiest couple she'd ever known, as in tune with one another as her parents had been before them. And they had adored their two daughters. Andrea and Beth, in turn, despite an occasional display of willfulness from Andrea, had loved them right back with a fierceness reserved for the very young and very loyal.

On those rare occasions when she felt that the world was too much with her, Elisha liked to retreat here for a few hours, to relax and recharge before venturing out again.

In all honesty, a few hours was all she could take, because along with the love was a slow pace that would have driven her up a wall if she had been part of it for any extended period of time. She knew that for a fact because when she'd broken her leg three years ago, Henry had insisted that she stay with him and the girls to convalesce.

She did.

For a week.

And then she went hobbling back on her crutches to the noise and breakneck pace that surrounded her Manhattan apartment. She needed the rapid pulse of the city, throbbing all around her, in order to feel alive. Slow and steady was wonderful if you were a turtle determined to beat a vain and slothful rabbit, but it definitely was not what she was about. So accustomed to moving fast, she even tossed and turned madly in her sleep. Or so Garry had claimed.

"What's all this?" Henry asked. He grinned and looked, for all the world, like a taller, male version of her, right down to the bone structure and coloring. He was eyeing the boxes she had in her arms. The ones she'd been struggling to keep from falling on the ground from the moment she had emerged from the taxi that had brought her from the city to his Long Island home.

"Tribute," she announced, willingly surrendering the booty into her brother's open arms. "Conscience gifts. Call them whatever you want. This is to make up for the dinner I missed."

"You don't have to try to buy us off," Henry told her, setting the pile on the side table.

"Sure I do," she contradicted. Elisha slipped off her coat and tossed it over the back of the sofa with the ease of someone who knew she was home. She turned to face him. "Besides, I just like buying you and the girls things," she told him for perhaps the hundredth time before her brother could protest again. "What else do I have to spend it on? I don't own a house with a pool, so I can't be lavishing all my money on a poolboy slash boy toy."

He looked thinner, she thought. As thin as he had right after Rachel died, when eating had ceased to be important to him.

Everyone around her at the office was coming down with something. She wondered if Henry'd had the flu. It was just like him not to mention anything.

The next moment, Beth came rushing up to her. At ten, the girl had dark brown hair and was slight for her age. Though brighter than her years, her maturity level had elected to remain happily ensconced in childhood for as long as possible. She still slept with a stuffed animal she'd had since she was two, a rabbit that looked every bit of his well-loved years.

Coming up a little past her waist, Beth wrapped her arms around the aforementioned body part and cried, "Aunt Lise," and "What d'you bring me?" in the same breath and almost at the same time.

"Beth," Henry looked at his daughter.

"She has a right to ask," Elisha said. "After all, it would be a terrible thing if I'd brought all those gifts and none of them were for her." She caught Beth's small heart-shaped face in her hand and tilted it up a little. "Right, kiddo?"

"Right," Beth agreed with a sharp nod of her head. And then she looked at her curiously. "What's a boy toy, Aunt Lise?"

Flashing a contrite glance in Henry's direction, Elisha still laughed as she looked down at her niece. "Something a looker like you is bound to find out in another five, six years." She laughed as she heard Henry groan. Looking at him over her shoulder, she said, "And you thought *these* were the tough years."

"No, I didn't," he answered. "I remembered what it was like with you."

She had the good grace to wince a little. There were no two ways about it. She had been a hellion at seventeen, slipping out at night to hang around with her friends. She never did anything that would have gotten her standing in front of a camera holding a placard with a long number against her chest, but she had come close a time or two. She didn't envy what lay ahead for Henry.

Taking two of the packages she'd brought, Elisha presented them to her younger niece.

Beth hurried off to the sofa, declaring, "Thank you," and "Can I open them?" even as she began to do so with the bigger of the two gifts.

"That's what wrapping paper is for, honey. To rip off." She watched the girl fondly as Beth made short work of the blue-and-white paper.

"Wow, thank you!" she cried once she was looking down at a popular video game and the latest imprint of a classic children's book. "I love them both."

"See?" Elisha turned to look at her brother. "One gift for the mind, the other for the soul." She picked up two almost identically sized gifts and handed both to Henry. "Open yours."

Though it looked as if he would have rather waited until after dinner, when things were a little more settled, Henry did as she asked. He'd managed to remove only a little of the tape on the first gift before Elisha gave it away. "It's Sinclair Jones's latest thriller. I know you like him."

"I do. Thank you."

"Open the other one."

"Why don't you just tell me what it is?" he teased. "Save me the trouble of tearing off the wrapping paper."

"You don't tear wrapping paper, Henry," she accused. "You 'remove' it. Like a neurosurgeon carefully working his way through a maze of nerve endings. You're supposed to rip it off. Like Beth." The ten-year-old looked up at her and flashed a smile before going back to reading the first page about a little girl who lived in the Swiss Alps.

"We all do things our own way," Henry told her. He slid open the side of the second gift. The appreciative smile that curved his mouth was worth waiting for. She'd scored, Elisha thought. *"The Life and Times of James 'Wild Bill' Hickok,"* he read aloud. "Thanks, Lise."

She paused to kiss his cheek. "You've very welcome. Hey, if I can't get good books for the people I love, what's the point of working at a publishing house?" She looked around. By now, they should have numbered four, not three. "Where's the other lovely member of the family?" Elisha asked her brother.

"Right here," Andrea answered. She walked in, her hands deep in the pockets of the jeans that had a tendency to reside on her hips rather than in the vicinity of her waist. "Hi." She brushed a kiss against Elisha's cheek, her eyes on the remaining two packages on the table. "Anything for me?"

"Sorry, these are for the mailman," Elisha told her, picking the packages up and holding them to her. Then she laughed and thrust them toward her niece. "Since he's not here, I guess you can have them."

But before Andrea had a chance to open even the first gift, her father asked, "Did you finish your homework, Andrea?"

The older girl's hand dropped from her gift. She held them against her with her other hand, her eyes communing with her shoes rather than looking up at her father. "Almost."

"How many pages in an almost?" Henry asked in a voice that held the echo of endless patience. With Andrea, he found that he had to be. And at times, even that didn't work. He knew she had a paper due in English the next day, a paper she'd been putting off writing for over three weeks now, ever since she'd gotten the assignment.

"Two."

He was familiar with the game. "Two pages to go, or two pages done?"

She didn't stick out her lower lip, but Andrea looked petulant. Fifteen was the age for it, Elisha thought. Again, while she didn't envy her brother, she did admire him.

"Two done." And then the girl, a carbon copy of her late mother with her delicate features and her long, silky blond hair, sighed dramatically as she went on the offensive. "I just don't get it," she lamented. "Why do we have to study Shakespeare anyway? Nobody talks like that anymore."

It was a familiar complaint. Not one that she had made herself, Elisha thought, but that was because she had fallen in love with the beauty of the written word only a little after she'd climbed out of her first crib. She'd taught herself how to read. Her mother had called her precocious. The real reason was that Elisha had been impatient. Too impatient to wait for her mother to read to her. So she'd learned how to sound things out on her own, asking any nearby adult to help her when she needed it. She was reading by four.

"They did once," Elisha pointed out. "And who knows, maybe no one'll talk like you do now in another hundred years."

The expression on Andrea's face was the last word in skepticism. "Yeah, right."

Now, *there* was a challenge if she'd ever heard one. "Nobody says *groovy* anymore or talks about the cat's pajamas," Elisha said.

On the sofa, her finger marking her place, Beth looked up and laughed at the expression. "Cats don't have pajamas."

Unless they're in cartoons, Elisha thought. "That's what they said in the forties."

Beth's face became solemn and thoughtful. She looked a great deal like Henry when she pondered things. "Cats had pajamas in the forties?" the girl asked.

Elisha did her best to keep a straight face. "It was a more innocent, less complicated time."

"Sounds boring," Andrea said. "Just like this play I have to do my report on."

Her interest piqued, Elisha asked, "Which play are you doing?"

"*Romeo and Juliet.*"

A section of the past came flooding back to Elisha. In high school, the drama class had put on the play and she had landed the role of Juliet. She had some very fond memories of rehearsing the kiss Juliet gave Romeo in an attempt to share the poison she thought he still had on his lips. Tommy Leonetti had some very definite ideas about just how "dead" Romeo was supposed to be at the time. She wondered if Tommy was still a great kisser.

Banking down her thoughts, she looked at her older niece. "You should be able to relate to that."

"Why?" There was almost contempt in Andrea's voice, but it was aimed at the Bard and the story she had to sludge through. "I wouldn't be dorky enough to get married at fourteen."

A little gentle education was called for here. Not to mention a helping hand with the report. Making up her mind to tackle both, Elisha looked at her brother. "How long until dinner?"

"Take all the time you need."

"Okay, then." Elisha slipped her arm around Andrea's shoulders, leading the girl back to her room. "What I meant by you being able to relate to this story is that Romeo and Juliet rebelled against their parents."

Andrea looked at her, a spark of interest entering her eyes as they left the room. "Cool."

CHAPTER 7

Henry said nothing on the subject throughout dinner, a simple but palate-pleasing pot roast. Neither did she. Instead, the conversation around the dining-room table centered on a variety of items that were of interest to the girls.

But as soon as Beth had run off to test out her new video game and Andrea had excused herself to talk to her girlfriends, Henry looked at her knowingly. "You did the rest of the paper for Andrea, didn't you?"

She knew better than to make eye contact with him. Henry had a way of staring a person down to the point where the truth just popped out of its own accord. She'd often thought he'd missed his calling as an interrogator, although as a lawyer, it did come in handy at times.

Elisha studied the delicate pattern on the white tablecloth as she said, "No, I guided her through the rest of the paper."

He sipped the last of his mineral water, his eyes still on his sister's face. "So the report is written?"

"Yes."

He laughed softly and shook his head. "You did it for her," he repeated.

Elisha looked up from the white-on-white swirls. Henry had her and they both knew it. "I didn't physically sit and write it." A grin quirked her mouth. "She types faster than I do."

"But you dictated."

It was an old game. She was determined not to cry uncle, at least not completely.

"Maybe some of the words," she allowed, then quickly followed up with, "Can I help it if she likes the way I phrase things? Really, Henry, she's a very bright girl, just a wee bit lazy when it comes to planting her bottom on a chair and doing the work." She knew she wasn't telling him anything new. No man was as up on his kids and their habits as Henry was. "Hell, I deal with that almost every day." Slowly, she began to gather up the dishes, stacking them on one another as she talked. "You have no idea how many writers talk a good book, but when it comes right down to sitting there and facing a naked page, or trying to get from point A to point B, they become like willful children. Anything'll distract them so they don't have to deal with that emptiness."

Reaching for Andrea's water glass, Henry placed it by his own. "Emptiness?"

"Of the page or computer screen," she elaborated. Elisha moved her own glass next to her brother's, then brought over Beth's to complete the set. "There are a lot of good words inside their heads, but they swirl together like alphabet soup and they don't think they have the wherewithal, or patience, or whatever to put it together so it makes sense." Dropping the silverware on top of the four dishes, she smiled. "That's where I come in."

He cocked his head ever so slightly, as if the information would transfer itself into his brain a little more swiftly at that angle. "You put it together for them?"

There were times when she was sorely tempted to toss out a page and put her own words down in its stead. But that was the easier way and the more dishonest way. Although she had to admit it was personally satisfying to see her words in print, even under someone else's name.

"I nag," she corrected him. "I push, I prod, I provide the encouraging word, sometimes over and over again." For her most insecure authors, she thought. With them, bolstering their morale was very much like trying to pour a given amount of water into a pail with a gaping hole in it. "Until they get it done."

Henry nodded at the explanation. "You had it right the first time. You nag." He grinned. "As I recall, you were quite good at that."

"I never nagged you."

"You most certainly did."

Stubbornly, she refused to give up any ground. "About what?"

He rolled his eyes, seeming more amused than frustrated. "Everything. You thought things had to be done a certain way—your way—and you wanted me to do it just that way."

From her point of view, she'd been altruistic, but she supposed she could see that from his position, her behavior might have seemed a little irritating. "I just didn't want you making my mistakes."

"Kids need to make their own mistakes," he told her quietly. He got up from the table, picking up the stack of plates and silverware. "That's how they learn."

He had a point and she was more than willing to concede to it. Henry was even a better father than theirs had been, and she had adored their father.

"Which is why you're the parent and I'm the editor. I wouldn't have the patience to stand back and let them learn on their own," she admitted honestly. "I'd just jump right in there and do it for them." Holding the glasses to her to keep from dropping them, she followed Henry into the kitchen. "You really have done a great job with the girls. They're wonderful."

Henry placed the dishes on the counter and opened the dishwasher. One by one, Elisha rinsed off the dinner plates and handed them to him to place on the rack.

"Yeah, they are, aren't they? Don't get me wrong, there have been a few rough patches, especially with Andrea, but for the most part, I've been pretty blessed." The last dish he took from her slipped through his fingers. It landed on the tile with a clatter. Because it was the everyday dinnerware, the plate didn't shatter.

Not looking in his direction, Elisha stooped down to pick up the dish.

"Never knew you to drop anything," she teased. "I'm the one who does that, usually because I'm moving faster than the speed of light."

When she rose back up, her grin froze, then abruptly faded the second she saw her brother's face. Henry was struggling to mask it, but she was positive she saw a glimmer of pain flash across his features. Something squeezed her heart.

"Henry, what's wrong?"

He did his best to look unaffected as he waved a hand at her question, dismissing it. "Nothing. It was just a twinge."

"A twinge of what?" she demanded. He made no answer, as if the question had no significance. Still looking at him, Elisha quickly pulled over a chair. "Here, sit," she ordered.

When Henry did as she asked, she became really concerned. Henry had never had a macho complex, but he just never showed any weakness. If he needed to sit down, something was very, very wrong.

She looked at his color again, thinking how pale he was. She could feel the foundations of her world weakening, as if she'd just found out that they were constructed of cardboard instead of concrete.

She placed a hand on his shoulder, trying not to feel at a loss, wishing she was that know-it-all big sister again, or at least could somehow channel her. "Maybe you need to see a doctor."

Henry raised his head and gave her an acquiescing smile. "I *am* seeing one."

"Seeing?" she echoed, picking up on the one telltale word. He hadn't just gone once and gotten a clean bill of health. "As in an ongoing process?"

This definitely didn't sound good to her.

"Don't make a big deal out of this, Lise. I just went in for a checkup."

"Why didn't you tell me?"

"Because I knew you'd make a big deal out of it. I went because I haven't been to a doctor for a while and I thought it might be a good idea to get myself checked over."

She wasn't buying that, not for a moment. "Women think like that," Elisha pointed out. "Men don't think like that." She was doing her best not to allow panic to cross her threshold. So far, she was succeeding. "Now, what's wrong?"

With the patience of Job, Henry stuck to his story. "Nothing."

She couldn't very well choke the story out of him. "How serious a nothing?"

Henry laughed, stood and reached for the dishwashing detergent. He added the appropriate amount to the machine. "You always were dramatic." He punctuated the statement with an affectionate laugh.

She sighed. The man was a veritable sphinx when he wanted to be. "And you were always closemouthed."

There was deep affection in his voice as he posed the question, "How would you have known? You were always talking. Or dictating," he added before she could defend herself. They knew one another very well. They always had. "I couldn't have gotten a word in edgewise. Mom and Dad wouldn't have even known I could talk if you hadn't had to go to kindergarten a few hours a day and leave me at home."

"You're trying to divert me, Henry. All right, if you're already seeing a doctor, what did he or she say?"

"It's a he. Dr. Steven Rheinhold," he said. "And he think's that it's probably just an ulcer. He wants to run some tests."

An ulcer would be consistent with someone who kept everything inside and never displayed any anger, she thought. An ulcer could be treated and managed.

"Tests."

He smiled and passed his fingertips over the furrow that had formed between her eyebrows, smoothing it out. "Don't say it as if it's a death sentence."

The second he said the forbidden word, Elisha rallied. She instantly forgot about her own reaction, her own concerns, and became the eternal cheerleader.

"No, of course not. Tests are good. They rule out things, put your fears to rest. Tell you what you should be doing." She looked at her brother pointedly. "Like resting."

He returned her look without flinching. "You'd be the one to talk."

With her, it was more a case of collapsing instead of resting, and she did so periodically. But this wasn't about her, it was about him. The only really important "him" in her life.

"Like you just said, brother dear, I always do." She sobered slightly, turning the dishwasher on for him. "You'll tell me the minute you find out anything?"

"If I can get through."

She knew he was referring to the last time. The woman on the switchboard had placed him on hold and immediately lost the connection.

"Call my cell," she told him. "And the answering machine."

"So in other words," he deadpanned, "you don't want to know."

"I'll answer it," she promised. "I don't want anything happening to you."

"Nothing's going to happen to me," he reassured her in the soft, patient voice that inspired confidence in all who heard it. "I've got too much to live for."

"Yeah, you do," she agreed. Pausing to kiss his cheek, she ordered, "Remember that."

"Yes, ma'am," he murmured, then laughed.

She loved the sound of his laugh. It made her feel better.

CHAPTER 8

"Okay, I quit. I quit, I quit, I QUIT!" Paula Reynolds shouted in a voice of full-blown, hair-pulling hysteria.

She ended her ten-year career by slamming the door as she left Rockefeller Randolph's spacious office.

Breathing fire, the now former senior editor pushed her way past Elisha. As she hurried by, Paula's eyes looked more than just a little possessed. "He's a monster!"

The pronouncement echoed in the hall, causing heads to turn and people to look out of their cubicles and small offices.

Bemused, Elisha knocked once on Rocky's door and then let herself in. Rocky was probably in the throes of recovering from whatever salvo Paula had fired in her wake. He did not do confrontations well and he was at his best when the good ship Randolph & Sons was sailing through tranquil waters.

Rocky's eyes rolled as she stepped over the threshold. The fine features of his face ceased looking so pinched.

"Thank God it's you." He breathed a heartfelt sigh of relief. "I thought she was coming back to strangle me. Never knew Paula was so emotional."

She was here to tell him that Sinclair had called earlier from the road to announce that the book tour was going well and that he had a spot on one of the morning shows, but she tabled that news for the time being. Rocky was obviously dealing with some crisis and that took precedence over friendly chitchat.

Elisha took a seat in his guest chair. "I take it that reference to monster she just yelled wasn't meant to describe you."

Rocky shook his head, then mentioned the name of the most famous and most difficult star in their stable. "She was talking about Ryan Sutherland."

A smile played across her lips. "Thought as much." The day was windy. From her window, she watched a bird in the distance struggling to fly to his intended destination. "What does that make now, three editors he's chewed his way through since Parks retired?"

Taking a deep breath, Rocky let it slowly out before answering, "Four. Milo Benson lasted a week."

"Right, Milo. I forgot about him." The young Harvard graduate had been Jason Parks's heir apparent, trained by the older man to eventually take his place. No one, however, had thought that "eventually" would turn into "immediately," but heart attacks don't follow timetables. Jason's had been entirely unexpected, considering how well the man cared for his health. In comparison to most, it had been a minor attack, but Jason felt it was a sign that he needed to retire to do something less stressful than deal with deadlines and prima donnas.

Left in the lurch, Rocky had handed the jewel of the Randolph lineup to Milo. The thinking had been that Milo would see to the demanding author while arrangements were made to transition the blockbuster author to another senior editor. The best-laid plans of mice and men and publishers often went awry. As in this case. Milo had left after a week to take a more lucrative offer with another firm. Or so he had said. Elisha had a feeling that the young man had said what he had in order to cover his pride and allow himself to make a quick getaway.

Because Rocky looked as if he needed to unwind and because

she possessed more than a healthy share of curiosity, Elisha asked, "So what's the complaint this time?"

"Paula called Sutherland a male chauvinist pig."

Elisha pretended to wince, not at the accusation, but at the term Paula had used. She struggled to keep the amused look off her face. She knew that at the moment Rocky wouldn't appreciate it. "Haven't heard that one in a long time. You would have thought that someone as modern and forward thinking as Paula would have come up with a more up-to-date term."

Rocky shrugged. "Sometimes the old standards work best." The comment was said more into his shirt than to her.

Elisha was instantly on her guard. "You're mumbling, Rocky. Does that mean you're going to ask me to do something I won't like?"

He sighed and shook his head. "You know me too well."

Elisha frowned. "And apparently you don't know me at all. Hello." Moving forward on her seat, she put her hand out to him. "I'm Elisha Reed. Perhaps you've seen my office. It's the one with the overflowing paper leaking out through the cracks and beneath the door." She slid back on her seat, her eyes never leaving Rocky's face. Surely he was kidding about what she thought he was going to ask her to do. "I already work a twenty-six-hour day."

"Twenty-four," Rocky corrected automatically. "There are twenty-four hours in a day."

"I know." She shot the zinger at him with the accuracy of a mischievous child with an old-fashioned slingshot. "I've been borrowing hours against the future. I'm up to the year 2025."

He did his best to sound upbeat as he tried to move forward. "Look, Elisha, I know that you're overworked..."

When he used her given name, she knew that the deck was

stacked against her and that she'd lost before the game had ever begun. "I've always loved your flair for understatement, Rocky."

"I can give the newer authors to Edlestein, free you up a little."

"To do what?"

Rocky sighed, a man between a rock and a hard place with no promise of a pillow anywhere in sight. "Don't make this hard, Elisha."

She looked at him sweetly. "Then don't say the words, Rocky."

"What words?"

She'd heard all the rumors and each time she did, she gave up a quick, silent prayer that she wasn't the one dealing with Sutherland. Now, apparently, she would be.

"The words condemning me to dance in attendance to a man who could serve as the poster boy for anger–management classes—the 'before' side."

"Lise, the man writes tremendous blockbusters for us. We need to keep him happy."

The stories about working with Sutherland were legion. None was uplifting. "From what I'd heard, I don't think the man is capable of 'happy.' Unless you mean allowing him to toss vestal virgins into a volcano. That might bring a smile to his face."

"Women find him charming."

Rocky was referring to cocktail parties. Sutherland had attended Sinclair's launch party. And had been mobbed as she recalled. "Women who don't have to be working with him."

Rocky tried to recall all the kind comments he'd heard leveled at the writer. "He's a man's man—"

"Fine, give him to some man." Her eyes widened as she thought of the perfect solution. Or at least a solution that would keep her off the hook for a while. "You, for instance."

The thought clearly horrified Rocky. He turned ash white.

"He'd break me in two—verbally. The guy's an ex–Navy SEAL among other things. I think he was also a mercenary for a while."

"Take a bodyguard and have him frisked before you start working together." Not that Sutherland liked or welcomed any input from anyone but himself. As far as she was concerned, that made him a walking ego.

Rocky rose from behind his desk and came to stand in front of her. Apparently begging was easier for him at closer quarters. "Lise, please, you're my only hope."

She hated when he looked so sad. "Don't give me those puppy-dog eyes, Rocky—"

"Rumor has it that he's thinking of leaving us, of going to Horizon Publishing. If I lose him, my father might decide to really come out of retirement and take over. That means he'll be looking over everyone's shoulder again."

The older Randolph showed up once or twice a week as it was, haunting the halls, nosing into people's progress and schedules. "To 'come out of retirement,' your father would have had to fully 'go into retirement.'"

Rocky fixed Elisha with a long, forlorn look. "Please?"

She sighed. "You've got nobody else?"

Rocky shook his head solemnly. "Nobody."

She thought of her assistant. This, she believed, would be perfect payback. The conniving woman wouldn't even know what hit her.

"How about Carole Chambers?" Elisha asked sweetly. "She's dying to sink her teeth into someone of renown and she's terrific at kissing up."

"She's very competent," he said seriously, "but she's not ready for someone of Sutherland's stature. She doesn't have your background or your expertise."

Elisha eyed him, her expression never changing. "And this

is the part where I'm supposed to jump to my feet and declare, "Give him to me, Rocky. I can do it."

"A little hammy but yes."

"You've been watching too many Mickey Rooney, Judy Garland movies." The man said nothing, he merely continued looking at her with eyes that silently pleaded for her understanding and compliance. After a beat, knowing she couldn't find it in her heart to turn him down, she sighed and shook her head. "Oh, all right. I don't have a life, anyway. And he *is* the biggest draw we have."

"The biggest," Rocky agreed.

"You know, for a man who runs a publishing house, you're not very eloquent."

For the first time since he'd made the request, he smiled. "I don't have to be, I have you."

"That remains to be seen."

His smile faded. "What do you mean?"

"I mean, if Sutherland starts giving me ulcers, I might have to go Paula's route and quit."

"I'll take him away before I'd let you quit."

She looked at him. Rocky had managed to surprise her. "You mean that?"

"Yes, I do."

"Okay, then we have a deal. Bring on the ex-SEAL. Maybe I can teach him to behave."

Rocky shook his head. "Not even you, Lise. I'm just hoping for some kind of semi-peaceful existence."

"Ah, Rocky, a man's grasp should extend his reach, or what's a heaven for?"

"Just make sure you stay out of Sutherland's grasp."

She looked at him. "Am I going to have to worry about that, too?"

"Don't worry, I'll handle him if anything gets out of hand."

She leveled her gaze at him. "All right, I will hold you to your word."

They shook hands on it. Elisha was pretty certain that the one Rocky kept out of her line of vision had its fingers crossed.

CHAPTER 9

"So, are you the latest sacrificial lamb they've decided to send into the arena?"

She had been braced for this all day. All week, really. Ever since she'd shaken Rocky's hand and agreed to take on Ryan Sutherland, Randolph & Sons' highest-drawing card, as her author.

She knew him, of course. It was hard to work for the publishing house and not know the tall, bombastic man who looked every bit the action hero he detailed in his books.

He moved into her office like a dark storm crouching on the horizon and inching its way across the sea. At approximately five-eleven, he was not an overly tall man, but he had a larger-than-life quality as well as an aura of danger that she sensed he was careful to cultivate. It was good for sales and good for drawing women to him. As if his celebrity status wasn't enough.

But they had never done more than nod at one another whenever their paths crossed, either in the halls of Randolph & Sons Publishing or at a book launch. She had been to several of his launches. He, in turn, had attended a handful of others for people he might not call friend but to whom he felt he owed some sort of allegiance.

Either that or it was a good excuse to imbibe alcohol, which he was able to do on a grand scale without looking the slightest bit inebriated.

Part of his SEAL training, no doubt.

Feeling a little like someone whose ramparts had just been scaled, Elisha forced her mouth to curve as she sat back in her chair. She slid off her glasses and took a good look at the man who was going to make her life a living hell.

"A sacrificial lamb? Now, that's an interesting metaphor, Mr. Sutherland. Do you see yourself as a gladiator or a butcher?"

Ryan smiled at his new editor. He hadn't expected a comeback. Most editors, particularly those of the softer sex, usually mumbled and laughed self-consciously. He threw people off-kilter and he liked it. "I see myself as someone who doesn't suffer fools gladly."

If he expected her to cringe, he was going to be disappointed, Elisha thought. She was more than up to the challenge he represented. "Judging by your last contract, I doubt if you suffer at all. I understand bales of money were involved."

He was accustomed to his editors bowing and scraping, had come to take it for granted. This woman looked as if she wanted to go fifteen rounds with him. He was in no mood for a sparring partner.

"Bales of money that wouldn't have appeared on Randolph's doorstep without the product of the sweat of my brow. Namely, my talent." He looked at the chair before her desk. "Mind if I sit?"

She gestured toward the chair. "Please." She waited until he had lowered what looked to be his still-taut body into the chair. Once upon a time, when she had thought about life taking a different turn, this would have been the kind of "hero" she might have invented for herself. But now he was just a writer, albeit a very successful writer, and her regard of him was in a purely professional capacity.

"Granted," she continued once Sutherland had placed his leather briefcase on the floor, "but as I hear it, half that money was spent on headache tablets and tranquilizers."

He looked at her, vaguely puzzled. They'd given him a babbler, he thought with a disgust he didn't attempt to hide. "I don't take tranquilizers."

No, but you do keep the companies who make them in business. "I was referring to all the editors you've chewed up then spit out in the last year."

Piercing blue eyes narrowed on her. He'd stopped by his publisher's, as was his habit whenever he was in the city. This time there had been more of a specific purpose to his visit. But he was beginning to regret it. "Did Rockefeller select you to antagonize me?"

"No, to work with you." She flashed him her best, most disarming smile, hoping to get them back on track. "Maybe we should get to know each other a little better before we leap into the creative process."

Ryan moved his torso forward as he slid to the edge of the chair. He gave her the impression of a commando about to jump from a plane and yell "Geronimo." His voice was so low when he spoke, it seemed to rumble in her chest first before she heard it with her ears.

"One, I neither need nor want to get to know you. I don't need to know the name of your parents, or that you called your first pet, a goldfish, Simon. None of that matters. You are what the publisher whimsically wishes to call my editor, not my intended mate. And two, *we* are not leaping anywhere, least of all into a creative process. That process is strictly for me alone. Your main job is to take what I have done and bring it over to the production department."

She stared at him, trying desperately to keep a poker face and not let the writer see that she thought he was just about the biggest egotist she had ever met. "Like a messenger."

His sardonic expression never changed. "You have a fairly good grasp of the language, I see."

She could understand why Paula had fled after three months of this. Paula thought of herself as the end product of a long line of incredibly intelligent women. To be regarded as a single-celled amoeba would have been difficult for her. She, on the other hand, was not about to allow herself to get rattled. She decided to think of this as a tennis game. She was going to hit back every ball the man lobbed at her.

She smiled, exuding a calmness that only went down to the first layer. Beneath that was an entirely different matter.

"I have an infinitely wonderful grasp of the English language," she replied, "which is why I am a successful editor. And for the time being, until God or Rockefeller Randolph tears us asunder, I am your editor, Mr. Sutherland. That means I will be editing." Her gaze never wavered as she looked him straight in the eye. "Undoubtedly lightly, but I *will* be editing."

He glanced down at the briefcase he'd brought. Inside were the fruits of his latest labor. Protocol dictated that he present it to his newest editor. No thought was given to its pages being marked up because that just didn't happen with one of his works. "Change one word of what I've written and you won't have to wait for God to tear us asunder. I'll do it myself. With my bare hands if I have to."

She read between the lines. "Editing isn't an insult, Mr. Sutherland. Even Hemingway and Fitzgerald had Maxwell Perkins."

The reference, coming out of nowhere, amused him. "And you fancy yourself my Maxwell?"

"I fancy myself part of the team that is putting out your books, Mr. Sutherland." Her mouth curved again, because what she said was true. "I am your first audience, devoid of the hero worship."

Thunder rolled across the plains again. The look in his eyes darkened. "You don't like my books?"

She'd found his Achilles' heel, she thought. Despite his bombastic manner, he felt a thread of insecurity about his books. Good, she'd make that work for her. "I never said I didn't like your books, Mr. Sutherland. But it's not my job to read them for pleasure."

His mouth twitched in dismissive disgust. "Perhaps you should. Everyone else who's plunking down their hard-earned money is going to be doing just that, reading for pleasure, for entertainment. For escape. Maybe you would better serve your employer and the public by remembering that and trying to implement those principles when you read the results of my efforts."

She didn't particularly like the way he'd lingered on the word *serve*. Sutherland undoubtedly viewed her as some sort of servant. If that's what he thought, man, did he have the wrong job description.

"It might have slipped your mind, but we're supposed to be a team," she reminded him.

"It never slipped my mind because it was never on my mind to begin with." His eyes were penetrating as he looked at her, pulling out her secrets. Making her feel that he had somehow been blessed with X-ray vision. It took everything she had not to shift uncomfortably. "The last 'team member' I had jumped out of a helicopter with me into the Indian Ocean at two o'clock in the morning. He didn't make it back."

"Was he reading one of your manuscripts at the time?"

Ryan opened his mouth to answer, then stopped. Instead of saying something, he began to laugh. It was a deep, rumbling sound, like the beginnings of an earthquake deep within the bowels of the earth.

He gave up the opposition. For now. "All right, tell Rockefeller you're acceptable."

She wondered if everyone wanted to pluck out every dark hair on his head within five minutes of the initial introduction, or if she was setting some kind of record. "He already knows that."

"To me," Ryan emphasized, not caring a damn what anyone else thought on the subject. He was the one who would have to deal with her, although he was determined to keep the contact down to a minimum. Maybe if she were more attractive, he might feel more inclined to interact with her, but she made him think of an old-fashioned schoolmarm, right down to the glasses atop her dark blond head. That had never been the type to pique his interest. "Tell him you're acceptable to me."

She knew that he was trying to make her look away. She stared back harder. And smiled wider. "He already assumed as much."

Ryan wasn't sure whether he admired her bravado or was annoyed by it. "Oh, he did, did he? And why is that?"

"Because he's never met an author who didn't like me." She was very proud of that. Rocky had once said that, if he had a worthwhile story to tell, she could probably get along with the devil himself. Obviously, he had decided to put that theory to the test.

Sutherland made no effort to mask his disdain. "You're not one of those needy types who needs people to like her, are you?"

"No." She didn't strictly "need" it. She did, however, like it. "It's just a happy by-product of my work." Maybe he'd treat her with more respect if she began to sound more like an editor and less like a verbal sparring partner, she thought. Elisha took out a pad from the middle drawer. "Now then, I see by the notes that Paula left—"

Sutherland looked away. His sneer seemed to fill up the room. "A thoroughly scattered female."

Maybe another editor might have tried to placate him by murmuring something in agreement, but she couldn't. She didn't even like Paula, but the woman didn't deserve to be reviled like

this. She needed someone to stand up for her and for lack of anyone else in the room, the lot fell to her. "She was a very competent editor until you peeled her like a grape."

He blew out a breath that was meant to dismiss not only Paula
and her theory, but Elisha, as well. "Her nerves were far too close
to the surface. If she'd been a Navy SEAL, she would have been
killed the second she entered enemy territory."

"In case you didn't notice, Paula wasn't a Navy SEAL, she
was an editor," Elisha pointed out, refusing to back down. "And
do you consider yourself enemy territory?"

His eyes held hers. Again she felt as if she were being
breached. "I am if you intend to invade."

She spread her hands wide in complete innocence. "I'm just
here to facilitate the tremendous effort it takes to produce the
blockbusters you write."

"Well, 'Max,' you can facilitate the 'tremendous effort'—and
you're right about that—by staying out of my way and letting
me do what I do best."

"Filleting those around you?" she guessed.

For the second time since he'd walked into her office, Ryan
Sutherland laughed.

"Only as a last resort." After a moment's debate, he picked up
the worn leather briefcase that was resting against his chair. After putting it on his lap, he withdrew a considerably large manuscript from within. Leaning forward, he placed the book on her
desk. "All right, here it is."

She eyed the offering, wondering if he expected her to bow
down before it. "Your first draft?"

"My *only* draft."

Shivers raced down her back. They weren't the kind she had
once welcomed. These were meant to warn her and keep her alive.

CHAPTER 10

It wasn't until well after lunch that Rocky ventured to stick first his head, then the rest of his lanky body, into her office. There was a hesitant expression on his face, as if he doubted the wisdom of even asking, but knew he had to.

"So." The single word hung in the air as he eased the door closed behind him, never taking his eyes off her face. Or possibly it was her hands that he was watching warily. Milo had thrown something at him before tendering his resignation. "I didn't hear any wild screams or robust cursing this morning. How did it go?"

As soon as Ryan had left, Elisha had barricaded herself in her office, determined to read his book from first page to last. She had initially wanted to just get a flavor for what he had written, but editing was second nature to her and the pencil had found its way into her hand by the time she had gotten to page ten.

She raised her eyes from the manuscript. "I'm surprised you had the nerve to show your face in my office."

Rocky frowned, looking mournful. "That bad, huh?"

As far as first official meetings went, she'd had better. Any one of her first meetings had been better. Ryan Sutherland made the hairs on the back of her neck stand up. Working with him was going to be a challenge.

"The man doesn't need an editor, Rocky, he needs a lion tamer. Ryan Sutherland gives new meaning to the word *hubris*."

She realized she wasn't saying anything new. Everyone who knew the man probably thought that. Except the bimbos he occasionally squired and only because they probably didn't know the meaning of the word. She sighed, indicating the manuscript she was working on. "Too bad he's talented as hell."

A spark entered Rocky's brown eyes. "Is that his latest book?"

Elisha nodded in response. "That's it."

There was nothing but sheer admiration and gratitude in Rocky's voice. She knew if the meeting had gone badly, Sutherland would have taken his manuscript back home with him, a bartering chip to be used in his demand for another editor. Rocky had to be congratulating himself for pairing them up.

"Well, you got more out of him than Paula did, that's for sure. When she asked to see the first few chapters, he refused to show them to her."

"But she was his editor, not to mention probably his type." The woman under discussion was tall, leggy and endowed. All the things she had once aspired to be herself, before things like that had taken on a lesser importance in deference to deadlines. And gravity.

"I don't know about his type, but he'd said something about her being more suited to parade around before the judges of a Miss America beauty contest than to touching, much less offering, a comment about one of his manuscripts."

Elisha sighed. "Sounds like the dear man." She shook her head. "I'm surprised she didn't threaten to sue him and Randolph & Sons for sexual harassment."

"She wanted to," he admitted, perching for a moment on the side of her desk like a sparrow ready to take flight at the first sign of danger. "And it was touch-and-go for a while. But I pulled a few strings and got her a job at Arlington Press—at slightly more pay. The executive editor there owes me a favor."

"And now you owe him one."

He shrugged, his thin shoulders rising and falling like a marionette whose strings had suddenly been pulled then dropped.

"It's what makes the world go around." Repositioning himself on her desk to catch a glimpse of Ryan's latest tome, he asked, "So, how is it?"

She nodded, looking back at what she'd been reading. "Good. Needs a little polish, but good."

"Tell Sutherland about the good part, skip the talk about the polish." He rose from her desk and moved over to the window. "I don't have time to attend another funeral this month."

She looked at him. "Rocky, the manuscript could be better."

He turned away from the window. There was a note of pleading in his voice as well as in his eyes. "And I could be taller, but I'm not. If the book's readable, and of course it is, we put it out." He drew closer to her. "Maybe you missed this part, but Sutherland doesn't exactly handle criticism well."

In her experience, no one liked to be criticized unless they were masochistic. However, good criticism served a purpose. It made you grow. Everyone could stand to grow a little, even Sutherland. Everything but his ego.

"Maybe he should learn."

Rocky stared at her as if she'd just told him to cut the author loose. Which was what her suggestion amounted to.

"He's the top-selling author we have, Lise. One of the top-selling authors in the country." His voice had risen several ranges. After clearing his throat, he tried again at a lower octave. "In other words, if it's not broke, don't fix it."

She frowned, her eyes pinning him where he stood. "Then why did you give him to me, Rocky? Why didn't you just take him on yourself if all you wanted was a rubber stamp?"

"Take him on myself?" he repeated incredulously. "Because

I'm already taking tranquilizers and Sutherland makes me nervous. Really nervous. Almost as nervous as my father does." He seemed to reconsider that. "Maybe even more. There's blood between my father and me. Sutherland was known for spilling blood in the days before he began to write. Besides," he protested, "you're good with people."

"People, yes, not demigods."

Drawing closer, Rocky watched her writing along the margins of Sutherland's book. His eyes widened. "What are you doing?" he asked in the same tone someone might have used to someone caught with a brush, hovering over a da Vinci painting.

She looked down at the page then back at Rocky. He was acting even more skittish than usual, she thought. "I'm making notes in the margin, why?"

Taking the manuscript and turning it so that it faced him, Rocky began to flip through the pages. "Were there others?"

Had stress made his mind snap completely? "What? Notes? Yes."

"In pencil?"

Elisha glanced at what she was holding to make certain. "Yes." He sighed with relief. "Good, you can erase them."

She pulled the manuscript back around to face her. Just in case he got any ideas and tried to undo her work. "I don't want to erase them. I want Sutherland to read them."

"Lisc," he began patiently, "the public would plunk down their money to read the man's grocery list."

She thought of the earlier meeting. Sutherland had created less than a stellar impression on her. She was pretty certain the feeling was mutual. "Then they'd be wasting their money. I doubt if Sutherland eats anything but nails."

"My point—" Rocky took her hands in his "—is that you give him his lead. I just need a figurehead who can last."

She could be stubborn when she wanted to and she wanted to. "I'm making it better."

"He won't want 'better,'" Rocky insisted. "He thinks he *is* better."

She drew her hands away from his and picked up her pencil again.

"Rocky, you made me his editor, and until you 'unmake me' his editor, I am going to edit. Now, this is a very entertaining book, just like his others, but, just like his others," she repeated for emphasis, "his main character could stand a little work, could be a little deeper."

He stared at her as if she'd just uttered a heresy. "He's an action hero, for God's sake. What kind of depth does he need? I haven't read it, but if it's like his other stories, the hero's a literary version of G.I. Joe. Fortunately, that's all the public wants."

She wasn't satisfied. "But is that all Sutherland wants? There's a depth to the man that could be in his work. Everyone can improve."

Rocky's expression changed from frustration to horror. "And you're going to tell him this?"

"Yes."

He sighed, shaking his head. "How long have you had a death wish?"

"My only wish," she enunciated carefully, "is to make each book I work on the best book possible. And this—" she moved the manuscript slightly "—could be better. I'd be doing Sutherland a disservice as his editor if I don't say so."

"You might be doing yourself a disservice if you do."

"Why? He's not going to burn me at the stake."

"I don't know. The man breathes fire when he's angry. You might just be burnt to a crisp once he gets going."

So Sutherland would rant and rave, that didn't worry her. She could hold her own in a verbal exchange. "Sticks and stones, Rocky, sticks and stones."

Rocky laughed shortly, his brow furrowing into grooves of concern. "He might have those in his arsenal, too."

After putting her pencil down, she pushed away from her desk and focused her attention on the man who was desperately trying to make her give up her principles. "Rocky, you know I have a great deal of affection for you—"

"But?"

"I was just curious. How is it you can continue to walk around without a spine?"

"It's a congenital thing. I taught myself how a long time ago."

She was about to comment on that when her cell phone began to ring. Elisha almost ignored it, then decided to take the call. Holding up her hand to indicate that she didn't want him to leave and that the conversation was not over, she took the phone out and flipped it open.

The name that appeared on the tiny screen was her brother's. Her pulse accelerated instantly. "Hi, Henry, what's the good word?"

"The test results came in today."

Her throat tightened involuntarily. She tried to glean some sort of hint as to the test's outcome from his tone and failed.

"And?"

"Can you come by for dinner tonight?"

The question rang in her head. *This can't be good.* But she couldn't get herself to ask. Her tongue had frozen against the roof of her mouth.

She didn't even hear the door close as Rocky slipped out to give her her privacy.

CHAPTER 11

Elisha stared out the rear passenger window of her taxi as familiar-looking houses moved by on either side.

There was only a mile left to go. A mile to Henry's house.

A mile before she knew.

She fought against this overwhelming urge to fling open the door, jump out of the cab and run the rest of the way, as if running on her own power could somehow get her there faster. But at the same time, an oppressive feeling of dread rose within her, willing the ride to go on indefinitely so that she would never arrive at Henry's house. Because until she heard the words, she could go on hoping that the news was good. That things in her life would continue just the way they had always been. With her existing in a madly spinning world that provided a trapdoor for her. A trapdoor that would open when she needed to touch upon the threshold of hearth and home and allow her to go see Henry.

Henry was not only her rock, he was her link to the past. Her link to the life that she'd had before the world had gotten so crazy. In Henry's eyes she could almost see her childhood.

The cab had stopped moving and the driver was looking at her expectantly. She realized that he'd said something, probably some inane thing like, "We're here, lady." He was waiting for his money. Digging through her wallet, she snared several bills and thrust them at him. More than the fare since he smiled.

Taking a breath, she opened the door and slid out. The air smelled like rain. The July humidity seeped into her soul. Her knees felt oddly disembodied as she walked from the cab to Henry's front door.

Please let him be all right. Please, God. I won't ask for anything ever again, I promise. Just let my brother be all right.

When he opened the door to her ring, Henry was smiling.

She felt her heart leap up, enveloping itself in armaments of hope.

It's going to be okay, she thought. Everything's going to be okay. People who had just gotten bad news didn't smile, right?

Elisha clung to that as she kissed Henry's cheek. "Hi."

He hugged her. She hugged back a little longer than she ordinarily did, breathing in the scent of the aftershave lotion that he used. The same one their father had used. Henry didn't believe in change. Neither did she. More than anything in the world right now, she wanted nothing to change.

"Hi, yourself," he said, releasing her.

"So—" Elisha tried to sound cheerful, but her voice failed her. It almost squeaked.

The next moment, she saw that the girls were in the room, standing directly behind Henry. Within earshot. His daughters looked cheerful. Happy. Nothing seemed different.

Was everything all right then, or hadn't he said anything to Andrea and Beth?

He hadn't, she suddenly realized. Henry hated to bring sadness into their worlds. He was always looking for that one ray of sunshine trying to push its way through a storm-filled cloud. Telling the girls about their mother's death had been one of the most difficult things he'd ever done. But he had.

And that was when it had dawned on her that her younger brother was so much braver than she was. Because she would have never been able to tell them. Being the bearer of bad news was just not something she could do.

Elisha looked at Henry, her eyes asking him a thousand questions. None seemed to register. They all bounced back to her as if she'd been looking at a painting of Henry instead of someone with a soul.

"Aunt Lise, come see what I did," Beth cried, pushing ahead of her sister.

Not bothering to wait for a response or for Elisha to follow her on her own, the little girl wrapped her fingers around her hand and began to tug her in the direction of the stairs.

"Come see," Beth insisted again, more loudly this time. "It's in my room."

Elisha looked over her shoulder at Henry, who waved her on as if he didn't have a care in the world. "Go ahead. We'll talk later."

Was it bad news, or good news that would keep? She didn't know.

All she knew for sure was that she had just been given more time to pray. More time to make deals with God, a God she visited on occasion in her mind but who she'd long since stopped having contact with on a regular basis. Church was a place that resided in her childhood. It had been years since she'd attended any kind of Sunday services. When she'd dropped out in the beginning, there was always an excuse handy. Until she no longer felt the need even for that.

It was agony, making small talk at dinner, pretending there was nothing on her mind. She was surprised that she wasn't doubled over by the weight of it. But she went along with the charade, knowing it was necessary.

But knowing didn't keep her mind from wandering. Wandering so that at times, when she got to the end of her sentence, she'd forgotten her train of thought.

She wasn't making sense and the girls were looking at her oddly.

"Been a long day," she murmured, taking refuge in the glass of chardonnay Henry had poured her. She wished it was stronger.

She wished she was stronger.

Finally, the meal was over and the girls scattered, as they always did. Andrea to her homework and friends who seemed to live online twenty-five hours a day, Beth to a miniature version of her big sister's existence.

Elisha waited, mentally counting to twenty to make sure that both girls weren't just out of the room but out of earshot, as well. If anything was wrong, she didn't want to take the chance of having either of her nieces learn something dreadful by eavesdropping.

She pressed her lips together. Henry was clearing the plates as if there was nothing more important in his life than loading the dishwasher.

Was that a good sign, or a sign of denial?

Playing hide-and-seek with the truth was draining her.

Taking up a second load of dishes in her hands, Elisha followed her brother into the kitchen. She put the pile down beside his on the counter. She stared at the back of his head, willing him to turn around. When he didn't, she couldn't take it anymore.

"Henry, if you don't tell me right this second, I'm not going to be responsible for my next move. What did the doctor say?"

"The test is positive."

She'd always believed that medicine was a strange world, where words like *negative* meant good and *positive* meant bad. The complete opposite of the way things were supposed to be.

Maybe Henry had gotten them confused. It would have been a natural mistake.

Her mouth felt as if it was sandpaper dry. It was hard to ma-neuver her tongue, hard to form the words. "Positive as in…?"

Her voice gave out. There was only a finite amount of strength in her body and right now, that strength was being channeled toward breathing and toward keeping her heart go-ing. Things like talking seemed to be of secondary importance.

"I have cancer, Lise."

He still hadn't turned around, so she circled around him un-til she could see his face. Elisha drew in her breath. For just an instant, Henry's face looked drawn and worn, as if the words he had just uttered had taken their toll on him.

She felt as if someone had just shot an arrow straight into her heart.

From somewhere deep inside her, a flicker of optimism came. "Hey, cancer can be licked, Henry. Lots of people are cancer sur-vivors. There's a woman living in my building…"

She was talking now. Talking as fast as she could, hoping that all the positive thoughts she was generating would somehow ne-gate or deplete the positive results of Henry's test. But even as she was talking, her brother was shaking his head. Her words were fall-ing by the wayside. Conquered.

"Elisha, I've got pancreatic cancer."

Pancreatic cancer.

All she could remember was that when she was a lot younger, she'd heard that an actor named Michael Landon had had it and he'd died. His face had been on the cover of *People* magazine. She could almost see it in her mind's eye. He'd looked much too young to leave this earth. Too young. The way Henry was too young.

She also remembered reading, or maybe she'd heard one of her parents say it, she couldn't remember. In either case, the words were chilling.

Pancreatic cancer was always fatal.

Elisha squared her shoulders, ready to do battle. Refusing to believe it. Refusing to allow Henry to believe it, either.

"Your doctor could be wrong," she pointed out with feeling.

Henry's face once more became composed. He was taking this a lot better than she was, she thought. "He's not wrong."

"He could be wrong," she insisted. "People make mistakes. Labs make mistakes. You read about it all the time." Why was he just standing there, taking it? Why wasn't he fighting it? "Embryos get mixed up, for God's sake, why wouldn't lab tests? It's not like yours was the only test being done at the hospital."

Henry's expression was in direct contrast to the turmoil she felt going on inside her. He almost looked serene, as if he'd accepted everything. As if the fight was all over.

Gently, he placed his hands on her shoulders. "I took the test twice, Lise. There's no mistake."

She took a breath, changing direction while going ninety miles an hour. "Okay, then we get you treatment. Whatever it takes. I don't care what it costs. I've got savings—"

Again, he stopped her. "Lise, I love you for caring, but I've made my peace with it."

Her heart twisted inside her chest, twisted so hard it almost took her breath away.

"Well, I haven't, dammit, and I'm not going to," she declared heatedly. "And neither are you." She was ordering him and begging him at the same time. She didn't want him just giving up this way. "Miracles happen every day, Henry. People who aren't supposed to live defy the odds and do just that. They *live*. Paralyzed people walk. Things that science and test tubes can't explain *do* happen and I'm not giving you up without a fight, Henry."

Her eyes were filling with tears. She hated that. Tears were a sign of weakness and she couldn't do battle like this. She was going to put all her strength into the fight. She was going to win. For Henry.

"Do you hear me?" she demanded, her eyes searching his face for a sign that she'd awakened the warrior within him. The warrior that was necessary to conquer this horrible condition.

CHAPTER 12

Henry looked behind her, anticipating an invasion by one or both of his daughters. His eyes shifted back to his sister's face. He knew where she was coming from but it didn't help. Nothing was going to help.

"Lower your voice, Lise. I don't want the girls to hear."

"Because you don't want to upset them—because nothing's going to happen," she emphasized. "See? You do think the way I'm thinking."

The expression on his face told her that he wished he could agree, but beneath the optimist had always been a pragmatist.

"No," he told her quietly as he resumed loading the dishwasher, "because I haven't found the right way to tell them yet. After losing their mother, this is going to be a doubly hard blow for them to deal with." He turned from the machine, his eyes intent on hers. "Will you take them?"

Frozen in place, Elisha swallowed before asking, "Take them where?"

He smiled sadly, knowing how hard this had to be for her. In his own way, he supposed he was as protective of her as he was of his daughters. But he had no one else to turn to. He'd lost touch with people after Rachel had died, devoting himself singularly to the girls and then to his work. That left no real time for friends.

"Into your house, into your life. Take them as your children." He took her hands in his. "Lise, I need this favor."

Elisha pulled her hands out of his grasp and took a step back. She wished she could be the brave soldier that he wanted her to be, but she was intent on offense, not defense.

"I'm not taking them anywhere because you're not going anywhere. Now, I know some doctors at New York Hospital...."

Her mind felt as if it was racing around like so many disoriented mice in a maze where all the avenues looked and smelled equally alike. She didn't know which way to run first, which way would lead her to where she ultimately wanted to go.

"I've got a top-notch doctor, Elisha," he told her. "His name is Samuel Epstein. He's an oncologist."

She tried to process the information. To use it as a building block. "So you're getting treatment?"

His shoulders moved up and down in a half-helpless shrug. "What's available," he allowed, "but he's not letting me get my hopes up."

She hated the physician immediately. What right did he have to take away her brother's hope?

"A positive state of mind is important, Henry. I've read that over and over again. The mind is a tool, it can—"

"Peace of mind is important, too," he told her, cutting in. "I need to know I can tell the girls you'll take care of them."

She sighed so deeply, it felt as if it was coming from her very toes.

"Of course I'd take care of them." The next beat, she was back to her mantra. To the mantra she wanted him to embrace. "*If something happens to you, which it isn't going to because you're going to lick this. Do you understand? You're going to lick this.*"

Henry's mouth curved in an indulgent smile. "Yes, ma'am."

He was humoring her. She didn't want him humoring her, she wanted him to believe it with every fiber of his being. They were going to conquer this. *He* was going to conquer this. "I'm your big sister and I've always known better than you."

He remembered those days very well. Days of being bossed around, of going along with whatever Elisha said because she was so forceful about her beliefs. "Whatever you say, Lise."

"Damn straight." She bit her lip to fight back tears. Emotion rose up in her throat, threatening to choke her. He couldn't be sick. He couldn't be. *I'll never forgive you if you take him from me,* she warned God. "I need you, Henry. I need you well, or some reasonable facsimile of that. I need you every bit as much as the girls do." She took a deep breath again and exhaled. "Maybe even more."

He took her hand again in his. "I'll hang around as long as I can."

"Longer," she told him in a whisper that was half an order, half an entreaty as she threw her arms around him. "Longer."

Elisha held it together the rest of the evening, although she begged off early. She remained stoic during the ride home from Henry's house to her penthouse apartment, not wanting to break down in front of a stranger, someone who, like as not, fancied himself a part-time psychologist by virtue of his job. In a way, because she was by definition and admission largely an emotional creature, she surprised herself by being able to hold on to those emotions for that length of time.

But the moment she flipped the apartment lock closed, the shaky walls of the dam inside her broke down.

There was no more strength left in her legs.

Her back against the door, Elisha slid down in one slow, boneless motion until she reached the floor. She remained there, huddled, her face buried against her knees, and cried. Huge, body-racking sobs echoed through the foyer as she tumbled headlong into a long abyss.

Time lost all meaning. She wasn't sure just how long she remained there, sobbing, feeling sorry for herself because her life might no longer contain one of the people she loved most in the world. She cried until she was beyond being exhausted, half past dead. The notion of remaining exactly where she was, wet, limp, disoriented, took on serious merit. She hadn't the energy to get up and go to bed. It no longer mattered where she slept.

But that would be giving up. And Henry needed her not to give up. Because he needed someone to be his cheering section.

She raised her head, brushing aside the tears with the heel of her hand. She couldn't give up.

The questions she'd asked Henry told her that he had more or less resigned himself to be vanquished by this hideous disease and if she lay here like some lump, even for a few minutes, then she was tacitly going along with that.

Going along with her brother's death sentence.

No, dammit, if there was some way in heaven—or hell—that she could find something, some procedure, some medicine, some*thing* to prolong Henry's life, to, please God, cure him, she wasn't going to find it lying here, feeling sorry for herself like some heroine out of an eighteenth-century melodrama.

With a shaky breath, Elisha pulled herself together. This wasn't the time to think about herself and what Henry's departure from this world would mean to her. She had to focus on Henry, on getting him well.

One hand on the doorknob, she pulled herself up to her feet. Just then, the phone rang.

Henry.

He was calling to tell her it was all some horrible mistake. An early April Fools' joke, something—

She'd kill him. After she finished hugging him, she promised herself, she'd kill him.

The word *Private* stared back at her on her caller ID as the phone rang again. Private. That could mean it was Henry, or it could be any one of a myriad of people who had decided to hide their identity behind the single, neutral word.

She lifted the receiver, hopeful. "Hello?" She'd almost choked out the words. The tears might have been gone from her cheeks but they were still in her throat, all but clogging it.

There was a pause on the other end of the line, then she heard someone gruffly ask, "Are you all right?"

The voice wasn't familiar.

This time, she cleared her throat before saying anything. "Yes." Rather than forceful, the word came out in almost a squeak.

"You sound like you're crying."

And then she recognized the voice. Or thought she did. Its pitch sounded as if it were emerging by being scraped off the bottom of a barrel.

"Mr. Sutherland?"

"Yeah," the voice on the other end of the line rasped in her ear. He sounded almost uncomfortable. Maybe he was one of those men who had no idea what to do in the face of a woman's tears. Or maybe that would be giving him too much credit, she amended. "Is this a bad time?"

Though she'd hadn't had very many dealings with him and only one as his editor, she'd never heard him sound hesitant before. Did he actually have a human side?

For a second, in the face of kindness, she almost came undone and answered his question in the affirmative. But the admission was much too private a matter and the last thing she wanted was to answer any more questions. If she started to talk about it, about what was bothering her, if his questions extended that far, she'd only begin to cry all over again.

And tears were much too personal to share with a stranger.

But Ryan Sutherland was not the kind of man who could easily be put off. So, taking note of the television program guide on her coffee table, she lied. "I'm watching a sad movie."

She heard him grunt and mutter something unintelligible under his breath. She could just picture the condescending look that was probably on his face. She hated contributing to what was undoubtedly his less-than-flattering view of women, but ultimately, this was better than having him pry into her life.

"A romance, right?"

Her back stiffened. She read a world of meaning into his tone and took umbrage at almost all of it. Rather than answer, she gave him a nonanswer and let him draw his own conclusions. Someone as opinionated as Sutherland would, anyway.

"Why are you calling me at home, Mr. Sutherland?" *And who gave you my phone number? Or did one of your ex–Navy SEAL pals steal it for you?*

"I'm calling you at home, Max," he said cryptically and she could have sworn she heard papers being shuffled in the background, "because Randolph sent a messenger over to my house with an envelope. Do you know what was in that envelope?"

She wasn't up to playing Twenty Questions. Her head was aching. "No, what was in the envelope?" she asked, displaying a patience she hadn't realized she had.

"My manuscript. My manuscript with notes penciled in the margins. Notes I didn't put there."

She held her breath, waiting for more.

And it came. Like a dreadful plague from God. "I want to talk to you."

No, Elisha thought, judging by Sutherland's tone, the man didn't want to talk to her, he wanted to vivisect her. Slowly. Over an open spit with flames shooting out. But after what she'd heard and gone through at Henry's tonight, whatever Sutherland was able to dish out seemed almost insignificant in comparison.

"Fine, how's tomorrow sound?" she asked.

"Tonight sounds better."

"I'm sorry," she lied. "I've got a previous engagement." There was no way she was up to facing the man tonight. Her asbestos suit was currently in the cleaners.

"With your TV set?" Sarcasm dripped from every syllable.

The flare in her temper surprised her. It wasn't fair that someone like Sutherland was lumbering his way through life like a bull in a china shop while someone as wonderful, as kind, as caring as her brother was given such a limited life sentence. She felt like reading Sutherland the riot act for intruding into her life at a time like this, but she knew she couldn't.

She did the next best thing. "I'm off the clock, Mr. Sutherland. I don't have to answer that." And for the first time in her life, Elisha hung up on an author.

She blew out a shaky breath, wrapping her arms around herself in an effort to remove the chill from her soul. She wasn't sorry she'd done that. There were larger things in this life to deal with than Ryan Sutherland's ego. Or if not larger, at least far more important.

CHAPTER 13

"You look like hell."

Elisha never batted an eye, even though Sutherland's declaration a beat after he opened the door to his apartment caught her off guard. She hadn't expected him to be *that* honest. Though she didn't doubt that his assessment of her was dead on. After all, the man seemed to have an eye for that kind of thing.

"I bet you say that to all the women you're trying to sweet-talk."

Inside, she looked around as she stripped off her coat in the small foyer. The living space was all wooden floors, scattered rugs and dark, massive furniture. And not much of the latter.

As far as apartments went, it was spacious. The man obviously loathed clutter or the appearance of it. There was one small mess on his coffee table, consisting of papers, several coffee cups and a few books and magazines, all fraternizing with one another to form a collage.

It was the following day, coming on the heels of an almost utterly sleepless night. She knew there'd be hell to pay with Sutherland after she had deigned to place pencil point to paper and edit his manuscript. With that, and keeping in mind what he meant to Randolph & Sons, she'd promised herself that she would treat the man with kid gloves. But at the last moment, the gloves just hadn't wanted to go on.

She was going to be polite but firm. In her bones, she knew

that he wouldn't respect a pushover and more important, neither would she. And right now, she needed to have something firm to grasp hold of. Her emotions were in a very precarious state.

For a moment, Elisha regretted coming and wished she'd gone with her first impulse—to call in sick. She hardly ever took a sick day and she was more than entitled to one. But if she hadn't come in, more than likely she would have spent the day the way she'd spent the previous night. In agony. She'd alternated between pacing, praying, feeling utterly helpless and surfing the Net. The latter she'd done in hopes of stumbling across solutions, across little-known instant cures. Hoping to find a miracle on the next Web site.

Even as she'd walked into work this morning, she was still debating turning around and going home. Perhaps with a manuscript tucked under her arm, preferably one that needed a great deal of her attention. It had been a viable plan.

But the first person she'd encountered after the receptionist was Rocky. The executive editor's pallor had brought new meaning to the word *pale*. He'd taken her by the arm, ushered her into her office and then closed the door behind them.

"Sutherland called me last night." The words had escaped from his mouth like a secondhand declaration of war.

She thought of the call she'd gotten herself. "A lot of that going around," she'd muttered in response. Very gingerly, she'd uncoupled herself from Rocky's grasp. "He called me, too. The man needs a hobby."

"He has a hobby," Rocky'd lamented, losing the battle to sound authoritative. "It's called skinning people who cross him."

Pity had stirred her overburdened heart as she looked at her boss and friend. "You do look a little the worse for wear."

He'd taken her comment the wrong way. "This isn't funny, Elisha. Sutherland said something about pulling his manuscript."

His eyes looked a little red-rimmed as he'd cried, "Do you know what that means? We've already counted his book in for the January lineup. We've got magazine space reserved, TV and radio commercials. Money invested… If he pulls his book, we have this gaping black hole…" Rocky's reedy voice had trailed off, lost as he obviously contemplated his immediate future. He looked a little green around the gills as he announced, "I'm going to have to talk to him."

He'd said it in the same voice as that of a prisoner having to face the firing squad. She couldn't let him do that. Rockefeller Randolph was not a man to hide behind. His physique was too thin.

"I did this," she'd told him, abandoning her plan for a quick retreat. It hadn't been very viable, anyway. "I'll talk to him."

The look in his eyes was that of a man who'd just gotten a call from the governor, staying his execution. "Oh, God bless you, Elisha."

"That remains to be seen," she'd muttered with little energy.

Only then had Rocky stared at her more closely. When he did, his face took on a look of concern. "Are you all right?"

Rocky was one of the closest friends she had, but she just wasn't ready to share yet. So she'd just nodded. "Yes, I'm fine. Just a bug going around. I think I might have caught it."

And now here she stood, in the middle of the three-bedroom apartment that Sutherland maintained in Tribeca. He kept it in order to dispense with the long drive home to his house on the island after a longer night out on the town. On average, he spent about five nights a month in the apartment.

Even as she tried to take in her surroundings, she felt disembodied. Nothing felt quite real. With effort, she tried to muster the words for an apology she just didn't feel was necessary.

An apology, she abruptly decided as she turned back to look at the author, that Ryan Sutherland just wasn't going to get. She *wasn't* sorry. She was doing her job. Letting the manuscript go into production as is wouldn't be doing her job. Not when she saw the potential for more.

Her voice was as emotionless as she could manage. "If you're attempting to intimidate me by glaring at me, Mr. Sutherland, I have to warn you that it's not going to work."

Sutherland waved an impatient hand at her statement. "Believe me, Max, if I wanted to intimidate you, I would and I could."

He was less than an inch away from her, standing in her space. Making her feel as if her back was to the wall when, in effect, there was no wall behind her. Elisha felt completely naked under his gaze, and yet, there wasn't anything sexual about it.

Or at least, not overtly. Subtly, though, she realized that she felt just the slightest, distant female-male twinge.

Maybe she was hallucinating. Sleep deprivation did things like that.

Ryan peered at her face. She wasn't the kind of woman who immediately snared a man's attention, unless he was into the prim, proper type, but she was pretty enough, he supposed. There was no question, however, that he had seen the editor looking a lot better. "You get any sleep last night, Maxwell?"

There was no point in lying, seeing as how he'd already made the verbal assessment that she looked like hell. "No."

He nodded at the information, as if he was absorbing it through his skin rather than the customary route, through his ears. If she hadn't known better, she would have said there was a flash of discomfort in his eyes, but that could have just been the lighting.

"Was that my fault?"

It took her a second to fathom what he was asking. Of all the pompous, self-centered... Did he think the whole world revolved around him? That one harsh word from his lips would send her into an all-night sleepless marathon of defunct TV sitcoms on double-digit cable channels?

"No."

He seemed not to hear her answer. Or maybe he just didn't believe it.

"Because if it was, I'm sorry." He bit off the word as if it was utterly distasteful in his mouth. Yet he did look sincere, she thought. Did he think she'd fallen apart, worried about her job, because she's incurred his literary displeasure?

"It wasn't," she said with more feeling than she'd intended. When he looked at her, one eyebrow arched in silent query, she added, "It's a personal matter."

He seized the word as if it was a battle cry. "So's my writing."

Good, they were getting away from her and on to his work. Elisha was in no small way relieved to get into something she knew like the back of her hand. In contrast, this pain she was feeling was something entirely new to her and she wanted it gone. In lieu of that, because she knew that it was hopeless to wish it away, she could try to bury it for the time being.

"Every writer feels that way. Moreover, they feel like every single word they put down is an integral part of them and if anything is done to that word, that line, that page, it's like taking a knife and skewering their heart."

One corner of his mouth lifted slightly in what might have been an amused expression. "Then you're familiar with the process."

"I'm familiar with improving things." They had gotten little farther than the foyer. Turning, she went toe-to-toe with him. "Are you willing to admit that nothing's perfect in this world?"

A glint of suspicion entered his eyes. "Never said it was."

"So if it's not perfect, that leaves an avenue open for improvement. The writing can be tinkered with."

He resented the word and made no bones about letting her see how he felt. Just what the hell did she think she was dealing with, some hack writer? "Tinkering is reserved for old-model cars left up on blocks in the garage. My manuscripts don't need 'tinkering.'" He loomed over her. "Do you even *know* how much revenue I bring in to Randolph & Sons a year?"

It wasn't easy, especially since she was in no mood to stand here, trading slings and arrows, when she could be home, looking for a way to save Henry. But she managed to force a smile to her lips. She did her best to make it seem genuine.

"I bet you know down to the penny."

His eyes narrowed, turning to dark, fearsome slits. "Damn straight I do."

She drew herself up. At her tallest, in her heels, she was five-seven. He was only four inches taller but seemed much more so. Like a shadow that stretches at first sunrise. She wouldn't let his size intimidate her. She was beyond that.

"This isn't about your book bringing in more money."

"Then what *is* it about? About your frustrated desire to be a writer? Do you think that the only way you can achieve it is by taking something that's already done and putting your stamp on it? Is that your master plan, Maxwell?"

For two cents, she could see herself punching him. It would undoubtedly sting, but it would also feel good. But getting fired wouldn't. She needed this job right now to keep her head straight. To keep from falling to pieces. So she answered his accusations instead of telling him where he could put them. "I have no desire to stamp your work, Mr. Sutherland. I just thought that you had it in you to be a really good writer."

She couldn't have insulted him more if she'd tried. His brow turned to dark thunder. "I *am* a really good writer."

He was breathing fire in her space. She didn't budge. "You write pulp, Mr. Sutherland. Good pulp," she allowed quickly before he could say anything about her choice of words. "Pulp that sells like hotcakes. But isn't there something inside you that wants to produce something memorable?"

He eyed her, wondering where she drew her bravado from. He wouldn't have thought her capable of it, looking at her. She irritated the hell out of him, but there was something inside him that did admire her moxie. "Not particularly."

Well, that took the wind out of her sails, Elisha thought. She retreated, feeling oddly saddened at the same time. "Too bad. Because you could."

Critics hated his books. Readers loved them. Critics got books for free. The public paid. As the old cliché went, he knew which side his bread was buttered on. "If it ain't broke, don't fix it."

Maybe she'd misjudged the man within. "I thought you liked taking risks."

"It's obvious that *you* do." His voice was almost malevolent, but his expression entertained another emotion. "Most people don't stand up to me."

"And you like that?" she asked, incredulous. "Being a bully?"

"I like having my authority recognized."

Elisha shook her head. "There's authority, and there's being a bully. Someone like you should know the difference." She took her coat from the rack where she'd hung it. There was nothing more she could do here. He wasn't going to discuss her changes, he was going to vanquish them, one by one. He didn't need her for that. "There's no point in my staying to talk over my notes. We both know you can go over my head and ignore them. Rocky wants you to be happy and to stay with the company."

He glared at her. "And you obviously don't give a damn."

She paused to look at him. "No, you're wrong there. I obviously *do* give a damn. Looks like you're not exactly that much of a judge of character, either." Turning on her heel, she walked to the door. "Don't bother seeing me out."

His voice trailed after her. "Wasn't going to."

CHAPTER 14

Every time she called Henry's cell phone, Elisha literally held her breath. Afraid that there'd be no answer.

It had been almost two weeks since Henry had dropped his bombshell on her and she still hadn't even begun to come to terms with the black specter that had been released into her life. In a way, she felt selfish, focusing on her feelings this way. After all, this wasn't about her, it was about him, about Henry.

And yet, all she could think of was what was she going to do without him. She couldn't even begin to imagine what life would be like without Henry.

She *refused* to imagine what life would be like without him.

The very notion that it could happen made her want to absorb him through every pore of her body. To memorize moments they spent together. He was her little brother. The last of her family.

Granted, there were the girls, but Beth, and even Andrea, were children. Not only that, they were the second generation. Henry was the last one who knew her when she'd had braces. When her hair had been a light blond instead of the descriptionless shade of dark blond it had evolved into. Henry knew her when she used to catch fireflies and put them in a jar, secretly believing that if there was ever a power failure, she could light up the world with them.

Impatiently, she looked at her watch, counting off the seconds. Where *was* he? If something had gone wrong, he would have called, right? Or had someone call for him. Fear began to scramble up the inside of her chest, lodging itself in her throat.

When Henry's voice came through on the other end of the line right after the fifth ring, she didn't bother hiding the sigh of relief.

"Hi, you're still there."

"Still here."

She could hear the smile in his voice. It warmed her. "Did you call that doctor I found for you?"

Patience embedded itself in the warmth. "Elisha, he's a holistic healer."

That was no reason to write the man off. The testimonials to the man had taken up three pages on the Internet. "And maybe he's on to something. What have you got to lose?"

"Time," he told her frankly. "I don't want to spend it chasing my tail. I want to spend it with you and the girls."

She'd been frequenting bookstores, looking through the alternative-medicine sections as well as hitting all the Web sites dealing with the latest medical breakthroughs. Somewhere in all that discovery, in all that rhetoric, there had to be something that would keep Henry on this earth a little longer. The stack of books and notes she'd accumulated were a healthy size. It was time Henry started going through them.

"Well, I'm coming up for dinner tonight, so you're getting that part of your wish." Elisha paused, searching for the right way to segue into her question. There wasn't one. But this was Henry and he was used to her jumping from topic to topic, so she jumped. "Have you told them yet?"

She heard him taking in a breath before answering. Was that just a coincidence, or was he hurting? She was afraid to ask that question. "Yes."

Okay, one hurdle down. She took the next, the one that

meant he was convinced he was going to win. "And did you also tell them that their daddy is going to lick this thing?"

Henry laughed shortly, but she couldn't tell if there was a smile on his face when he said, "Yes, I told them all the appropriate lies, Elisha."

She knew he always wanted to be truthful with the girls. But he wasn't militant about it. The truth took on many shapes and he would never knowingly strip his daughters of their safety net.

"They're not lies, Henry. Dammit, I told you that you have to believe that you're going to get well, otherwise, it won't work."

"This isn't an old stage production of *Peter Pan*, Elisha. You don't just clap your hands and make Tinker Bell live. I'm afraid that this is a little bit more involved than that."

"Faith can move mountains."

"It helps if you have dynamite on your side."

This time she did hear the smile in his voice. It heartened her a little. "That's what I'm looking for. Dynamite."

"Keep looking, Lise. I'm not trying to discourage you."

"Good, because you can't."

That was for the wee hours of the night, when she'd lie awake, staring at her ceiling, feeling hopelessly overwhelmed. Wondering why things arranged themselves the way they did. Why they couldn't be the way she wanted them to be.

Elisha thought of the pile of books and articles on her coffee table at home. "I've got some more things I found for you."

"I look forward to seeing them."

Her mouth curved even as she shook her head. Some things didn't change. Henry was still the one trying to comfort her instead of the other way around. Even during that awful period when his wife had died, Henry was the one who'd ultimately wound up comforting everyone. Her, the girls, Rachel's best friends. When did he get the privilege to break down?

Elisha caught her lower lip between her teeth. She didn't want to think about it.

"Okay, then it's settled. I'm coming over tonight. Don't go to any trouble, by the way. Since I'm inviting myself over, I'm bringing dinner."

"Pizza?"

She laughed. "I'm too predictable."

Henry was nothing if not supportive. For just a second, it felt as if the other thing, that darkness that loomed over their lives, was just a lie. "Hey, don't underestimate that. It's nice to have some things to count on. Seven?"

The receiver nestled between her ear and shoulder, she was already looking through her BlackBerry for the number of the pizzeria she called that was near Henry's place. "Earlier if I can get away and the traffic doesn't make a saint cry."

"See you then."

"Bye."

She was just hanging up the receiver when her phone buzzed. Henry's light hadn't gone out yet, so the call was coming in on her second line. Elisha paused a second as the words suddenly hit her.

Henry's light hadn't gone out yet.

And God willing, it won't, she thought before she switched to the second line. Locating the number for the pizza parlor, she placed the BlackBerry on her desk and turned her full attention to the call.

"Elisha Reed."

"Elisha, this is Sinclair. I'm just back from my tour. My head is still spinning." The deep chuckle rang in her ear. Sinclair sounded very pleased with himself. The tour must have gone very well. With any luck, he could live off the fumes of all that goodwill for several weeks. Long enough to guide him into his new project. "This is New York City, right?"

"Right. All eight million of us, stuffed onto a little island."

"Which brings me to my next point," Sinclair said. "Are you free for lunch?"

These days, she didn't seem to have an appetite. Eating was a low priority. She'd intended on spending lunch today the way she had the last two weeks, checking all the sites she now knew by heart, looking for something new to have been put on since the last time. That one new thing that might point her to the right path that would eventually lead to arresting her brother's condition, or perhaps even, please God, sending it into remission.

She was making deals with God on a daily basis now, bartering for time, just a little more time. Every new day was precious.

On the other end of the line, Sinclair seemed to interpret the silence in his own way. He, like everyone else, was aware of how hard she could work.

"Because if you're not free for lunch," he continued, "I'll bring lunch to you. Or if it's a matter of another author sucking up your time, I'm feeling too good to sulk about it. I'll just take you out to dinner."

To Sinclair, dinner before eight wasn't civilized. By then she intended to be well into her visit with Henry and the girls. "I'm afraid that dinner's not possible, Sinclair."

She heard him make a disparaging noise. "Dinner's always possible." And then his voice brightened, taking on a hopeful note. "Unless it's a hot date."

The man was like a favorite grandfather. One who believed that God had intended the people of the world to exist in pairs. He'd even attempted to play matchmaker once, until she made it perfectly clear that her single status was not something she lamented but, for the most part, enjoyed. If he'd had the slightest inkling that it was by resignation, the man would have been off and running, searching for possible mates for her.

"I'm seeing my brother and his daughters tonight." It wasn't necessary to say anything more, even if she was able to.

"Ah, family. Very important, family. Don't know what I'd do without mine." And then he chuckled. They both knew he had a family that at times made the Addams Family appear normal in comparison. "Of course, I like keeping them at arm's length because as wonderful as having family around is, not having them around at times is pretty damn wonderful, too." Dropping the topic, he reconnoitered. "So, is it settled? Lunch?"

She supposed that the Internet wasn't going anywhere. Besides, there was that old adage about a watched pot. Maybe by tonight, there would be something new on it worth reading.

"Lunch," she agreed.

"I'll come by to pick you up at eleven-thirty. Brace yourself, I intend to tell you all about my adventures, especially about the woman who wanted me to autograph all the copies of my books that she had in her den." This time, the chuckle was very earthy.

"Sounds like someone had a very good time," she commented, doing her best to sound enthusiastic for his sake.

She genuinely liked Sinclair. He'd been her first author of renown and she found him very easy to talk to. When he wasn't going through a crisis about writer's block, he was very entertaining. Riding high on his success, she had no doubt that he would sound just like an animated version of one of his books—chatty, fast-paced and exuberant, with a dash of mystery thrown in every so often. With any luck, she'd give him his lead today and he would do all the talking for the rest of the meal.

Elisha closed her eyes, suddenly feeling exhausted. Since Henry had told her his diagnosis, she'd been averaging only four hours of sleep a night. With the least little bit of encouragement, she could easily just fall asleep.

When her eyes drooped down a second time, she forced herself up to her feet. She had an hour before Sinclair came to take her away to lunch. An hour in which she had to get some kind of work done. She hated not being productive. With a sigh, she rose to her feet and headed out of her office, down the hall to the newly renovated ladies' room.

Work had been completed three weeks ago, but the area still smelled faintly of paint. She tried not to notice. Paint gave her a headache.

Elisha turned on the faucet and cupped her hands beneath it to catch the water. Taking in a breath, she brought the water to her face. All it succeeded in doing was washing away the minimal makeup she'd remembered to put on this morning.

For a second, she looked at her reflection. The lighting in bathrooms was designed to make everyone look like a wraith, she decided. She really did look like hell, she thought, recalling Sutherland's less-than-heartwarming greeting the last time she'd seen him.

She hadn't heard a peep out of him since then. Was that a good sign? To hell with signs. Right now, she didn't care. All she cared about was that Henry would be around to help her celebrate her birthday next April.

And after April came, there'd be another goal to meet. She intended to continue updating goals indefinitely, until Henry wound up outliving her.

Stranger things had happened.

CHAPTER 15

"Is something wrong?"

The question came from behind her. Raising her head and looking into the mirror, Elisha realized that one of the bathroom stalls had been occupied when she'd entered. Carole came out, doing her best to summon a look of concern on her perfectly made-up, heart-shaped face.

Dammit, she should have checked first to make sure that she was alone. Not that she'd cried, thank God. But she looked as if she had been crying and heaven only knew what Carole would create out of this nothing of a scene. Elisha had no doubt that if there was a way, the woman would attempt to use this to try to advance herself. She had no idea how, but then, she'd never wanted to further her career by walking on top of dead bodies.

Elisha took a deep breath, peeling back a smile so far, the corners of her mouth hurt. "Not a thing." And then, because women didn't just throw water into their faces for no reason, she had to say something. "I'm just a little tired, that's all."

Instantly, the woman in the tight, powder-blue power suit took her cue. Though they were standing practically hip to hip at the counter, their eyes met in the mirror. "Well, if you like, I could take over a few things for you, free you up so that you can go home early and get some rest." Carole turned her head to look at her directly. Triumph lit her eyes. "You really do look as if you need it."

"What I need," Elisha replied cheerfully, not the easiest feat to accomplish through clenched teeth, "is to get back to work."

Like a shark on the scent of blood, the nubile blonde refused to back away. A confidential note entered her voice. "Mr. Randolph told me he thinks you really should delegate more."

She wasn't going to let the little witch get to her, Elisha promised herself. Carole obviously smelled a moment of weakness and was trying to move in for the kill—or at the very least, move in.

Sorry, honey, no vacancies, not today.

"Mr. Randolph says a lot of things," Elisha replied with a calmness she didn't feel. She could see the way the would-be senior editor was looking at her, as if Carole was waiting for her to admit to having one foot in the grave.

Elisha slanted a glance at herself in the mirror. She was losing weight, not by design, and her clothing was beginning to hang on her frame. This was definitely *not* one of her best days. Apart from better-fitting clothing, she really did need to learn what to do with makeup so that she didn't resemble someone from the cast of *Night of the Living Dead*.

On her way out, Elisha paused to give Carole one last, phony smile. "I wouldn't take Mr. Randolph's words to heart if I were you." She turned away and crossed to the outer door. "Provided you can find your heart." The last was said under her breath as she made her exit.

Elisha returned to her office, determined to get something done in the hour before Sinclair arrived. She supposed she couldn't really fault Rocky if he'd actually said what Carole claimed he'd said to her. The man meant well, he just didn't understand what kind of person Carole Chambers was. Being born the heir apparent to Randolph & Sons Publishing, Rocky had no idea about the kind of back-stabbing melodrama that could and did go on in the business world.

The literary world was no different, given the wrong set of people. For the most part, Elisha found that she got along very well with the other senior editors. Happily, that extended to most of the rising editors and assistant editors, as well. But every species had its piranha and Randolph & Sons had Carole.

Well, Carole Chambers wasn't going to be feasting on her flesh anytime soon, Elisha silently promised herself as she slipped back behind her desk.

Especially not while she was still breathing.

Sinclair Jones stuck his leonine head into her office at exactly eleven-thirty. His blue eyes shining and nearly lost in the depths of his smile, the author strode in, slightly larger than life despite his five-ten stature, and lifted her up out of her chair. Elisha found herself folded into a big, grandfatherly hug with absolutely no preamble or warning.

If she was given to heart attacks, she might have had one.

"There's the world's best editor," Sinclair declared heartily. His snow-white beard grazed her cheek a second before he brushed a chaste kiss against it.

Trying to catch her breath, Elisha returned the man's hug in kind as best she could. When he was in the throes of enthusiasm, Sinclair lost track of his own strength. On occasion, ribs were bruised.

She tried to match his smile. She really did like the man and enjoyed his company, both professionally and personally. But these days her heart did not go easily into things without effort. She was still reeling, still ricocheting between being wildly hopeful and incredibly frightened, neither of which meshed very well with the nature of her work.

"You're only saying that because it's true."

He laughed, stepping back, but not before catching her hand

in his. Gently, he began to draw her over to the doorway. "I hope you're hungry because I'm ordering everything on the menu. We'll share."

She knew how he could get. Like a child with a sweet tooth let loose for the first time in a candy store. Her eyes met his. One of them had to be the grown-up here. "What did the doctor say about your cholesterol?"

He chuckled. "That it's alive and well and so am I." He tugged on her hand. "Come, don't spoil this, Elisha. I'm fresh from an absolutely fantastic high." In the middle of his entreaty, he stopped to share his latest discovery. "Did you know I have fans in this funny little place in New Mexico called Truth or Consequence? I've never heard of the place. The show, yes," he clarified quickly, "but not the place." And then he positively beamed. "But apparently they have heard of me."

She didn't wonder. The publicity department had gone all out, getting Sinclair's face in a dozen different ads. This was going to be his biggest blockbuster. Albeit not like Sutherland's, but then Sutherland was in a category by himself.

"That's because you're famous."

His grin got wider, spreading out the white whiskers even more. "I am, aren't I?"

Like a kid tempted to pinch himself in order to prove to himself that all this was true, he stared for a long moment at the outer trappings of his success. In this case, his five-hundred-dollar designer jacket. He raised his eyes to Elisha again.

"I still can't really believe it. I mean, I know it's true because they were lined up at all the bookstores, waiting for my autograph, and I see those royalty checks that come in twice a year, but sometimes, I just step back and shake my head in wonder. Inside—" Sinclair tapped his barrel chest with a closed fist "—I'm still that guy cleaning out the saloon in Waco, Texas. Dreaming of better things."

She patted his hand. "Well, you don't have to dream anymore. It's all true."

"It wouldn't have been if you hadn't rescued that first manuscript of mine out of the slush pile. That manuscript that had gotten a thousand rejections."

Her mouth quirked in amusement. "Remember what I told you about exaggerating?" It was one of the few things that she red-lined in the margins of his manuscripts. He had a tendency to go overboard.

"I'm not exaggerating," he protested. "I've got the rejection slips to prove it." He sobered just the slightest bit, a twelve on the Richter scale going down to an eleven point nine. "To keep me humble in case I ever get a big head."

"Big heart." Standing beside him, Elisha affectionately patted his ample chest area with her hand. "You have a big heart, Sinclair, not a big head," she assured him. "If your head hasn't gone up several inches in the last fifteen years, I'd bet even money that it's never going to."

She flashed a smile at him with far less effort than the previous one had taken. "Now, where is the man who used to clean out a saloon in Waco, Texas, planning on taking me for lunch?"

"Anywhere you want to go," he told her expansively. "The sky's the limit—and I mean it," he added.

Sinclair sounded as if he wanted to make an afternoon of it. But one of them still had several things to see to before the close of day. Elisha looked at her watch and slowly shook her head to the unspoken part of his offer. "I've only got an hour. The sky's going to have to be close by."

Undaunted, he agreed with feeling. "Close it is. I know just the place."

He crossed to the rack by the door where she'd hung her suit jacket this morning. Sinclair took it off the hook and stood waiting to help her slip on the outer garment.

Her back to him, she let him play the gentleman. "You know, courtly manners like yours went out a long time ago."

She turned to face him again as he answered, "They should make a comeback. Men like to treat women like ladies."

Elisha had no idea why Sinclair's comment made her think of Sutherland, or the way the other author had stood there, like a huge, uncouth bore, telling her that he wasn't about to bother showing her the way out of his apartment. Not that a safari guide was in order, but a drop of gallantry would have been nice. Sutherland could stand to learn a thing or two from Sinclair.

After buttoning her jacket, she picked up her purse and smiled at him. "You're a rare man, Sinclair."

"I like to think so." Slipping his arm around her shoulders, he ushered her out of the office. "So, did I tell you that I have a brand-new idea for a mystery?"

She paused long enough to pull the door closed behind them. "No, but I knew you would."

He laughed dryly. "That makes you one up on me, Elisha. I always think that the last book I wrote will be *the last book I wrote*," he said with emphasis. "And that there aren't any more ideas left in my head."

"I don't believe you for a minute," she informed him lightly. "There are lots of ideas left in your head, Sinclair. And they'll come when you summon them to come."

"That's why I love having you in my life, Elisha. You make me feel so confident."

"Part of my job, Sinclair. Part of my job." And then she did smile. "As well as my pleasure."

"Mine, too."

His booming laugh rang out as they stepped out in the hallway and walked toward the elevators.

CHAPTER 16

"What do you mean you can't stay for a meeting?" Rocky stared at Elisha. "You always stay," he protested.

This was the third late-afternoon meeting in as many days. Twice she'd reluctantly put things on hold and remained, to pilot the meetings as well as participate in them because Rocky liked handing the reins over to her. But not tonight. She couldn't. Who knew how many more evenings with Henry she had left?

She hated the thought, but running from it accomplished nothing and robbed her of precious time. "I know. But I've got a family emergency."

"What kind of emergency?"

She really, really didn't want to go into it. So far, she hadn't shared news of Henry's condition with anyone. "Dinner."

Rocky seemed baffled. "Dinner's an emergency? Lise, you're not making any sense. Now, I know that it's a little late to be calling a meeting without any warning, especially since I'd said yesterday that there wouldn't be another one today, but this really wasn't my idea. My 'won't-stay-retired' father wanted all the senior editors to get together for a little brainstorming session. Seems he thinks that adding another line to the stable is a good idea and he wants to see what you all come up with."

This time she intended to remain firm. Her resolve was

stronger than Rocky's and they both knew it. "My brain doesn't storm after five o'clock anymore, Rocky. It just lies there."

His look told her that he wasn't buying. "I know this is the third meeting in a row, Lise, and I'm really sorry about it. But if you're going to come up with an excuse, it has to be a better one than you're not up to brainstorming. We've all seen what you can do. Hell, I've seen you work practically around the clock that time we needed John Spencer's book in the lineup after Randall flaked out on us," he said, mentioning one of their former editors.

"That was a onetime event," she pointed out. "I don't do that on a regular basis. I'm not a robot." She realized that she was beginning to sound a little testy and she didn't mean to, not with Rocky. Despite his title, he was just the messenger here. It wasn't his fault. "Besides, I really do have previous plans."

Leaning his posterior against her desk, Rocky crossed his arms before his shallow chest and looked at her, a shadow of a man dressed in black. "The dinner."

"The dinner."

Rocky softened slightly. "With a guy?"

She almost laughed out loud. That part of her life was behind her. "Rocky, there hasn't been 'a guy' in my life in the way you mean for a very long time. It really is family."

"So, if it's family, it can be put off."

"No," she said firmly in a tone she never used with him, "it can't."

"Elisha, what's going on? Something's up and you're not leveling with me."

She looked away. "Nothing's up."

"Lise, I'm a hell of a lot more intuitive than the average man on the street, certainly more so than my father ever was. I'm too damn sensitive for my own good and my sensitivity level tells me that something's wrong." He turned her face toward him.

"Now, out with it." And then he stiffened. "Oh, damn, are those tears? Tell me those aren't tears."

She measured the words out evenly. Anything else and she would have choked. Emotion had come swarming out of nowhere to overwhelm her. "They're not tears."

Rocky frowned. "I don't believe you."

One tear trickled out. Annoyed, she rubbed it away with the back of her hand. "I'm just repeating your own damn dialogue, Rocky—"

He caught her hands in his and forced her to look at him. "Okay, I'm not your boss, not the guy whose head is going to be on the chopping block if I don't deliver my best senior editor to the meeting—"

Elisha was clutching at straws, trying desperately to divert the conversation from the direction it was headed. "You never called me your best senior editor," she sniffed. She hated herself for giving way to tears when she was trying so hard to be strong. So hard not to think of anything beyond the single moment she was living in.

"Didn't want you to get a swelled head," he told her gently. "But you are. And stop interrupting." He resumed his speech, "Don't think of me in any professional capacity at all. Just think of me as your friend. Someone you've known for twenty-four years. Someone who cares about you." When she began to turn her face away, he inclined his head, peering at her. "Someone who's shared his own traumas with you."

And then, because she couldn't hold them back any longer, the words just burst out, almost on their own. "Henry has cancer."

"Is it serious?" His tongue felt thick in his mouth. "I mean, of course it's serious, cancer is always serious. But it can be treated, right?" He watched her carefully.

"I keep hoping…" And then, just for a fraction of a second, Elisha's hope deserted her. "It's pancreatic cancer."

The air stood still around them. The street noise below grew distant. His eyes intent on her face, Rocky said nothing and seemed stricken.

Finally, he drew in a breath, as if that could somehow protect them both. "How much time…?"

Elisha shook her head violently, not allowing him to finish the question. Not wanting him to. "I haven't asked him. I don't want to know," she confessed. "I just want every minute I can find to count." She looked at him, knowing he understood even if she was being incoherent. "So, you see, I—"

"Go," he said, waving her toward the door. "Go see your brother. Be with him."

She lost no time in gathering up her jacket and purse, then stopped. She *was* leaving him in the lurch and as much as she wanted to leave, she hated to do that to him. "What about your father?"

"I'll deal with him."

He'd said that way too cavalierly. She smiled at him, gratitude in her eyes. "Rocky, you're afraid of your father."

Sparse shoulders shrugged beneath the burgundy cashmere sweater. "So, I'll let him bully me around a little bit. He won't do it in front of the others. Thank God he's got this thing about maintaining decorum before 'the troops.'" His mouth twisted in an ironic smile. "You would have thought the man was a career soldier instead of someone who'd donated a little time to the army reserves in his twenties." And then Rocky tried to smile, offering Elisha what he hoped was some kind of positive energy. "Let me know if there's anything I can do."

Miracles were out of Rocky's realm. Still, she was grateful for the offer. "I might need a shoulder."

"I've got two." As if to emphasize the fact, he raised and lowered his in an almost comical fashion. "They're not too wide and they're kind of bony, but they're yours if you need them."

She could feel the tears coming again. She needed to leave before they materialized. Once was more than enough. "Thanks, Rocky."

She was almost at the door when he called after her. "Wait."

Elisha turned around, afraid that his fear of his father had gotten the better of him. Afraid that she was going to have to ignore any last-minute plea that might be rising to his lips. She really needed to see Henry tonight. It had been three days since the last time and those were three days she wasn't going to be able to recover.

A sense of fatalism warred with her natural tendency toward optimism. "What?"

"Henry lives on the island, right?"

"Right."

"So—" he crossed to her "—you're going to need transportation."

"I'm getting a cab." That was the one thing she could always count on. The city was always full of taxis looking for a fare.

But Rocky was shaking his head. "Forget the cab. We have a limo at our disposal." He wasn't telling her anything she didn't know. The limo was used to pick up out-of-town authors at the airport, as well as to chauffeur them around when they were visiting. In the off times, Rocky used the limo to take him to and from his apartment. "I'll have Tom drive you."

"You don't have to do that."

"Sure I do. I just cost you time, arguing about coming to this afternoon's meeting." She knew Rocky felt bad about what she'd told him. This was his way of trying to help. "Besides, Tom is a genius when it comes to maneuvering through traffic. You'd swear you were on a motorcycle instead of in a limo. And he knows more shortcuts than Rand McNally. I guarantee he'll get you there faster than any cabdriver. And in comfort, too. You won't spend half the ride to the island trying to figure out 'what that smell is.'"

"Comfort's not very high up on my priority list, but okay. I'll take you up on your offer." Impulsively, she kissed his cheek. "And thanks."

Caught off guard, Rocky brushed his long, thin fingers along his skin where her lips had touched him. The look on his face told Elisha he wished he could do more. "Don't mention it."

Giving her an encouraging smile, he took out his cell phone and pressed the preassigned number that would connect him to his limo driver.

Behind them, in the hall, senior editors and an assorted number of staff members were beginning to file by, on their way to the conference room. Rocky purposely kept his back to the doorway.

CHAPTER 17

Elisha discovered optimism only went so far. Even hers. In their second or third meeting, Ryan Sutherland had accused her of being a terminal optimist, saying that the only cure for that was reality.

She hated the fact that the man was right.

As the days and hours of the past month had dried up and blown away, she had begun to feel like someone addicted to pistachio nuts who had been presented with a bag filled with them. And none of the nuts had an opening, not so much as a tiny, split crack that she could pry apart in order to get at the green meat housed within.

None of the doctors she'd had Henry go and see had anything encouraging to say.

It was like living in a world stocked with an endless supply of futility.

Henry, being Henry, had decided to continue living his life by going to work, treating each day as just that, a day. A single day in his life. He wanted to go on working at the law firm for as long as he was able.

Though he was a hell of a lot braver than she was, she believed that a part of her brother had to hope that by continuing as before the diagnosis, by putting little importance to this devastating sentence, this hideous six-letter plague would somehow just wind up fading back into the darkness from whence it had emerged.

Henry might have continued with his life, but things changed for her. She still went in to work, but she lit candles, she prayed. She made endless deals with God in which hers was the only voice that was heard.

"It's okay," she said as she deposited into an envelope yet another check for one of the myriad charities that sent letters of entreaty to her. "You don't have to move the earth, or send a dove past my window to show me you're listening. Just make Henry get better. That'll be my sign."

Never heavy to begin with, Henry began to lose weight and it showed, really showed. Elisha stepped up her prayers and contributions. She couldn't outrun the nervous, restless feeling that tumbled throughout her body like a malfunctioning dryer.

At the end of the month, she told Rocky she was taking Friday off in order to turn it into a three-day weekend. Her intent was to surprise Henry and the girls by whisking them off to Walt Disney World in Orlando. Rocky had insisted on lending her his father's private plane and paying for the accommodations at the Disneyland Hotel.

She didn't argue.

The trip was hard on Henry physically, revitalizing emotionally. Being Henry, he'd soldiered on without complaint, pretending not to be as tired as he was. Like her, he wanted this to be a memorable outing for Andrea and Beth.

The entire time they were at Walt Disney World, Beth hung on to his hand as if someone had dropped a tube of superglue between them. Her ten-year-old enthusiasm bubbling up, she dragged her father off first in one direction, and then another, wanting him to see the same exciting things that she did.

He saw them through her eyes and loved it.

He loved it all, even the lines. Because he was with the three people who mattered most in his life and he was all the richer for it.

Elisha could see her brother's pleasure, his satisfaction in his drawn face. Though she knew the trip was tiring for him, she honestly felt that this was a great deal better for him than staying home, keeping a death watch.

In contrast to Beth's exuberance, Andrea was almost eerily quiet, observing it all like a section of background scenery. It was easy to see that she was torn between denial and dreaded acceptance of her father's fate. Having fun almost made her feel guilty.

But, because it meant so much to Henry, the girl did her best. They all did.

Pretending for one another, Elisha noted. Pretense was all they had. That, and the moment.

They spent two nights at the Disneyland Hotel in a major suite. Rocky had insisted on that, too. She smiled to herself, the only genuine smile since she'd swung by early Friday morning to pick the three of them up and take them to the airport. In the limo that Rocky had provided. There was no doubt about it. Rockefeller Randolph was one in a million.

Too bad that all the good guys were either taken or gay, she thought. If Garry had displayed half the thoughtfulness, half the sensitivity that Rocky did most of the time, she would have proposed to him on their first date. But there were no princes in her world. No one to ride up on a white charger to whisk her away to his castle in the sky. That was something she'd come to terms with years ago. But being subjected to Rocky's generous spirit inexplicably made her ache for what she once had believed was possible.

Dammit, there she went again, thinking of herself. She wasn't the major player here, Henry was. She was just a lesser, supporting character. And she was going to be as supportive as she possibly could be.

Elisha looked at her brother sitting beside her on the plane. After three days, they were finally on their way home. Henry looked wan. Maybe she should have made the minivacation for only a day or a day and a half at the most. With each passing day, his strength left him a little more, dribbling away like tears of heartbreak. She didn't want to be the cause of any more depletion.

She caught her bottom lip between her teeth. "Was the trip too much for you?"

Sitting in the seats directly opposite them, Beth had fallen asleep more than fifteen minutes ago, her head leaning against Andrea's arm. Andrea sat perfectly still, her eyes staring straight ahead at her father and yet, through her father. Her face was expressionless. She looked like an ice sculpture.

Andrea worried Elisha.

"It wasn't too much for me," he assured her, stopping to take a breath in the middle of his words. "Nothing's too much for me as long as I spend the time with all three of my favorite girls." His mouth quirked in a fleeting smile. "Thanks for doing this for me."

She moved her fingers in the air, as if to stir away the thanks.

"You don't have to thank me, Henry. I wanted to do this. I've been meaning to get away and visit the Mouse for some time." And then she lifted and lowered her shoulders in a halfhearted shrug. "But you know how it is. Time just had a way of getting away from me."

He turned his head to face her. "Yes, I know how it is. And I can say this to you. Don't let it," he said with feeling, though it was hard for him. Someone was shooting arrows into his stomach. Large, pointy, stinging arrows. "Don't let time slip through your fingers, Lise. Don't retreat from life. And, above all, don't live it through the books you work on."

"I don't," she protested, then lowered her voice when Andrea looked in her direction. She thought of the two books she had worked on last and then laughed at the idea of vicarious living. "Besides, I don't exactly see myself as an aging sleuth or a gungho ex-commando, scaling the sides of villas in Switzerland," she said, mentioning both Sinclair Jones's and Ryan Sutherland's most famous characters.

Trying to picture her as one or the other, Henry started to laugh. Almost immediately he began to cough, clutching his abdomen.

Her entire body was on alert as fear scissored through Elisha.

"Can I get you anything?" she asked, ready to summon the steward that Rocky employed on board. "Water? Um—"

Words dried in her throat.

Helpless, she was utterly helpless and she hated it. Henry was right in his assessment. Somehow, without fully realizing just when it had happened, she had slipped off to the sidelines. There she had allowed life to whirl madly out of control around her while she handled one literary emergency after another. In the meanwhile, the big picture, her life, just went on evolving without any thought to it on her part, without any intervention on her part whatsoever.

That had to change. But later. Not now. Now belonged to Henry.

Getting himself under control, determined not to allow the sharp pain he felt to overwhelm him, Henry waved back her concern.

"No, I'm fine. Really," he added, trying to muster more feeling into his voice because Andrea was watching him with wide, frightened eyes. "Really," he repeated, smiling at his oldest daughter. "Just drew in a little air and saliva, that's all," he explained. "Went down the wrong way."

Exhaling, he settled back in his seat once more and allowed

Elisha to fuss over him for a moment because he knew she needed to. He smiled as he watched her adjusting the blanket that she'd thrown over his legs. "I'm not some infirm old man, Lise."

"I know that," she said sharply. "Can't a big sister fuss over her little brother once in a while?"

"This would be the once, not the while," he teased.

Elisha didn't much feel like teasing back. Not when all this adrenaline was coursing through her veins like molten lava flowing down the mountainside from an erupting volcano.

Sitting back, she looked at him. "Maybe you should take Monday off," she suggested. When she saw the protest rising to her brother's lips, she quickly headed it off. "After all, it's not like they're going to fire you for skipping a day." And then she smiled at him. "You're too important to them."

"They'll get along fine without me." He raised his eyes to hers and added softly, so that Andrea could not hear, "You all will."

"No," she replied as fiercely as she could without waking Beth, "we won't."

There was nothing but kindness and understanding in his eyes. He remembered how he had felt when Rachel had died. Like the world had ended. But it hadn't. It went on. It was something Elisha and the girls would learn, too. "You're going to have to."

She stiffened her shoulders. "Don't tell me what I have to do," Elisha retorted, then she softened, fussing with the blanket again. "Just because you're not feeling well right now, Henry, doesn't mean you get to boss me around."

"So if I ask you to thank Rocky for me for all this," he bantered, "you won't do it?"

She blew out a breath and then laughed lightly. She'd already thanked Rocky. Several times. But this time, it would be coming from Henry. Rocky would appreciate that. "That I'll do."

Henry settled back, a wistful expression slipped over his face. He wasn't going to see his girls grow up, wasn't going to see them fall in love. Wasn't going to see them get married. Wasn't even going to be able to see that happen for Elisha.

He turned his head to look at his sister's concerned face. "He would have made a great guy for you. Too bad he's gay."

She laughed, really laughed, the tension breaking for a moment. It was uncanny how much they thought alike. "I was just thinking the same thing."

CHAPTER 18

"What the hell makes you think that you have the slightest idea about what goes on in a black-ops world?" Ryan Sutherland demanded as he strode into her office without so much as a knock on her door. He slammed the same door in his wake.

The vibrations, or maybe it was the gust of wind he'd created, made the remainder of her cold coffee slosh dangerously in her mug. Had her cup been full, it wouldn't have stayed that way one second into his dramatic entrance. And the pages she'd spent half the morning working on, reading and rereading because her mind insisted on wandering instead of absorbing, would have been rendered a disconcerting shade of deep brown.

Elisha was just hanging up the telephone receiver after a lengthy forty-five-minute conversation with Sinclair. Though she loved him dearly, both on the page and off, he was, until Sutherland had been tossed into her life, the most taxing of all her authors. Her part of the conversation had consisted of trying to reinflate the man's suddenly roadkill-flat self-esteem.

Between talking up Sinclair's flatlining ego and sparring with some very dark thoughts about her brother's swiftly deteriorating condition, Elisha felt completely drained. There wasn't an upbeat, friendly bone left in her body. Certainly not any words that might remotely lead a person to believe that she was capable of sustaining that mood.

The last person she felt like taking on right now was Ryan Sutherland. But wishing him away wasn't about to work. Glancing at her cup to make sure no damage had been done, she then raised her eyes to her intruder. Better to end her silence than allow his fuming to continue.

"Because I have expertise and an imagination, not necessarily in that order," she said, answering the question he'd just shouted at her. Sporting what appeared to be a week's growth on his face, Sutherland looked more the part of an angry backwoodsman than an author who regularly occupied the first slot on the *New York Times* best-seller list. He also acted the part of the aforementioned backwoodsman. "Didn't your mother ever teach you how to knock?" The question came out sounding more tart than she'd intended, but she wasn't sorry.

Sailors at sea watching an approaching squall were privy to more sunshine than she saw now on Sutherland's face. At the mention of the female contributor to his gene pool, the man's expression had gone from highly annoyed to a place she had no way of describing.

"My mother didn't teach me anything," he informed her angrily.

His voice seemed to be coming from a deep, dark place. It occurred to her that she had absolutely no knowledge of his background. All she knew about Ryan Sutherland was that he was forty-eight and had been a Navy SEAL. Speculation had it that at one time or another, one of the alphabet-soup government agencies, one that wasn't widely known by the public at large, had used him as a covert operative. Others said he'd hired out as a mercenary for several years.

But as to Sutherland's origins, if he had any family, or what he did to unwind, none of that was common knowledge to her. She'd been remiss, Elisha suddenly thought, upbraiding herself. She knew everything there was about her other authors—their birthdays, their marital status, what teams they followed and what they liked and disliked, but nothing about Sutherland. But then, Sutherland had been shoehorned into her life at a time when her emotional world had been set on its ear, and he hadn't exactly been a font of information himself.

Besides, the man irritated the hell out of her.

"Sorry to hear that," she finally murmured. Rallying, she flashed a somewhat less-than-sincere smile. "Then let me be the first to tell you, doors are for knocking on if they're closed."

Elisha was surprised to see something like a half smile emerge on Sutherland's lips. They were sensual, she caught herself thinking. The man had great luck when it came to women, she'd recalled hearing. Part of it had to be that smile. It certainly wasn't because of his charming manner.

Looking at it, she couldn't tell if the smile was sarcastic or if he was amused. If it was the latter, it was undoubtedly at her expense—as in she'd forgotten to wipe away traces of the jelly doughnut that had been her breakfast from her mouth, or worse, from her cheek.

Trying not to be self-conscious or obvious, Elisha brushed her fingers first along the outline of her lips, then against her right cheek. She bided her time before she brushed them against the left one.

She got her answer in the next moment. "According to what you edited, you would have been blown away in your first five minutes as a black-ops agent."

"Maybe not."

For the life of her, Elisha had no idea where the retort or the feeling behind it had come from. She was as suited to his former life as she was to being the lead ballerina in the Bolshoi Ballet.

Less.

But there was something very galling about Ryan Sutherland's brand of supremacy. Try as she might to ignore it, exposure to Ryan raised a very real, overwhelming desire within her to put him in his place.

"Lady, there's no way that you could have survived in my world. You couldn't have handled it." Ryan turned the idea of her existing in his world over in his mind and then laughed. "Hell, you couldn't have even handled the recreation part."

"Drinking and whoring?" she heard herself asking. "I'd take a pass on the whoring, but I can hold my own drinking." It wasn't something she had even remarked on once she was out of college. What was it about this man that suddenly made her want to compete with and best him?

Ryan's eyebrows rose like dark crescents on his forehead.

Amusement, it was definitely amusement that she saw there, Elisha thought. He was laughing at her, damn him. If it wouldn't have meant defeat, she would have marched out of her office into Rocky's to demand that he place Sutherland with some other poor soul as his editor. But that would have been crying uncle and she wasn't about to give Sutherland that satisfaction.

"Poker," he counted.

Lost in her own thoughts, she wasn't sure she had heard him correctly. She stared at him. "Excuse me?"

This time, the smile went a little deeper into her. Like a second layer of skin toning. "We played poker to ease the tension."

Poker. Memories came flooding back. Memories like one endless, hot summer when her father had taught both her and Henry the fine art of the game. Taught them that winning at poker wasn't just about luck but about skill. Mostly about skill. His intention had really been to teach Henry, but her sense of competition had won her father over and he'd taught her, as well. And she had become the better player because it meant more to her to win than it did to Henry.

Henry had always been more noble than she was.

She looked at Ryan now, thinking how much she'd like to wipe some of that smugness away. "I play poker."

The amusement on his face grew. He leaned over the desk, close enough for her to taste his words as he asked, "Sure you're not confusing it with gin rummy? Or old maid?"

Something went very rigid inside her. Paula had been right. The editor's last words as she'd stormed out of Rocky's office had been to peg Sutherland. A male chauvinist pig. Not very original, but damn accurate.

"Poker," Elisha repeated with feeling, her voice low, her eyes never leaving his. "Five-card stud, Texas hold 'em, Omaha, five-card draw, you name it, I've played it." Atlantic City with its casinos had been a favorite place for short, usually profitable vacations, when she'd had the time for them.

The smirk on his face was a thing of the past as Ryan regarded her with genuine interest.

Looks were obviously deceiving, he thought. At least in her case. He'd been away from his old world too long. Otherwise, this wouldn't have been a surprise to him.

"You're intriguing me, Max." He cocked his head slightly, still making up his mind. "Or are you just lying to impress me?"

She rose from her chair, five foot seven of indignation in small, stacked black heels. "In the first place, I don't lie—"

Everyone lied. But she looked so sincere, he decided to play along. "Ever?"

"Ever," she retorted with feeling. "And in the second place, I have absolutely no desire to impress you, Mr. Sutherland. The only thing I want from you is for you to reach your full potential as a writer."

She was back to insulting him, and Ryan banked down a flare of annoyance. "I have."

"No, you haven't."

He blew out a breath, struggling to keep his cool.

"And those notes you scribbled down in the margins of my manuscript—'take this a step further,' 'what's he thinking at this point?' garbage like that—" it took effort to keep his language clean when he wanted to vent, but one thing he had schooled himself in was restricting his profanity to the company of men "—that's going to make me a better writer." It wasn't so much a question as a jeer.

"In a word? Yes."

Pacing around her office to let off steam, Ryan laughed at her. It was either that or breaking his word to himself about the use of profanity in mixed company.

His steps brought him back to her desk where he stood in silence and glared at her for a long moment. "Are you up for a little bet, Max?"

"I'm listening."

"I'll bring you in on my poker game. I get together weekly in the city with a few of the men I used to work with." Ryan could just hear some of the comments he was going to get for even suggesting the idea. But Murphy and Finn would understand. Conway would grumble, but he was a decent sort. This was going to be for a good cause. To teach this annoying female her place. "And if you hold your own there—" He congratulated himself on saying that with a straight face.

"You'll work with my edit?"

He wasn't about to go as far as to give her a blanket promise. "I won't ignore it."

"What does that mean? Exactly?"

She was getting cold feet already, he thought. Good. Feeling magnanimous—and confident that she didn't have a snowball's chance in hell of holding her own—he said, "That if it doesn't completely turn my stomach, I'll take it the step further that you want."

"Can't ask for more than that."

"No," he said pointedly, "you can't."

She had no idea why she felt as if he was putting her on notice. After a beat, she put her hand in his, sealing the bargain.

A small part of her felt as if she'd just made a deal with the devil. But the cast-iron doors had just slammed shut behind her and there was no backing out. Not without seriously burning her posterior.

CHAPTER 19

1:59 p.m.

Elisha had lost track of how many times she had looked at her watch in the last half hour or so. Each time she did, it seemed as if the minute hand had gotten glued in place and that she was stuck in some endless science-fiction time loop that had doomed her to repeat the same action over and over again forever.

It was because of Sutherland. Sutherland and the damn poker game. It was on for tonight. Just thinking about it caused the adrenaline to rush through her veins.

Outside, the weather was teasing the windowpanes, alternately covering them with sheets of rain and then droplets. The sun had made a few futile attempts to break through, succeeded once for ten minutes and then surrendered to the inclement conditions. She stared at the rain as it came down, her mind elsewhere.

She was both looking forward to and dreading the poker game to which she had more or less challenged Sutherland. Dreading it because it had been a long time since she'd played those versions of the game she'd rattled off so easily. There was no doubt in her mind that she was rusty, and she hated making a fool of herself.

In order to practice, she'd tried to get just the barest of games going with Rocky. She'd won every hand she played against

him, but her success didn't raise her confidence. The man's fa-
cial muscles were completely incompatible with the term "poker
face." She could almost see each hand Rocky held in his eyes.

She was looking forward to playing against Sutherland because
it was going to be exciting in a nerve-racking sort of way and, try
as she might, she couldn't remember the last time that she had
done anything even remotely exciting.

Despite its hectic pace, her life had gotten far too predictable.
She glanced at her watch again.

2:00 p.m.

It was still a good four hours before she was supposed to show
up at Sutherland's Tribeca apartment, where he and his poker
cronies, or whatever he chose to call them, gathered for their
weekly game. She sighed, slipping her sleeve back over her wrist.

The minutes were crawling by on the back of a sloth whose
feet were stuck in molasses.

She needed something to get her mind off the pending game
and the wager she'd somehow gotten into.

Right, Elisha laughed at herself. As if that were possible. Despite the load of work on her desk—no different than any other
day at the office—she couldn't wrap her mind around anything
else except the poker game.

"The meeting's starting, Ms. Reed." Trina Wilcox, the admin-
istrative assistant, stuck her head into the office. Two perfect
rows of teeth flashed in a smile as she delivered the reminder.

The second the words were out, Elisha remembered that
Rocky had scheduled a staff meeting at two. It was right there,
on her calendar, not to mention that she'd entered it into her
BlackBerry and it was also on the electronic schedule she had
on her computer. How could she have forgotten? Rocky had told
her about it himself.

Maybe she was slipping into the early stages of Alzheimer's.

The very thought of Alzheimer's sent a very cold, very sharp shiver down her spine. Though, as far as she knew, no one in her family had ever experienced it, she had a very real fear of the mentally disabling disease. Coming down with it guaranteed that she would feel and be even more isolated than she already felt at times.

She frowned, glancing toward her reflection in the window, watching the rain wash over it on the other side. She was getting carried away again.

Alzheimer's. Why was she thinking the worst? That wasn't her style. It wasn't even *a* style. She didn't have Alzheimer's. What she had was brain overload and there really wasn't very much she could do about that, not with the kind of fast-paced life she led.

Until science found a way to take the mind and deliver it up to the next level, make it capable of doubling its size and functioning on a much greater plane, there was just so much that could be stuffed into a human brain. Right now, hers had the most recent articles on the treatment of pancreatic cancer that she'd downloaded and that was vying for space with the updated rules for Texas hold 'em.

Currently, her nine-to-five duties as an editor were coming in third. Staff meetings didn't even make it to the list.

Elisha suppressed a sigh. She hated slipping up and she knew that if the ever-even-tempered Trina was here to remind her about the meeting, Rocky must have sent the woman. So far, he had been more than understanding about her preoccupation. He'd even encouraged her to take some time off.

But she didn't want it to appear as if he was playing favorites. Which was exactly what people like Carole Chambers would do, noting it down and using it as ammunition for some perverse purpose. Like blackmailing Rocky in order for her to get an unmerited promotion.

It wasn't going to come to that, Elisha swore. She owed Rocky too much for him to be chewed out by his father because of her.

After closing the drawer she'd forgotten she'd opened sometime earlier, Elisha rose to her feet. She selected a notebook. Others used tape recorders to take down their notes for them; she still liked putting pencil to paper and jotting things down. The very act created tiny cells of thoughts in her head, thoughts she could later apply to the books she was editing.

She forced herself to smile at the woman. "Tell Mr. Randolph I'll be right there, Trina."

Her cell phone cut into the latter part of her sentence. She immediately drew it out of her pocket. Ever since Henry had told her about his diagnosis, she'd taken to carrying the five-ounce silver camera phone somewhere on her person at all times. Except when she was in the shower and then it sat on the counter next to the stall, its ringer set on loud.

Dutifully, Trina remained in the doorway.

About to wave the younger woman on her way, Elisha opened the cell phone and placed it to her ear. To create some measure of privacy, she turned her back to Trina and the open doorway.

"Hello?"

There was a man on the other end of the line, a man whose voice she didn't recognize. "Ms. Reed?"

If this was some telemarketer, sneaking in under the banner of "out of area," she was going to verbally vivisect him.

"Yes?" she asked impatiently.

"Ms. Elisha Reed?"

This time her response was testy.

"Yes?"

"This is Joshua Lambert. I'm one of the EMTs who responded to a call from your brother's house."

Anger drained out of her instantly. Her head began to spin

as every nerve ending in her body tightened in anticipation of something awful. In less time than it took to draw in a long breath, she'd slipped out of her world into some kind of frightening twilight zone.

"Why?" she wanted to know. "Why was my brother calling you?"

"He wasn't," the man on the other end corrected politely. His cadence was slow, clear, as if he had all day to explain. "His daughter was. Andrea," he clarified before she could ask. "Mr. Reed is at Walker Memorial Hospital."

It was both good news and bad. She clung to the good. "Then he's alive."

"Yes, ma'am, he's alive. He's the one who asked me to call you. I—"

"Thank you," she cried, not letting the paramedic say anything else before she shut the phone.

Henry was alive, that was all she needed to know. Anything more might counterbalance that one precious piece of information.

Walker Memorial. Elisha rolled the name over in her head. She was vaguely aware of where the hospital was located. Somewhere on the tip of the island, just before the expressway threaded into the city.

A taxi driver would know exactly where it was, she thought. Her mind was scattering in a hundred different directions, like a box of beads that had been dropped on the floor.

She couldn't focus.

Elisha was aware that Trina was watching her as she moved first to the door, then back again. Not once but twice.

She had to double back to pick up her purse and then again to grab her raincoat. Each time she nearly walked right over Trina.

The small-boned woman sashayed first to one side and then the other, trying politely to get out of Elisha's way. "Can I…?"

But Elisha shook her head. Not in answer but in dismissal. She didn't have time to listen to a question. She had to get to the hospital. Now. Later held too many possibilities within its boundaries. Possibilities she refused to even attempt to explore.

On her third effort to get out of the office, Elisha finally flew by the assistant. "Tell Mr. Randolph I had to go to the hospital. Cancel anything that's on my calendar this afternoon." She threw the latter over her shoulder as an afterthought.

Henry was all right, she silently insisted as she punched her index finger against the down button. A small light sprang up around the button in response. He was all right. The paramedic said that he had made the request, asking him to call. That meant he was all right.

Her mouth curved as she struggled to push back tears. How so like Henry. Making requests instead of demands. Anyone else would have made demands. She knew she would have.

She made one now as she got into the elevator.

You keep him alive, you hear me, God? You keep him alive.

It was half demand, half plea.

CHAPTER 20

It was a struggle not to cry.

All the way to the hospital, Elisha fought against the urge to break down and cry. Fought against even shedding a single tear.

She knew if she did that, there would be no stopping the torrent of tears that was rising dangerously high behind the emotional dam she'd managed to construct. And she couldn't cry. She had to be strong.

For Henry.

Who would be going home soon, she promised herself fiercely. One of those multidegreed, high-priced physicians was just going to have to fix Henry, that was all there was to it.

She wasn't about to accept anything less.

Mercifully, the cabdriver had given up attempting to engage her in conversation after three unsuccessful tries. Instead, he concentrated on getting her to the hospital as quickly as possible, especially since she'd promised a fifty-dollar tip if he could do it in under an hour.

The rain was pelting the roof, sliding down the sides of the windows. Heaven was crying, but she wouldn't.

Elisha realized that she was sitting on the edge of the passenger seat, straining against the seat belt as far as she could go. Her hands were planted on either knee and she was rocking. Unconsciously trying to find some kind of comfort in the motion.

She needed to get hold of herself. To pull herself together. Removing her hands from her knees, she saw that she'd been clutching them so hard, all ten imprints of her fingertips were clearly discernible. That was going to bruise, she thought. She always bruised so easily. Her skin was a great deal fairer than Henry's.

Henry.

Oh God.

With effort, she forced herself to breathe regularly. And all the while, within the confines of her mind she silently kept repeating, *It's going to be all right. Henry's going to be all right.*

But he didn't look like someone who was going to be all right. Not when she saw him.

There was a battalion of machines on either side of his bed, all measuring something different, all speaking a strange, whirling, beeping language like invading aliens from another planet. A monitor to Henry's right displayed four horizontal lines, each a different color, each with a different wave function. Some were arrhythmic, others had a symmetry to them. She cheered the latter on, praying the uniformity was catching. There was comfort in uniformity.

It was crowded there with the machines and the bed. Hardly enough room for her prayers. Glass walls separated Henry's room from the others within the Intensive Care Unit.

She edged over to his bed, trying not to bump into anything, trying not to set any alarms off.

Henry looked as white as the crisp sheet that was beneath him. As white as the blanket that had been thrown over him. White was the color of surrender. She wished someone had thought to make everything red. Red was a fighting color.

An oxygen tube snaked its way across Henry's face, allowing

him to breathe better. She strained her eyes, trying to see some kind of movement from his chest. It took more than a moment for her to finally satisfy herself that he was breathing.

She wanted to cheer.

And then his eyes fluttered open and she offered up silent thanks to God.

Forcing a smile, Elisha took her brother's hand in hers. His skin felt cool to the touch. She resisted the urge to rub her hands over his, to get the circulation going the way she used to when they were children and he would complain about being cold. It had been a chore to her then, an imposition that held her in place when there were things she wanted to do. Things that didn't include an annoying little brother.

Now, she couldn't think of anything she would have rather done than stand here, rubbing his hand. Making sure that Henry's circulation kept doing just that. Circulating.

"Can't say I care very much for your new look," she told him softly, nodding at the tube that created the impression of a transparent mustache.

Her heart ached as she saw Henry struggle to smile at her.

Think of yourself for once, Henry. Complain. Tell me where it hurts. Stop being so brave.

"I…waited…for you," he said to her in a voice that sounded so weak, she could feel her throat closing up just hearing it.

He'd waited for her. She didn't understand. Her mind was a complete utter blank. "Were we on for dinner tonight?"

He tried to move his head from side to side. There was barely a perceptible movement. "No…I mean…here… I was… waiting…for you…to come here… To…the…hospital."

There was this tremendous pressure in the middle of her chest. As if a boulder had suddenly been dropped there, dead center.

Don't say it that way, Henry. Don't say it as if you are barely hanging on to life. You're going to be fine, do you hear me?

"I got here as soon as I could, Henry." It was hard to talk, hard to keep her voice from cracking. "They didn't have your name listed at the information desk. I had to threaten the volunteer with bodily harm before he sent for someone to pull up the latest list so I could find you."

She felt his fingers flutter a little against her hand. She tightened hers around them.

Stick with me, Henry. Don't go. Don't go.

There was just the slightest trace of amusement in his eyes as he looked at her. Amusement and affection. "You...can't...threaten...everyone...Lise."

"It got me here, didn't it?" *I'm not going to cry, I'm not.* Elisha looked at her brother and shook her head. "An ambulance ride. Having a paramedic call me. I never knew you had a flair for the dramatic."

"Neither...did...I." The words were light, reedy, as if he didn't have the strength to project them any farther than just the small area surrounding his pillow. Elisha leaned in closer in order to hear him better.

As she did, she saw Henry wincing. She knew, because of what she'd read and not because of anything Henry would admit to her, that there was a great deal of pain associated with his condition.

"Are they giving you anything for the pain?" Weakly, he moved his head from side to side. "Well, dammit, they should be." Agitated, she looked around for a nurse to summon. Someone to buttonhole and demand that they come to Henry's aid. "Where's the nurse?"

"I...told them...not to... I...didn't...want to be fuzzy when...you...got here."

She could feel her eyes stinging. The struggle almost undid her. "Fuzzy's good. My favorite bear was fuzzy, remember? Mr. Fuzz-bear."

She was talking nonsense, she thought. Her mind was jumping from the present back to her childhood. Back to when things were safe and rugs weren't ripped out from beneath her. Back when there was no pain and everything was all right because their mother and father were there to protect them.

I want to go back. I don't want to be an adult. Not anymore.

Henry was looking at her. Looking into her eyes. Her soul. "You…you'll…take care of…the girls?" Every syllable looked as if it cost him.

She wanted to make him stop talking.

She wanted to make him talk forever. Because if he was talking, he was still with her. And she wasn't alone.

"You'll be getting out of this hospital bed and taking care of them yourself," she insisted with feeling. The lump in her throat kept getting bigger. "Not today, maybe not tomorrow, but you will. You will." She could see her words weren't changing anything. "Henry, you have to. Do you hear me? You have to get better. You have to come home. I'm not ready for this to happen."

"Lise—"

"I'm not," she cried, desperation vibrating in her voice. "You can't leave me, Henry. I can do a million things, juggle a thousand balls in the air, but I need to know that you're there, somewhere in the background, with your patient smile and your endless good humor. I need you."

She pressed her lips together to keep back the sob that was choking her. After a moment, she continued, "I'll tell you a secret, Henry. One I never told you before. When you were born, I tried to get Mom to take you back." She could hardly see. Tears were swimming in her eyes, refracting the light. Distorting everything. She brushed them aside so that she could see her brother. So that she could see him still breathing. "I wanted a dog. Or at least a sister, not some dumb brother."

He tried his best to smile. "I...know...Mom...told me."

"Well, I changed my mind, Henry," she told him fiercely. "I don't want a dog or a sister. I want you." And she was losing him, she thought. "Please, Henry."

"If...I...could stay...I...would."

That's all she needed. For him to will himself to remain in this life. "You can. You can. You just have to try harder. Please. Try harder. You've got to try harder, Henry."

But each breath that he took sounded thinner, more shallow than the last. Elisha just held on to his hand more tightly.

"Henry," she whispered, afraid that if she tried to speak in a normal voice, it would break completely apart. "Henry, I love you."

She saw his lips moving, but there was no sound.

Elisha leaned in closer. "What? What is it, Henry? I can't hear you."

"I...love...you...too."

She felt his breath on her cheek.

And then nothing.

Raising her head to look at him, Elisha saw that her brother's chest had stopped moving.

The barely wavy colorful lines on the monitor beside his bed gradually flattened out. A mournful, droning filled the air around her.

"Henry! Henry, come back. Please come back!"

But there was no response. As she knew there wouldn't be.

Elisha's eyes filled with tears, instantly overflowing. She touched her fingertips to her cheek, trying to press in the breath she'd felt there. Trying to preserve the last bit of her brother that she had.

"Say hi to Mom and Dad for me," she whispered before her voice broke.

CHAPTER 21

"Code Blue! Code Blue!"

A disembodied voice shouted the call to action somewhere in the vicinity as an alarm sounded the moment that all four of the wavy lines on the monitor beside Henry's bed became linear. Within the next minute, the small enclosure exploded with activity as hospital staff came rushing in, determined to wrestle back another soul from death's grasp.

The crash cart bumped against Elisha's hip as a nurse angled to get it into position for the attending physician.

Like someone standing on the sidelines, watching a nightmare unfold, Elisha began to back away. The fight before her was a futile one. She knew that in her soul. Everything was going on around her in a blur of sounds and colors, none of it making any sense.

Her brain was numb. Her body was numb.

Henry was gone.

And then suddenly, behind her, she heard a small, high-pitched wail, "Daddy!"

Beth's cry halted Elisha's headlong spiral into a bottomless abyss of despair. There wasn't just herself to think of. She couldn't give in to the destructive clawings of grief.

Turning around, she saw that both Andrea and Beth were being ushered in by a distressed-looking Asian woman she vaguely recognized as someone who knew Henry. But no name came to her.

Andrea was holding tightly on to Beth's hand to keep the little girl from pushing through the ring of blue-uniformed people and flinging herself onto her father's bed. Elisha recognized the look on the older girl's face. Andrea was as numb as she was, as disbelieving in what had transpired.

They were both waiting, Elisha thought, for a commercial break to be announced, after which programming would resume as usual and life would return to its normal boundaries. Boundaries within which Henry was still among the living.

Sobs racking her small body, Beth shifted her deep blue eyes to her, as if she expected her to make everything all right. As if she had the power. "Aunt Elisha?"

For a split second, Elisha couldn't move. Couldn't offer any words of consolation.

You're not alone, Lise. You've got nieces to take care of. Henry's girls. They need someone to lean on. It's up to you to be that someone.

And who did she have to lean on? she wanted to cry. Who?

The answer was as self-evident as the emptiness that was still tugging for possession of her soul.

No one.

The lump in her throat still made it impossible for her to speak. But she could act. Elisha opened her arms to her nieces.

Without hesitation, both girls flung themselves into the embrace.

"Is he…?" Andrea couldn't bring herself to finish the statement.

Elisha knew exactly how the girl felt. She bypassed the word that neither one of them wanted to hear. The word she couldn't say. Not yet. Instead, in Henry's honor, she focused on the one positive aspect in the otherwise horrible event.

"He's not suffering anymore."

"But we are," Beth sobbed, her small fingers clutching on to her raincoat as she clung to her waist. Her tears dampened the material.

Henry, think like Henry, Elisha schooled herself. "He wouldn't want us to."

Beth raised her head, her soft cheeks wet with tears. "Then why did Daddy go? Why did he leave Andie and me?"

"He didn't want to, honey. He didn't want to, but he didn't have a choice." Elisha dropped down on her knees beside the child she was trying to comfort even as her own heart was breaking. Even as her own heart selfishly asked the same questions. "And all of him didn't leave, Beth. He's still here."

Wiping her face with the back of her hand, Beth blinked, confused. The father she adored was still lying prone on the hospital bed, despite the actions of the people around him. "Where?"

"Here. In your heart." Elisha lightly tapped the little girl's chest. "And in here." Her fingers brushed against Beth's temple. "Your daddy will always live on there."

Beth shook her head. It wasn't enough. "But I want to see him. Talk to him. Go for a walk with him and have him hold my hand."

So do I, baby. So do I.

"Just close your eyes, Beth." She had no idea how she was saying this, how she managed to push one word out after another and not have it sound like babble. "Whenever you want to see your daddy, just close your eyes and you'll be able to picture him. He's never going to leave you," she told the little girl with feeling. "A piece of your father will always be inside of you and inside of Andrea." She glanced up toward the older girl. Tears were sliding down Andrea's face. "And he'll always be watching over both of you. Because that's the kind of man your daddy was."

Behind her, activity around Henry's bed had halted. The

nurses wilted away in defeat. The physician set down the paddles that had failed to restore a rhythm to his heart. His expression was perfectly stoic as he looked at the young intern beside him. "Call it."

The latter looked at the clock on the wall directly behind the bed. There was a note of distress as he said, "Three-eighteen."

Three-eighteen.

From somewhere in her head, a voice arose, much like the voice of a media commentator delivering an endless stream of news: *At three-eighteen the world lost a good person it could ill afford to lose. Henry Reed. We'll not see his like again.*

Trembling inside, Elisha rose to her feet again. She put her arms around Beth, holding the little girl to her.

Her eyes met those of the woman who had ushered in the girls. There were tears in her eyes. She was clearly distressed over Henry's passing. Welcome to the club, Elisha thought, her arms tightening around Beth who had begun to sob again.

"I just took the girls to get the something to eat. He told me I should. Henry," she added in a disoriented voice, in case there was any question as to whom she was referring. "I didn't know…" The woman's voice trailed off as she looked at her helplessly.

"You couldn't have known," Elisha replied, trying to absolve her of any feelings of guilt. Henry knew he was dying, would die in the next few minutes. That's why he sent the girls away. He didn't want them to see that. She took a breath, trying to steady a voice that kept wanting to crack. "I'm sorry," she apologized. "I can't seem to remember your name."

A slight smile quirked the woman's small mouth, indicating she understood. At a time like this, nothing made sense and names of acquaintances were lost in the shuffle. Words gushed out in an effort to make the introduction and subsequent explanation as short as possible.

"I'm Anne Nguyen. I live next door to Henry and the girls. Andrea came to me when Henry collapsed. When the paramedics arrived, they would only let Andrea accompany Henry to the hospital. They said that Beth was too young to ride along, too. Something about violating the rules, so I took Beth and followed the ambulance to the hospital."

As she spoke, Anne looked toward the bed. They all did.

Henry seemed serene. Almost as if he was just sleeping instead of breaking three hearts and leaving behind a hole that could never be filled. An orderly was taking away the crash cart. There were other patients to treat, other patients to stand vigil over, poised to go into action. Henry didn't need it anymore.

"I didn't even know Henry was sick," Anne confessed to her.

"Henry never liked to talk about himself," Elisha murmured. Her mouth curved in a fond, sad smile as she thought of her brother. "Said he didn't want to bore people."

The physician turned from Henry's bed and looked from one woman to the other, obviously trying to address someone about the man he had failed to revive. After a beat, he crossed to Elisha.

"Are you Mrs. Reed?" he asked Elisha.

"Ms.," she corrected. "I'm his sister. Henry's wife died five years ago." Still holding Beth to her, she placed her other arm around Andrea's shoulders. They were rigid, she noted. As if the girl was holding everything in by sheer willpower and if she bent, even a little, she'd shatter. *I know how you feel, Andie.* "These are his daughters, Beth and Andrea."

The physician frowned ever so slightly, as if this was more information than he wanted. As if this would make everything more personal than he intended it to be.

"I'm very sorry for your loss, Ms. Reed." He looked somewhat ill at ease with the situation, avoiding eye contact with the girls. "The nurse will be here to help you with the arrangements."

"Arrangements?" Elisha echoed. What was he talking about? Right now, it was all she could handle just to remember to breathe in and out.

His voice softened. "To have your brother's body removed."

"For the funeral," Anne prompted from behind her when she said nothing.

Funeral. Henry's funeral. She hadn't even thought that far ahead.

Because she never wanted this day to get here.

She nodded woodenly. "Right. The funeral. I, um…" She tried to think, to remember where Rachel was buried. Henry had handled all the details for Rachel's funeral and burial. Grieving, he had still managed to take care of everything. Because he had to.

And now it was her turn. Her "had to." There wasn't anyone else to do it. She certainly couldn't hand over the responsibility to Andrea. Aside from being cowardly, it wouldn't have been fair.

She cleared her throat, then nodded. "Of course. Thank you. I'll speak with her."

"Fine." The doctor was already standing in the doorway. He nodded his head quickly, taking his leave. His eyes drifted over to the bed, then retreated and focused on her face. "Again, I'm sorry for your loss."

Elisha could feel her chest constricting, could literally feel her heart aching.

Not nearly as sorry as I am, Doctor.

CHAPTER 22

Looking back later, Elisha could only describe the hours after Henry's death as sheer hell.

In an effort for self-preservation, she disassociated herself from what she was doing. She was vaguely aware of watching even as she was doing. Aware of standing on the sidelines, watching herself as she somehow managed to go through the paces, going from point A to point B as she set about getting things organized.

The pain was endless.

With Beth clinging to her and Andrea moving like a shell-shocked soldier beside her, Elisha followed the ICU nurse to the tiny office designated to the Social Services Department. It was restricted to just one person, Jennifer Mendoza.

Jennifer found chairs for all three of them and encouraged them to sit. She had a soft, comforting voice and kind eyes. Information about Henry, his time of death as well as his home address, was already on her computer screen. She'd pulled it up the second the ICU nurse had given her Henry's name.

Within minutes, Jennifer helped her get in contact with a respected mortuary on Long Island located close to the cemetery where Rachel had been buried. Elisha had remembered that Henry had reserved the space beside his wife the same time he had made arrangements for her funeral.

That was Henry, Elisha thought. Always prepared. For everything but this.

"Are you sure you'll be all right?" Jennifer asked as Elisha rose to her feet. Elisha had given her best trouper smile. The woman seemed to see right through her. "Here's my card." She plucked a white business card embossed with several numbers. "Call me if you need to talk."

Elisha remembered pocketing the card as she walked out. She didn't remember which pocket. Didn't really remember the ride to Henry's house that followed, only that Beth had leaned against her, crying again. Anne had insisted on remaining with them while Elisha talked to the woman at social services and then drove all of them home.

"I'll stay with the girls while you make arrangements for the funeral service," Anne volunteered as she pulled up in the driveway.

The house looked dark. She fully expected to see Henry throwing open the door, calling out a greeting. But the door remained closed.

"Do you have a license?"

She realized that Anne was asking her something. "Excuse me?"

"A driver's license," Anne clarified. "Do you have one?"

"Yes, but I don't have a car. I can get around faster on foot in the city." She helped Beth out of the car. It suddenly occurred to her that she had no idea why the woman was asking her that. "Why?"

"You can take mine. To go to the church," Anne prompted when Elisha said nothing. "To make arrangements for the funeral service."

This is your department, not mine, Henry, Elisha thought. When their parents had died, Henry had been the one who had stepped up to the plate and handled all the arrangements. Because she just couldn't. She'd always been a whiz at multitasking. She'd been doing it ever since she could remember, but handling death and everything that went with it was something she just couldn't make herself face.

Gotta do it now, Lise. No way out.

"Thank you." Elisha took the keys that Anne offered. "I'll be back as soon as I can, girls," she promised. Bracing herself, she drove to the church where Henry and Rachel had gotten married. The church where final words had been said over Rachel's coffin and now, they would soon be said over Henry's.

Fresh tears sprang to her eyes as she made her way down the street.

The pastor at the church that Henry and the girls attended on Sundays was very upset to hear about her brother's passing. He offered Elisha tea and sympathy. She passed on the first, dutifully listened to the second even though it didn't help. To her relief, arrangements for Henry's funeral services were made quickly and simply.

Walking her to her car, the pastor repeated the words that the woman from social services had uttered. "Call me if you need anything."

I need Henry back. What can you do about that?

But she managed to smile as she accepted the card that he had pulled out of his pocket. "Thank you, you've been very kind."

"My Boss expects it," he replied as he closed the car door.

She didn't remember the drive back to Henry's house. Only that it was lonely. Drained, she walked into the house, setting the car keys down on the table in the foyer. All she wanted to do was slip into a coma. But there were still more things to do. A line from Frost drifted through her brain.

And miles to go before I sleep.

She looked at Andrea. "Did your dad keep an address book?"

The response was monotone, as if the personality that had been Andrea Reed had been completely drained out of her. "On the computer, why?"

"I have to notify his friends." *Now, there's a ghoulish task. Hello, I'm calling about your friend Henry Reed. He's dead.* "They'll want to come to the funeral."

Andrea frowned, then shrugged carelessly, as if it made no difference to her if anyone came to the service or not. "Whatever."

Alarms went off in Elisha's head. Like all teenagers, Andrea had her ups and downs, but this was more than a step beyond that. "Andrea, do you want to talk?"

Something dark and moody flared in the girl's brilliant blue eyes. "No." Her lips pressed down firmly, forming a barrier, locking away any communication.

Elisha tried anyway. "Honey, this was a terrible thing that happened. We're all hurting right now and it's going to take time for things to settle in—"

"Are we going to have to go to an orphanage?" Beth was suddenly in front of her, clutching at her imploringly. Elisha looked down at a trembling lower lip.

The only nodding acquaintance Beth had with the term *orphanage* had arisen out of watching a stage production of *Annie* last year. The girls in the play had been forced to work hard. That was probably the image that was replaying itself in Beth's head now, Elisha realized.

"Oh no, sweetheart, no. You'll both come to live with me."

"No." The word, expelled vehemently, came from Andrea.

Elisha turned to look at her, stunned by the force of Andrea's rejection. Was this part of the grief she was experiencing or was there something more behind it? She couldn't deal with this, Elisha thought. She wasn't equipped to become an instant parent.

"Don't you want to live with me?" she heard herself asking.

"Not in the city," Andrea retorted heatedly. "All my friends are here."

And "here" was where she intended to stay, if body language was any indication.

"Mine, too," Beth piped up. The next moment, she began to cry all over again.

Overwhelmed, Elisha sank down on the sofa in a heap. It felt as if she were a balloon and someone had let all the air out of her. With what seemed like her last bit of energy, she covered her face with her hands, completely at a loss as to how to handle this. All of "this."

"Oh, God."

She hadn't thought about the girls needing to transfer schools, needing to transfer their lives in order to move to the city with her. Everything seemed to have so many repercussions, so many strings that ran out like plant runners. How had Henry managed to keep all the strings untangled?

More important, how was she going to manage keeping them separated?

She didn't think she could.

This isn't fair, Henry. They need you. I can't do this.

Both girls stared at her, waiting for some kind of answer. She could feel Andrea's hostility. Andrea was *never* hostile toward her.

She did the only thing she could at a time like this. She stalled.

"Okay," Elisha announced. "It's too soon to talk about moving or not moving. Right now, we need to get through this funeral, then we'll talk about the rest of it."

Anne Nguyen had purposely let Elisha have some time with the girls when she walked in. She'd made herself useful by tidying up the kitchen, where Henry had collapsed, knocking over some things on the counter. She peered into the living room now, sympathy emanating from every pore.

"I can have the girls stay at my place tonight if you need a little time to yourself."

Yes, I'd like that. I'd like that very much, thank you. It would have been the easiest way to go, so that she could have some time to grieve once she got the phone calls over with. Phone calls to people she didn't know to come pay their respects to a brother who no longer had any need for things like that.

But the living did, she thought.

She looked at the girls. Beth had her arms around her as far as they would extend, her small body drooping into hers. She squeezed even harder when Anne made her offer. Elisha slipped her arm around Beth. Andrea moved farther away from her. In the blink of an eye, life had become impossibly difficult.

"No, that's all right, Anne. I think the girls want to sleep in their own beds tonight." In response, Beth nodded her head vehemently, still not loosening her hold. "But if you don't mind, you can help me spread the word around here."

"Of course." Anne sat down beside her for a moment. "Where will the funeral services be held?"

Her mind went blank. She'd just come from there, she upbraided herself. How could she have forgotten? She reached into her pocket to take out the pastor's card.

Andrea beat her to it. "St. Theresa's. My dad insisted we go every Sunday. A lot of good that did him, huh?"

When they became adults, Elisha thought, Henry was always the more religious one. He seemed to be able to find serenity by attending the weekly services. A serenity that had eluded her.

"Actually, I think it probably did." Elisha forced herself to return Anne's smile. "It'll be there." As if a cloud lifted from her brain, she remembered the address and recited it. "The service will be on Saturday at ten. Until then, he'll be at Amos Brothers Funeral Parlor."

Getting up, Anne nodded. "I'll let people know." Taking her hand, Anne squeezed it. "And you let me know if you need anything. I'm just next door."

"You've been very kind," Elisha told her.

"It's the least I can do. Henry was a great guy."

"Yes," Elisha whispered. "I know."

The front door closed as Anne let herself out after saying goodbye to the girls.

Busy, she had to get busy, Elisha thought. She couldn't just sit here, letting the depression sink into her soul any further than it already had.

"Andrea, if you could turn on the computer for me, I'll get started."

Andrea looked as if she was going to say something cryptic, then nodded. "Sure."

Elisha rose to her feet with Beth still holding on to her like a baby possum holding on to its mother for dear life. Elisha put her arm around the child, drawing her closer.

"It's going to be all right, baby." Elisha wasn't entirely sure if she said the words to comfort herself or the girls, but neither of them answered.

Her ear hurt. For the last hour she'd been holding the receiver to it, saying the same awful words over and over again, letting people know that Henry had died. She'd fielded the questions as best she could, congratulating herself each time for not breaking down the way she sorely wanted to.

But now she was finally finished with the calls, finally finished holding herself together. She glanced over to the battered old sofa that had once been in her parents' living room and that

Henry had claimed for his den, citing sentimental value. The leather was cracked in at least half a dozen places, but Henry wouldn't hear talk about getting rid of it.

She could remember sitting there with him when they were children. Right now, Beth was curled up on it and Andrea was beside her. Both had fallen asleep. She was torn between just leaving them there or herding them off to their beds. She didn't want to wake them, but their necks were going to ache tomorrow.

It would match their hearts.

Her cell phone began to ring. Startled, she pulled the phone from her pocket and looked at the incoming number. It wasn't one that she recognized. Getting up, she went outside the den to keep from waking the girls.

She flipped open the phone. "Hello?"

"I knew you'd lose your nerve at the last minute."

She recognized the voice instantly.

CHAPTER 23

"I knew you'd lose your nerve at the last minute," Ryan repeated when she failed to respond. "But I thought you'd at least have the decency to call and make up some lame excuse why you couldn't cancel. Something like the dog swallowed your car keys, or there was a power failure in the building where you live and you were afraid to climb down twenty-two flights of stairs in the dark without a flashlight, which you couldn't find because it was too dark."

She heard the words, but it was difficult for her to process them. Beyond exhaustion, her brain was completely disoriented. Every thought she possessed seemed to be existing on its own island, just out of range of any other thought.

Unable to give him an answer immediately as to why she'd never showed up at his apartment, Elisha focused on the last thing Sutherland said. The word *how?* rose up in her head.

"How do you know I live on the twenty-second floor?"

She heard him make an annoyed sound on the other end of the line. "I make it my business to know things and don't change the subject."

She was far beyond being bullied, or trying to make nice for the sake of the firm or because some egotistical writer needed to have his self-esteem stroked.

A sentence fragment he'd uttered some time in the past replayed itself in her head. Making him a liar. "When I said we should get to know each other, you said you weren't interested."

She heard a slight dry laugh, as if he was telling her that he knew where she was going with this even if she wasn't all too clear about the path herself. "In anything you might have wanted to volunteer. I have my own set of questions and I like finding things out on my own, not by hearsay or through secondhand information."

What did that mean? Had he followed her? Or was he just trying to perpetuate some aura of mystery? She had no time for games or for men who hadn't grown up and still wanted to play spy.

"And you're not going to move me off the track," Ryan said. "You forfeited the bet by not showing up. I'm sending over a fresh copy of my manuscript by messenger. Forward it to whoever does your printing. I know how damn confused they get if there's anything on the page to distract them." And then he issued his warning. "You're not to put one mark on this copy. Nothing. It's my story and I tell it my way. If you don't like it, then our so-called association, such as it is, is terminated."

Her head hurt. Elisha began to massage it. She made no response to his statement.

"Nothing to say?" he queried. "All right, then I'll just—"

"My brother died." The words, festering in her chest all this time like a fast-growing tumor, just suddenly exploded from her lips. At the same time that the tears materialized. She angrily wiped them away with the back of her hand. She wasn't sure she was going to be able to recover, be able to meet the challenges in front of her, immediate and down the road, large and small. She just wanted to run somewhere and hide.

"What did you say?"

The man was probably good at torture, she caught herself thinking. When she opened her mouth to answer, the hostility that suddenly materialized was hard to suppress. "My brother,

Henry, he died. Today. I'm sorry if I didn't remember our bet, Mr. Sutherland." Her voice rose and she struggled to contain the hysteria that rose with it. "But when the hospital called me, I forgot about everything else, including your illustrious poker game." She paused for just a second to drag air into her lungs. "Now, if that wounds your pride, I'm sorry, but working for an inside straight so that I can jump through the hoop you're holding just in order to do my job didn't seem to be all that important at the time."

He seemed not to hear her tirade, or notice the anger that had flowed his way. Instead, he asked, "Was it sudden?"

The question threw her. She had to stop to think, to try to pull together the threads that were unraveling so quickly.

"He had some warning, but all in all, yes, it was sudden. Henry never had a sick day in his life. At least none that he ever mentioned," she qualified because Henry always kept his problems to himself. It was the one thing about Henry that drove her crazy. "We used to kid him that germs thought he was too nice to attack."

Stopping suddenly, Elisha pressed her lips together. Her voice felt as if it was going to crack and the last thing in the world she wanted to do was break down in front of Sutherland. Even if it was over the telephone.

"He was too nice," she finally concluded.

"Did he have a family?"

"His wife died five years ago. Henry has—had," she corrected herself, hating the way the past tense tasted, "two daughters."

"Young?"

"Fifteen and ten," she recited automatically. Her patience frayed, she couldn't take it any longer. "Why are you asking me all these questions?" Elisha demanded angrily.

Ryan didn't answer her question. Instead, he asked another one of his own. "What's going to happen to your brother's daughters?"

Did he care? No, that wasn't possible. Then was he just pretending to be polite? No, that wasn't the Ryan Sutherland she was acquainted with. Besides, the tone behind his questions wasn't polite. He was shooting them out at her like rubber bullets. They weren't harmful, but they still stung.

"I'm going to take care of them," she informed him tersely. Not that it's any business of yours, she added silently.

Only then did his voice soften ever so slightly and lose some of its accusatory tone. She had to admit that to her ear, he also sounded a little skeptical. He probably didn't think she could do it.

That made two of them.

"That's a big responsibility," he said to her.

Oh God, yes.

But aloud, she kept her doubts to herself, kept her emotions so tightly wrapped that she sounded almost monotone as she answered. "I don't see as how I have much of a choice. I'm all they have."

"There's another choice," he told her. His voice was distant, as if the wires in their connection had just gotten frayed.

"Social services."

Her first thought was of the woman in the tiny little office. Jennifer. The one who'd helped her at the hospital. But then she realized that he meant a different branch. The branch that concerned itself with children who had no one to care for them.

"Foster care?" she cried incredulously. How could he even think that? Just what kind of callow, selfish bastard was this man?

"Yes." He said it as if it was a final verdict handed down by a judge. "Then the responsibility wouldn't be yours anymore."

She felt a flash of temper. Who the hell did he think he was?

He could play God with the characters who littered the pages of his book, but he had no business butting his nose into her life.

"But the heartbreak, not to mention the guilt, would be my responsibility," she shot back. "Look, Mr. Sutherland, you don't seem to think much of me as an editor and you seem to think even less of me as a person." She dragged her hand through her hair, trying desperately to bank down the growing helplessness she felt. "God knows I'm not going to be up for the award of Mother of the Year anytime soon, but these girls need me and I love them. And somehow, I'll find a way to do right by them." *Even though I haven't a clue what I'm going to do next.*

There was silence, and then he finally spoke. "Very impressive."

Damn him, he was the spawn of the devil. "I wasn't trying to impress you."

"I know."

All right, she was willing to admit that she had to be hearing things. Because she could have sworn she heard a smile in the man's voice. The man didn't smile. Not physically and certainly not emotionally. She was overwrought, that's what it was. Thinking she heard a smile in his voice was just the result of her nerves being stretched to the very limit and then pulled five inches farther.

"You need anything?"

She scrubbed her hand over her face. Okay, now she *knew* she was hearing things. To prove it to herself, she asked him to repeat what she knew she couldn't have heard. "What did you say?"

"Do you need anything?" He enunciated every syllable slowly, as if she was mentally impaired.

And maybe she was, Elisha thought, struggling not to come unglued.

I need a million things. Someone to take over my life and make it run right. Or, better yet, someone to give me back my life the way it was two months ago.

"No, but thanks for the offer."

There was a long pause on the other end of the line. So long that she thought he'd hung up and for some reason, the dial tone hadn't kicked in.

And then she heard him say, "We can reschedule the poker game if you'd like."

He was rescinding his mandate about his manuscript, going back to square one of their so-called agreement. Elisha passed the back of her hand over her forehead, checking to see if she had a fever. When she could detect none, she wondered if she was asleep on the sofa. Had she dropped off beside the girls? Was this some dream she was having?

No, she thought, she ached too damn much for this to be a dream.

Blowing out an emotion-laden breath, she answered, "I'd like."

"Good."

She wasn't sure if the connection gave out at that moment, or if the man had hung up. Most likely the latter. Sutherland had clearly been raised by wolves, but one of those wolves must have had a heart and passed it on to him. She didn't have time to contemplate what made his train run. She had nieces to see to. Closing her cell phone, she slipped it back into her pocket. She glanced into the den.

Beth and Andrea were just where she'd left them. Asleep and leaning against each other.

As it should be in life, Elisha thought.

With a sigh that was way past weary, she went off in search of blankets. She was going to cover the girls and leave them where they were. They looked too peaceful to move and God knew they needed the rest.

CHAPTER 24

The next few days kept her far too busy to sit down in a corner and cry. From the morning following Henry's death until the day of the funeral, Elisha found that every spare moment of her life was crammed with activity.

People came from the area and from the law firm where Henry was a partner just to pay their respects and to tell her what she had known all along: what a wonderful man her brother had been. Henry's neighbors invaded the house, to cook, to talk, to let her know that there were other life-forms close by who shared her grief and were available to trade stories about Henry at any given time.

She hardly knew any of them but she was grateful to them nonetheless. As a group, they kept her from sinking into herself. From giving in to the darkness that wanted to possess her.

They also took the edge off focusing on the girls. She didn't have to worry how they were bearing up to the wake. There were always at least several younger people who she took to be Andrea's friends at the funeral parlor.

She was concerned about Andrea.

Though the girl maintained a stoic expression, Andrea looked as if she was sleepwalking through everything. When her friends spoke to her, she hardly answered. Andrea was alone in the midst of everything.

In contrast to the girl's big sister, Beth clung to her. Even when the little girl wasn't hanging on to her for dear life, she was watching Elisha's every movement. Everywhere she went, she could feel Beth's eyes on her. She wasn't accustomed to this kind of restriction. It made her feel almost claustrophobic. At the same time, she felt guilty for harboring the feeling that she just wanted to flee.

And all the while, she nodded and smiled at the people who filed by.

"How are you holding up?"

The sound of the familiar voice behind her had her wanting to sob with gratitude. Elisha swung around. She'd never welcomed the sight of Sinclair Jones as much as she did at this very moment.

"As good as can be expected," she admitted once hugs had been exchanged. "What are you doing here?" She hadn't notified anyone other than Rocky about the wake. But even as she asked, the answer occurred to her. "Rocky called you, didn't he?"

Sensing she needed a moment away from everything, Sinclair drew her aside to a less populated corner. "Yes, but he wasn't the first to notify me about your loss. I am very, very sorry, Elisha."

Dammit, there was that lump again. She was going to have to get better control over herself than this. She forced a smile to her lips.

"Thank you." And then curiosity stepped up to the plate. She supposed that was a good sign. It meant that she wasn't completely dead inside. "Who called you before Rocky?"

"Sutherland."

She stared at Sinclair, not quite computing his answer. Maybe the low drone of voices had distorted what he'd said. "*Ryan* Sutherland?"

"You know anyone else by that name?" And then, before she could answer, he interjected, "Besides the actor, of course. And there's his father, as well," he recalled. "And that opera singer, Joan, I believe…"

Elisha tugged on his arm to stop the free-flowing word association. She knew that Sinclair's wealth of trivia could take him in directions that were miles from the subject at hand. She wanted to make sure he hadn't made a mistake.

"Ryan Sutherland called you?"

"Yes. Yesterday. Said something about knowing that I was a friend as well as your author and that I might not know about this." Gray-tufted eyebrows drew together over a nose that was distinctly Roman in structure. "Why didn't *you* call me?"

Because the words hurt too much. Because I was afraid I'd cry if I talked to a friend.

She shrugged her shoulders in a helpless manner. "It's been so busy…"

He merely nodded at the information, his manner telling her that he sensed she was shying away from the true answer. But that was her right and he wouldn't rob her of it.

"Well, I'm here now." He presented himself before her like a superhero arriving to right wrongs and vanquish evil. "What do you need me to do?"

Threading her arm through his, she smiled. It was nice being in the company of a friend. "Just stand here. Just be you."

He nodded again, ready to become her guardian of choice. "I can do that."

Rocky arrived at the funeral parlor not long afterward, grumbling about traffic. The disgruntled words faded the moment he saw Elisha. Without a word, he went to her and embraced her, enfolding her in his long, thin arms. She almost lost it then. Only the sight of several of her other authors approaching forced Elisha to tough it out.

"If you want to cry, let me know," Rocky whispered, releasing her. "You can retreat into my limo. Nobody'll see you."

"Thanks," she murmured.

Squaring her shoulders, she went to greet the others. After she fielded the well wishes and accepted condolences, a quick inventory told her that everyone had received the same phone call. Sutherland, it seemed, had been busy. He'd spread the word to all of them, leaving messages on answering machines that made it sound as if their presence was obligatory.

Yet he himself was nowhere to be seen, she noted.

"As if I wouldn't have come once I knew. Why didn't I know?" Frances Mitchell, another one of her authors, asked, squinting myopic eyes behind her tinted designer glasses. The prolific creator of Emma Wales, an amateur sleuth that had caught the imagination of the reading public, had a voice that sounded like whiskey being poured over gravel. It was the by-product of a wilder youth than the average great-grandmother could usually boast about.

"I didn't call anyone," Elisha explained. "Just Mr. Randolph." She nodded toward him. "I just said I wouldn't be in for a few days."

Having stepped away for a moment, Rocky made his way over to the cluster around Elisha once he heard his name mentioned.

"Funny thing was, Sutherland called me, too, to make sure I knew," he told her. Taller than those around him, he scanned the crowded room. To no avail. "I expected to see him here, too. Has he come by?"

"If he did, I never saw him."

Nor did she expect to. But then, she hadn't expected Sutherland to send flowers either, but he had. A huge arrangement that rivaled even Rocky's. It arrived at the funeral home the morning after he'd called her about the poker game. Looking at the wreath, she speculated that it had to have deprived every florist in a three-mile area of their white roses. White, for purity, she thought. It somehow seemed appropriate.

Just when she felt she had a handle on Sutherland, he ruined it all by doing something nice. And then not showing up to take any credit. If anyone marched to a different drummer, he certainly did.

But his thoughtfulness in rounding up her authors and in sending the flowers touched her. The man defied any kind of label. She had a feeling that he probably liked it that way.

"I want you to take as much time as you want," Rocky told her the next time he had the opportunity to get her alone. When she looked at him quizzically, he smiled, obviously realizing he hadn't been clear. "Getting back to work," he explained. "Don't worry about a thing. I've got Carole covering for you."

Carole. The barracuda understudy who was waiting in the wings for her chance to chew the leading lady to bits. Elisha's mouth quirked.

"Not exactly the most comforting thing you could say to me at the moment." Or any moment, she added silently.

Overhearing, Sinclair was quick to add his support. "Not to worry, Elisha. The woman doesn't hold a candle to you."

But she'd like to, Elisha thought, nodding a greeting at someone else who had come to pay their respects. There was no doubt in Elisha's mind that the younger woman wanted to hold a candle to her so close that she'd set her on fire, thereby successfully eliminating her from any and all daily dealings at Randolph & Sons Publishing.

"Thanks," she murmured to Sinclair. "I can always count on you."

"Yes," he told her firmly. "You can."

* * *

The sun was out the morning of the funeral.

It seemed all wrong to Elisha. It should be raining. Everything in nature should have been weeping, the way she was inside. She wanted rain to show her that the angels were grieving as much as she and the girls were.

As always, Beth was at her side. Even Andrea seemed to cleave closer today, her attitude shed by the wayside, at least for the time being. She had to remain strong. For their sake. Just as Henry had remained strong at his wife's funeral.

A great many good things were said about Henry. Eulogy after eulogy was given, with each person sharing a bit of their time with Henry for the benefit of the rest of the mourners. It was clear to his daughters that he would be greatly missed.

But then, they already knew that. Because they were missing him something fierce themselves.

"He sounded like a great guy," Sinclair whispered to her as yet another person walked up to the pulpit.

"He was," Elisha replied with feeling.

When it was her turn to give a eulogy, she did so on legs that felt oddly shaky. Afterward, she didn't remember speaking. Rocky told her she did fine. She took his word for it.

"I am—was—five years older than Henry. That made me his big sister. Big sisters are supposed to protect their little brothers. But in reality, our roles were reversed even before he grew taller than I was. Henry always tried to protect me. He was like that with his wife, his daughters. Everyone he knew. That was the kind of person he was. Bighearted and caring. You felt safe around him. No matter what was wrong, when you were around Henry, you knew it would work itself out. He was a great optimist and you couldn't help but be one, too, when you were around him. Without him, some of the light has gone away. If you're looking down, Henry," she said, looking up toward the vaulted ceiling, "I just want to tell you that I miss you, little brother. More than I can ever say."

After the service, everyone came back to the house. People clad in black mingled with people wearing far brighter colors in honor of the way Henry had embraced life. Wholeheartedly.

His spirit seemed to permeate the gathering. Everyone talked about him. Everyone had a Henry story to share. It did her heart good to listen. She fervently hoped that it had the same effect on the girls. But by and by, people began leaving, going back to their lives, leaving Elisha and Henry's daughters to try to reconstruct theirs as best they could.

"Remember, I'm right next door if you need me," Anne Nguyen told her as she shepherded her own three sons, all under the age of fourteen, out the door. Her husband stood in the background and took the boys home.

Elisha smiled and nodded her thanks, then turned from the door. There was no one left in the room except for Rocky. Everyone else had left. Left her to tend to Andrea and Beth. To take over the reins as head of the family, a role she knew nothing about. She squelched the recurring panic as best she could.

She smiled at the man, grateful for his blatant show of support. "You don't have to stand guard over me, Rocky. I know you have to get back."

He shook his head. His intent was to remain for as long as she needed him to. "They can't fire me, I'm the boss's son, remember?"

"But the boss can read you the riot act," she reminded him. And they both knew how much he hated that. How much he dreaded it.

Rocky shrugged, attempting to appear nonchalant. "Nothing that hasn't happened before."

In response, she got behind him and placed both of her hands against his back. "Go." Gently, she pushed him toward the door. "I'm going to be all right."

Closing the door, she turned from it. Panic dashed through her. *No, I'm not.*

CHAPTER 25

It had been almost two weeks. Two weeks since the world had stopped. She wanted to go back to work. To do what she'd done when Garry had left her with a huge, gaping hole dead center in her heart. She'd thrown herself into her work. God knew there was always enough of it to submerge her. Unlike some other careers where things fluctuated between feast and famine, her line of work and her level of responsibility provided a feast, a tremendous, gluttonous feast.

But now, getting near the table was no longer a matter of simply showering, dressing and sailing out of her trendy apartment. Then the most difficult part of getting to work involved finding a cab.

Now there were layers of responsibilities to impede her progress. She couldn't just get herself ready and go. For one thing, she was too far away. Trains and cabs needed to take her from Henry's house on the island to the heart of the city, where Randolph & Sons lived.

And more important than that, she was no longer alone. There was more than just herself to account for. While Andrea was old enough to come home from school and be left alone for several hours, Beth was not.

She needed a system.

The realization occurred to Elisha at approximately two

o'clock in the morning, as she lay awake, watching shadows from the oak tree outside her bedroom window chase each other along the textured ceiling.

More than that, she needed her life back. A life where she was accountable only for herself, not for two other lives.

Can't run from it now.

"There's always boarding school," Rocky had told her the day before when she'd called in to say that her plan was to come back on the following Monday.

His suggestion about the school had come on the heels of his query regarding what arrangements she'd made for the girls while she was at work. His question had thrown her for a loop because she hadn't even considered that arrangements *had* to be made. The moment he'd asked, she realized something had to be done soon.

"Boarding school?" she'd repeated. Visions of unhappy children wearing uniforms and marching to class, flashed across her brain. It would be a way out for her, but definitely not for them.

"Yes. There are plenty to choose from. Any one of them would be willing to send you a boatload of brochures." He made a slight, derogatory sound, then went on. "My parents sent me to one right out of preschool. Addams Academy in Massachusetts. I spent the first twelve years of my academic life calling the janitor Dad."

His tone confirmed her thoughts on the matter. "You're not really recommending that, are you?"

He laughed. "Only as a last resort. But I am recommending a nanny."

"A nanny?" She turned the idea over in her head. If she could find someone who was equal parts Mary Poppins and Mrs. Doubtfire, she'd be home free.

"Or a housekeeper," Rocky had amended. "Someone to be there for the girls when they come home." Then he paused before adding in a strained, hurried voice, "Unless you intend to give up your career and stay home with them, at which point you can read about my suicide on page six of the section dealing with local news."

She'd disregard the dramatic portion of his statement and concentrate on the one kernel of information he'd yielded. "A nanny, huh?" The best way to proceed was to get a recommendation. Since it was his idea, she'd asked Rocky first. "Do you know of any?"

"All my nannies have long since departed this earth but I'll ask around, see if I can find the names of the best agencies."

"That's all right, I'll handle it myself." Then, hungry for news, to touch base with what grounded her, she asked, "How's everything going at the office?"

"Didn't my threat of suicide if you don't return give you a clue?"

She'd laughed then. Rocky always knew how to lighten a mood. "I thought you were just stroking my ego."

"I'll stroke anything you want," he promised, "just tell me that you'll come back."

She'd worked too long and too hard to give it up just like that and they both knew it. In Rocky's case, she had the feeling he was counting on it. "Why, Rocky, this is so sudden. I thought I wasn't your type."

She could hear the warm smile on his lips as he answered, "If I was batting for the other league, you would be my first choice."

"Consider my ego stroked."

And now she lay here, trying to make plans for the swiftly approaching day when she would return to her desk at Randolph & Sons. Anxious, overwrought and fighting madly to stay one step ahead of the depression that losing Henry had created, she realized the amount of sleep she'd managed to get came to a grand total of two and a half fitful hours. During that time she'd managed, from all indications by the way the sheets were twisted, to do a fair imitation of an old-fashioned spinning top.

She remained in bed for another hour, then gave up. She spent the next hour or so planning on how to break the news to the girls. She wasn't sure what to expect. During her visits to Henry, the girls had been on their best behavior, each vying for her attention. Now she was no longer the visiting aunt but the substitute parent and that brought with it an entire new set of ramifications. There might be warfare on the horizon.

"A nanny? Why can't you just stay with us?" Beth asked when she'd called the two together to tell them about her newest decision.

Not letting her answer Beth's question, Andrea protested sullenly, "I'm too old for a nanny. You've got to be kidding."

She took the questions in the order in which they came. "I am staying with you, Beth, but I have to go to work. And no, I'm not kidding. A nanny will be here when you get home from school, here to give you a snack when you're hungry."

"You don't have to work," Andrea pointed out. "Didn't Dad leave you enough money for us?"

It was a rhetorical question. Andrea had a pretty good idea how much they were worth. She and all her friends liked to compare notes on what their fathers did for a living and approximately how much money was involved in the effort.

The girls knew that she'd gone to Henry's lawyer to find out about his will. To her surprise, her brother had left a sizable estate to be held in trust for his daughters. There were no worries as far as finances were concerned. There was also enough to see to everything more than comfortably.

"Yes, he did," she answered patiently, "but I still have to work."

"Why?" Beth turned up her face toward her like a morning glory seeking the sun.

It had been a long time since Elisha had had to explain herself or to justify her actions to anyone. She was rusty at it.

"Because I do." She cringed inwardly as her words echoed back at her. That argument was as effective as every parent's "because I say so," she thought. This wasn't the foot she had wanted to start out on with the girls, especially Andrea. She tried again. "Because being a senior editor at Randolph & Sons is who and what I am. I love my work."

"Don't you love us?" Beth asked. Elisha noted that her eldest niece didn't seem interested in the turn the conversation had taken. She was looking off sullenly, as if she was counting the moments until she could leave the room.

"I love you both very much," Elisha assured them, although only Beth seemed to care. "But it's a different kind of love than I have for my work, honey," she explained. "I need to do this in order to be happy."

"Instead of being miserable, saddled with us," Andrea interjected sarcastically.

Elisha could only stare at Andrea. "No, that's not true. I'm not 'saddled' with you. I'm blessed." She thought it was the best thing to say under the circumstances. She seemed to have convinced Beth. Andrea rolled her eyes.

"Look, you don't have to go to any trouble, hiring a nanny or housekeeper or whatever," Andrea insisted. "I can take care of Beth."

It was a little akin to the argument about getting a puppy, Elisha thought. Great promises were made at the outset, at the bargaining table. Promises that were rarely, if ever, kept.

"And what if you want to go out?" Elisha asked. "You're fifteen. You've got friends. You'll want to hang out."

Andrea shrugged as if she didn't see the conflict. "No problem. I'll just take Beth with me."

She wasn't up to arguing about this. She knew that there were light-years between good intentions and actual occurrences. She'd been a teenager once herself. A million years ago. "My way's better."

"Why?" Andrea challenged angrily. "Because you say so?"

She had two degrees, one in English, one in communication. Neither one of them did her any good right now in fashioning a snappy comeback. "Yes, because I say so."

"Whatever." Throwing up her hands, Andrea stormed out of the room.

Rising, Elisha was right on her heels. She stopped at the bottom of the stairs.

"Andrea, come back here," she called up after her niece. Instead of obeying, Andrea slammed the door to her room in response. "Or not," Elisha mumbled under her breath.

So far, she thought, this new mother thing was not going swimmingly.

CHAPTER 26

Slipping off her glasses, Elisha rubbed the bridge of her nose. She'd been interviewing potential nannies all morning long and so far, no one had stood out. Several of the women had been extremely competent, but those had failed in the most important category. There had been no spark, no warmth emanating from them. She wanted a woman who was not only efficient, but likable.

Was that too much to ask?

Eventually, she began to think that it might be. Initially, she'd begun the interviews with both girls in the room with her. Andrea's patience was in short supply, especially since she was completely against inviting a total stranger to stay in the house in the first place. After the second applicant had left, so did Andrea, her expression a testimony to both her boredom and her annoyance over the whole event.

But Beth remained with her, listening intently. At the end of each interview, Elisha would glance in the little girl's direction to see what she thought of the current woman sitting before them. And each time, Beth would shake her head, her silky dark brown hair bouncing back and forth against her rounded cheeks.

They were down to their last potential nanny when Elisha took Beth aside. "You had to have liked at least one."

Beth remained firm. "Not as much as I like you."

So, this is what they mean by prisoner of love, Elisha thought.

"Thank you, sweetie, I appreciate the compliment, but we're just going to have to find a runner-up soon. I'm supposed to get back to work on Monday, just like you have to get back to school."

Beth made herself comfortable on the well-upholstered arm of the chair Elisha was sitting on. She looked Elisha in the eye and delivered her argument. "I don't have to go back to school."

"Yes, you do, it's the law." Thank God, she added silently. "You don't want the police to come here and arrest me, do you?"

Beth, apparently, had given this more than just a little thought. "No. But I could be homeschooled. You can teach me."

Elisha laughed at the idea. Threading her arm around the slim shoulders, she pulled Beth onto her lap. Beth curled up as if she belonged there. "Look, my brilliant little scholar, you already know enough that you could actually homeschool me."

Beth was more than willing to entertain the idea, if it would keep her aunt home. "Okay."

"That wasn't a suggestion." Giving Beth a hug, she scooted her off her lap. "We'll get through this," she said with a great deal more enthusiasm than she actually felt. "Okay, who's next?"

"Just one," Beth told her. "Samantha Wentworth." Frowning, she looked up at her aunt. "I don't like her name."

At this point, a note of desperation was beginning to set in. She had to find someone. Some of the first applicants she'd interviewed this morning were starting to look pretty good to her.

"We'll give her a chance anyway," she told Beth. "If we hire her, we can call her Sam. You like the name Sam, don't you?" Thinking it over, Beth nodded. "Okay, then, let's bring in Sam."

Beth went to the door and called the woman in from the kitchen.

As it turned out, Samantha Wentworth was the best of the lot. During the interview, she looked at Beth several times, addressing her comments to her as if the little girl was on the same level as she was, rather than just an annoying charge she was going to be taking care of. That impressed Elisha and she could tell that it wasn't lost on Beth.

The references the woman had brought with her appeared to be impeccable. Each family listed on the sheet she'd had prospective applicants fill out had given Samantha a letter of recommendation, praising her qualities as both a housekeeper and a nanny.

The woman also did windows.

Nonetheless, Elisha made a mental note to give every family listed a call to ask questions firsthand. Letters could be forged.

God, when had she gotten so cynical?

"We'll be in touch," she promised at the conclusion of the interview as she walked Samantha to the front door and then outside to the woman's small economy car. For the first time that day, she actually meant the line.

"I'll be looking forward to it," Samantha replied. She'd addressed the sentence to Beth.

Exhausted, Elisha walked back into the house with Beth. "I think I like her."

"Yeah," Beth agreed slowly. "I think I do, too."

Elisha's mouth curved. Beth sounded like a little old lady. "Let's tell Andrea." Going toward the stairs, she stood at the bottom and called up, "Andrea, could you come down here, please?"

"She's not home," Beth told her.

For the last few days, Andrea had hung around the house. She'd come to expect that. That she'd gone out without saying anything made Elisha feel uneasy.

"She's not home?" Elisha repeated, fighting a wave of distress. "Then where is she? Do you know where your sister is?"

Beth raised and lowered her small shoulders as she said, "Out."

It was a large world outside the house. "That covers a huge amount of territory."

"That's all she said when she walked by me," Beth told her.

She should have been paying more attention to Andrea and less to the women she was interviewing, Elisha upbraided herself. None of the applicants had measured up, anyway. Not like Samantha had.

It was broad daylight and this was a nice neighborhood. There was no reason to feel this uneasiness that was setting in, Elisha told herself. It was just that she had no control beyond the walls of the house.

Don't have much control inside the walls of the house either, not when it comes to Andrea.

She looked down at Beth. "Where does your sister usually go when she goes out? Who are her friends?"

To both questions, Beth shook her head and replied, "I don't know. Andrea doesn't tell me their names. Says that's her business."

That didn't sound very encouraging, Elisha thought. This being responsible for someone else really was the pits. Along with the feeling of uncertainty and being trapped, the parental role brought with it a helplessness that made it difficult to function.

All sorts of things began popping up in her head as she thought about what Andrea might be doing. Each more negative than the last.

Elisha suddenly found herself wishing that her mother was alive so that she could apologize to the woman for what she knew she had to have put her through during her own teenage years.

Being the parent in charge was damn rough.

"You got your wish, Mom." She'd lost track of the number of times her mother had uttered the age-old line Wait, wait until you have children of your own. You'll see. "I've got children now, Mom. Henry's children."

She could only pray that she wouldn't make a mess of things.

* * *

By six that evening, by her own admission, Elisha was clos-ing in on becoming a basket case. She had no one to turn to in her circle of friends. They were either childless or clear across the country.

Desperate, with Beth in tow, she finally went next door and rang Anne Nguyen's doorbell.

There was a great deal of noise coming from inside. Her anx-iety growing to proportions she could barely manage, Elisha tried knocking on the door. Loud. As it was, she was about two steps removed from calling the local hospitals to see if any of them had had a teenage girl brought in recently.

Anne swung open her door even as she was issuing a warn-ing to her oldest to turn down his music or spend the rest of the evening in the garbage. Her son took this as an opportunity to begin negotiations for an iPod.

Taking one look at Elisha's face, Anne waved her son into silence.

"What happened?" Anne asked, drawing Elisha into her house. Like a faithful puppy, Beth followed behind her. "You look awful."

"I'm just worried." This would probably sound stupid to Anne. The woman had three children and she seemed to be jug-gling all three of them just fine. Meanwhile, *she'd* misplaced a fifteen-year-old girl. "Andrea went out."

Anne ushered aunt and niece into her kitchen. "She's a teen-ager, they do that." Without asking, she poured a cup of coffee for her guest and placed it in front of her. Beth had gone off, en-ticed to play the latest video game by one of Anne's younger sons. "Do you know where?"

Taking the cup gratefully, Elisha shook her head. "I'm not even sure when." She took a sip of coffee and realized that she hadn't eaten since breakfast. God, she had to get better organized than this. "I was interviewing nannies," she added quickly, not wanting Anne to think that she was completely oblivious to what was going on in the house.

"Nannies," Anne repeated with a knowing nod. "That would explain it."

"Explain what?"

"Why Andrea left the house." Anne sat down beside her, her own mug of coffee in hand. "The dynamics of her life are changing. She's trying to regain some control. The only thing she has control over is herself, so she took herself out of the equation. Went someplace familiar so that she could feel better about everything."

The only problem was, it might have been familiar to Andrea but not to her. It had been a lot easier when she could just sit on the sidelines, watching Henry be the parent. She didn't like the fact that Andrea was off in some unknown place.

Beth and Anne's son Eddie came running into the kitchen. "Mom, can I have some chocolate-chip cookies? For Beth."

"Well, as long as they're for Beth," Anne allowed, getting up. She went to the rack where the batch she'd just made were cooling.

"You bake?" Elisha asked.

"On occasion."

Elisha groaned. "All I do is heat things up that come prepared. Either that, or dial out for pizza."

"Pizza's good, too," Anne said, placing a dozen cookies on a plate and handing them to her son. "Bread, cheese, tomato, covers a lot of the food groups."

Beth's eyes shone when she saw the cookies. She might have had the brain of a high-school sophomore, but she had the cravings of a full-fledged adult woman. Elisha had a feeling the cookies were going to have a very short life span.

Clutching the coffee cup between both hands, Elisha brought it up to her lips. Seeking the familiar.

Like Andrea, she supposed.

Little by little, as she sipped, the agitation drained from her. She looked at Anne. "How do you do it?"

"Do what?"

She nodded toward the family room, where Eddie and Beth were playing a video game. Unable to play for lack of an extra set of controls, Anne's youngest son, Richard, was cheering them on. "Make it all work."

Anne smiled and sighed. Deeply. "It's a learning process."

That sounded a great deal like school. "When do you graduate?" Elisha asked.

"About five minutes before you die."

This time it was Elisha's turn to sigh. "Something to look forward to."

Anne set down her mug and placed her hand on top of Elisha's. "My mother gave me one piece of advice when I had my first baby. She said the journey was the important thing, not the destination."

"No offense, but your mother was probably thinking she was finally going to have her revenge for what you put her through as a kid."

Anne laughed, picking up her mug again. Somewhere in the background, something fell with a crash. Closing her eyes, Anne winced but remained where she was. "You're probably right."

CHAPTER 27

Andrea finally came home a little after ten that evening.

The time between when she'd put Beth to bed and Andrea's arrival had stretched out before Elisha to form an eternity. She'd spent the entire time vacillating between being furious and praying that the girl was safe. Several times, she'd picked up the phone to call the police, then replaced it. She knew all the excuses she'd get, that teenagers lost track of time, that they ran away from home. In either case, the police didn't involve themselves. Not unless she was willing to file a missing person's report. Because of Andrea's age, one couldn't be filed until she was missing for twenty-four hours.

So she waited. And paced. And swore under her breath at Henry for dying and leaving this all in her lap.

The second she heard the key in the door, Elisha raced toward it.

"Are you all right?" she demanded as Andrea entered.

The same remote, unresponsive expression she'd seen earlier was on the teenager's face. "Yeah. Why?"

Why? It took effort not to explode. "Because I just spent the last seven hours worried about you, that's why."

Andrea began to walk past her. "You didn't have to."

Stunned, Elisha made a grab for the girl's shoulder, swinging her around. Andrea shrugged her off. "Yes, I have to. I'm responsible for you. Look—" she struggled to hold on to her temper "—I don't want you leaving without telling me where you're going."

Andrea's eyes were sullen and accusing as they looked at her. "What is this, prison?"

God, was this what Henry had put up with? There was no way of knowing. Henry never complained about anything. "No," Elisha answered tersely, "it's a home. But if I'm going to turn my life inside out for you, you're going to have to throw me some crumbs here, Andie."

Andrea crossed her arms before her, the absolute prototype for defiance. "You're hiring a nanny. Doesn't seem like you're turning very much inside out to me."

"I'm hiring a nanny because someone has to be here for you in the afternoon since I'm still keeping my job." *If not my sanity.* "My commute is going to be more than twice as long as it was so that you can go on living here where your friends are."

The information caught Andrea off guard. Some of the defiance momentarily left her face. "You're not selling the house?"

"No." She never would have sold it. As far as she was concerned, the house was part of Henry's legacy to the girls. It was just living here that presented the problem. But she was going to have to deal with it, at least for now. "You and Beth have already gone through a lot, I can't take you away from your home and friends, as well."

Obviously surprised, Andrea shifted from foot to foot. A little of the girl she once knew returned as the words reluctantly emerged from Andrea's lips. "Okay." She frowned, then continued, "I'll let you know where I'm going."

Score one for the child-rearing challenged. A smile rose to Elisha's mouth. "Thank you. I appreciate it."

Andrea tossed her head. "But you're going to have to let me know where you're going, too."

The salvo the girl delivered had come out of left field. "What?"

Andrea smiled, clearly pleased to be in the driver's seat. "It works both ways. You said you'd worry if you didn't know where I was. Well, Beth'll worry if you're gone too long. She'll probably think another adult abandoned her."

Elisha looked at her, trying to keep the knowing expression from her face. It wouldn't be cool for Andrea to admit that she might be the one who was worried.

"Wouldn't want Beth to think that." Elisha smiled, putting out her hand. "Okay, you've got a deal."

Andrea took the offered hand, still looking a little rebellious, but relatively satisfied that she had won some kind of point. "Deal," she murmured.

Elisha was asleep probably ten seconds before her head hit the pillow. She was beyond tired, close to dead. It felt as if everything had been drained out of her over the course of the day. So when she became aware that the phone was ringing, her first impulse was to ignore it. Anyone who had something to say to her could say it to her answering machine and she'd deal with whatever it was in the morning.

But when the phone rang the third time, always long enough to deliver four rings before disconnecting, she knew there was no peace to be had until she spoke with whoever was on the other end of the line.

Probably Rocky, assuring himself that she was coming in on Monday, Elisha thought darkly, reaching for the receiver. She wasn't feeling very friendly.

"This better be an obscene phone call to make it worth my while." That would shake him up, she congratulated herself.

"Would heavy breathing do or do you actually require verbal scenarios?"

Her eyes flew open as every sleeping bone in her body instantly woke up. She scrambled into a sitting position, adrenaline rushing around without a clear-cut enemy or reason for defense. She had no idea why she reacted that way to Sutherland when, if it had been any of her other authors answering with that quip, she would have continued lying in bed.

"Mr. Sutherland?"

"You recognize my voice?" She thought he sounded mildly amused.

"No one else's voice sounds as if it's coming from the bottom of a three-hundred-foot oil well." *Think, Lise, think. Don't babble.* Thoughts began to emerge and solidify. "I'm told I have you to thank for spreading the word about my brother's passing."

He shrugged off her gratitude the way he shrugged off everything else, with a note of indifference that completely mystified her. "Don't know about thanks, but I thought you might need the support."

Maybe there was more to this man than just commando training. "I did. Thanks." She paused, trying desperately to lift the fog from her brain. "And thanks for the flower arrangement." Thinking of it, she smiled. "It dwarfed everything else." She had a feeling that it was supposed to. The man liked to think of himself as larger than life.

"I'm glad you liked it."

The room felt chilly. This was a colder autumn than most. She pulled the covers closer. "I was surprised you didn't come, since you told everyone else about the wake. I kept looking for you."

There was a long pause on the other end. "Funerals are not my thing. I've seen too many good men put in the ground already." He gave serious thought to hanging up before she could probe further, but he hadn't gotten to the reason for his call. "So how's it going?"

Was he being actually friendly? She glanced at the clock on

the nightstand. It was almost midnight. Was there a full moon out? Was that the reason for this show of civility? "You want that blow by blow, or a *Reader's Digest* summary?"

"The latter."

Elisha smiled to herself. She would have put money on his choosing that version.

"Rough, but I'll make it." Even as she said it, she didn't whole-heartedly believe it. But Sutherland wasn't someone she'd be willing to pour out her innermost insecurities to. The man respected strength, not weakness. Then, because she felt she had to say something, she added, "I've been interviewing nannies all day."

"Sounds like you didn't find one."

She tried not to notice that having his distinctly male voice rumbling against her ear was stirring something within her. Probably had to do with the fact that she hadn't been with a man for so long, she was no longer sure which end was up. And though she hated to admit it, Sutherland did have a sexy voice.

"Actually, I did," she told him. "I just need to check out her references."

"What's her name?"

"Samantha Wentworth. Why?"

It was clear by his tone that he didn't like explaining himself. "I probably have a lot better sources than you do."

"For checking out nannies?"

"As long as they come under the heading of human beings," Sutherland said crisply, cutting short any further speculation on her part. "How soon do you need to know?"

Okay, we'll talk your language. "ASAP."

"I'll see what I can do."

It was as good as a promise and she knew it. One less thing to worry about.

Settling back against the pillow, she slowly wound the cord around her finger. Curiosity got the better of her. "Why did you call, Ryan?"

There was a long pause on the other end of the line. She wondered if it was because she'd called him by his first name. Had she crossed some imaginary line she shouldn't have? She half expected to hear a click. Instead, he answered her.

"To see if you've thought about rescheduling your appearance at the poker game. I've got one going this Friday."

Friday. She'd missed the game two weeks ago. God, had it been two weeks already? Two weeks since Henry had died? It felt like aeons, and at the same time, like just yesterday. Without work to serve as her guide, the days somehow seemed to meld into one another without form or designation.

When she made no answer, he was all set to shrug it off. "All right, maybe it's too soon. I'll—"

"It's not too soon," she interrupted. "Besides—" she smiled to herself "—as I remember, the fate of your manuscript lies in the balance."

"No, it doesn't," he contradicted, his voice as sober as a judge doling out a death sentence. "My manuscript is just fine."

Somehow, they were back to the same argument. She had no idea why, but it made her smile. Probably because she missed familiar ground. "Oh, it'll sell, Sutherland."

"Damn straight it'll sell."

"But," she continued with feeling, "it'll sell more copies and gain you a measure of respect if you do it my way."

He exhaled in what she could only take to be exasperation. "Still cocky even after everything."

I am so far from cocky, you'd need a road map to find your way back to the first C. But it wasn't anything she would readily admit to him. "Hey, if it works…"

Sutherland wasn't about to listen to anymore. "Okay, the game'll be at my house on the island." Then, in case she didn't have it, he gave her the address.

All the phone numbers where she could reach him plus his two residences were already entered in her BlackBerry. What she wasn't prepared for was that he was holding the game at his house rather than his Tribeca apartment. "I thought your friends liked to play in the city."

"No," he contradicted with a touch of impatience, "I said my friends played when they were in the city. But I've decided to relocate it this time." Then, before she could get a chance to ask him why, he told her. "So that you wouldn't be too far from the girls."

Thoughtful. Ryan Sutherland was being thoughtful. It had to be some kind of trick. The man was setting her up for something.

She was still waiting to find out what that something was when he hung up several minutes later.

CHAPTER 28

"You going on a date?" Andrea asked incredulously that Friday when Elisha asked her to stay with Beth in the evening.

She hadn't called it anything at all, but if she had, it wouldn't have been a date. Dates were for people who still nurtured the hope for a social life. She'd given that notion up after Garry left.

"It's not a date. I'm going out to play poker with some friends."

The game didn't seem to matter to Andrea. The destination, however, did. The teenager eyed her. "In the city?"

"No, just a few miles away, actually." She'd had no idea that Henry and Ryan Sutherland lived so close to one another. She hadn't made the connection until she'd looked it up on her BlackBerry this morning and the address had sunk in. The world was a grab bag of constant surprises to her. "I need you to stay home with Beth until I get back." She didn't estimate that it would be too late in the evening. She'd win, put Sutherland in his place and be back by eleven. Maybe eleven-thirty.

Andrea looked at her moodily. "Why don't you hire a sitter?"

"I am," Elisha said brightly. "You." She'd babysat for the neighbors when she was younger than Andrea. There was no reason why the girl couldn't stay with her sister.

Andrea lifted her chin defiantly. If she was stuck, she was going to make the most of it. "Sitters get paid."

She'd expected something like this. Maybe she was getting

better at the game. Still, she asked, "You want money for watching your sister?"

Andrea blew out a loud sigh. "No, I want money to make up for my not going out tonight. I can't do that if I'm going to be here babysitting."

She supposed Andrea had a point. And if she went along with it, she'd at least seem as if she was willing to compromise. That had to earn her some points with the girl. "Well, since I'm spoiling your plans for the evening, I'll pay you for watching Beth." It had been almost thirty years since she'd babysat and had no idea what the going rate was. "How much?"

Andrea shrugged. "For you, I'll take five bucks an hour."

Fifty cents had been the going rate when she had sat for the O'Hara twins. It should have been fifty cents an hour plus combat pay. In comparison, sitting for Beth was a walk in the park.

"I'll make sure I'm not gone too long," Elisha promised.

Andrea stood back and gave her the once-over in slow, sweeping glances. And then she laughed dismissively. "Looking like that, you should be back before you even leave."

Elisha narrowed her eyes. She saw nothing wrong with the casual pants and loose, nondescript blouse she was wearing. She wasn't sure if this was the outfit she was ultimately going to wear, but the look on Andrea's face made her feel insecure. "Looking like what?"

"Lame."

Elisha glanced down at her outfit. It was neat, clean and the colors didn't clash. It was a poker game, for God's sake. "You think this is lame?"

The small noise Andrea made had definite rude overtones. "Well, not for a grandmother." And then she frowned. Elisha saw that her niece was looking at the glasses that she'd shoved on top of her head. "You gotta wear those glasses?"

"Only if I want to read the numbers on the cards. I've gotten rather blind when it comes to close work."

Andrea's expression said she didn't think much of the excuse, but she'd let it slide. For now. "Okay, then how about your hair?"

Instinctively, Elisha put her hand to her hair, as if to protect it from any insults that were coming. "What about my hair?"

Andrea had begun to circle her like a drill sergeant in the middle of a major inspection. "Well, for one thing, it hasn't seen fit to come out of the nineties."

Elisha turned her head so that she could keep her niece in her sights. "Excuse me?"

"Your hairstyle, very yesterday. And the color's dull." Having come full circle, Andrea stopped to stand in front of her again. Judging by the girl's expression, she hadn't passed whatever test Andrea had subjected her to. "Like your clothes."

Back to the clothes again, Elisha thought, just a little annoyed at all this critiquing. "I'm going to play cards, Andie, not try to seduce somebody."

"Good thing, because you sure wouldn't be able to, not unless it was some guy with a seeing-eye dog."

Elisha pretended to wince. "Ouch." The comment had been harsh, but she wasn't about to let Andrea see that it had hurt her. That made her too vulnerable.

"Sorry, I call it as I see it. You've got to get with it," Andrea insisted. "People know you're my aunt now."

"And you have an image to maintain," Elisha guessed.

Her expression said the conclusion was self-evident. "Well, duh."

Elisha looked over her shoulder toward Beth. The little girl had been standing there, listening to the entire exchange. Might as well have the peanut gallery put in their two cents' worth, she thought.

"How about you, Beth?" She beckoned the girl forward. "Do I look bad to you?"

Crossing to join them, Beth raised her face up to her. "You look like Aunt Elisha."

Beside her, Andrea stifled a laugh. Elisha wasn't sure if Beth's comment was a good thing or a bad thing. It certainly did nothing to bolster her sagging morale. She'd been doing fine until she'd gotten the once-over from Andrea. Of course, they moved in different worlds, she and Andrea. But she had to admit that the woman looking back at her from the mirror over the fireplace did look a little, well, matronly.

When had that happened?

When had she stopped looking hot? She could remember looking hot once. Could remember hearing one of her boyfriends refer to her that way. And she could remember when her appearance had been all-important to her.

It stopped being important to her the day that Garry left.

After that, she got too tired, too wrapped up in her growing career at Randolph & Sons to really care what she looked like as long as it was presentable. Her eyes widened as she looked, really looked at herself, perhaps seeing herself for the first time in years.

Somehow, she'd allowed herself to slide into the stereotype of a middle-aged woman without even realizing it was happening. Certainly without putting up a fight to prevent it.

Elisha suddenly glanced down at her midriff. Well, at least she'd lost those annoying pounds that had seen fit to sneak up on her over the years, although she wouldn't have recommended the method that had brought her to this lighter weight.

Exhaling a cleansing breath, she looked at Andrea. "Okay, what do you suggest?"

Andrea struggled not to look as smug as she felt. "Let me do your hair and makeup."

Given some of the things that passed as acceptable in the under-thirty set, she wasn't altogether sure if that was such a good idea. Especially since Andrea suddenly looked eager. "Whoa, are you still mad at me?"

Andrea paused to consider the question. Right now, they were living within the boundaries of a tentative treaty. "No, I guess not."

She would have preferred hearing more enthusiasm in the girl's voice, but she supposed she would take what she could get.

"Okay, then I guess you can have access to my face and hair." Andrea was already grabbing her by the hand and leading her up the stairs to her room. "If I like what you do," Elisha qualified, "I'll go with it."

"What can I do?" Beth wanted to know as she hurried up the stairs behind them.

Thank God she still had one of them in her corner. She looked over her shoulder at the little girl as Andrea led her into her room. "You can tell me if she's messing me up."

Beth seemed more than happy to be accommodating. "Okay," she chirped.

Andrea's room was a compilation of piles. Piles of clothing, piles of books, piles of DVDs and CDs. Somehow, to the teenager, there was order in the heart of the chaos. Andrea brought her over to a chair and gestured toward it.

Elisha had no idea why she was even concerned about the way she looked. She'd always made sure that her clothes, suits mostly, were always cleaned and pressed. But beyond that, she no longer gave her wardrobe much thought.

Yet it seemed important to look good tonight. She supposed she wanted to look her best while delivering the death blow.

"All right, Andrea," she said, sitting down. "I'm all yours." It was a swivel chair and she pivoted it into position. "Just be gentle."

Andrea rolled her eyes even as she went into her bathroom to retrieve her arsenal.

* * *

Ryan stood in the doorway, one hand leaning on the doorknob. He was staring at the woman who had just rung his bell.

This was his editor?

There'd clearly been some kind of change since he'd last seen her. The woman had on a leather jacket with a red turtleneck peering out from the top, but what had actually caught his attention was the pencil-slim black skirt she was wearing. It ended several inches above her knees.

He hadn't even realized that Elisha Reed had skin above her knees. She'd always made him think of some kind of prim, proper stereotypical spinster who'd given herself over to a career in letters. Obviously, he was going to have to rethink his initial conception of the woman in light of her appearance now.

The skin above the knees looked quite appealing. She had nice legs, he decided. And cleaned up a hell of a lot better than he thought she might.

He raised an eyebrow, not finished with his perusal. "Max?"

She stifled the urge to tug on the edge of Andrea's skirt. She wasn't used to anything so short, and the way Sutherland was looking at her was making her nervous. He was probably trying to rattle her so that she wouldn't play well. Well, she was on to him.

As if to show him that, she tossed her head. The hair that Andrea had spent the better part of an hour and a half lightening and working over moved in response. Rather than wearing it up and away from her face, the way she ordinarily did, it fell in waves just a little shy of her shoulders. She wasn't sure if she liked it yet, but it was different.

"Yes."

Sutherland stepped back, admitting her into the house. She

was very aware that he was giving her a very slow once-over. "You do know that it's regular poker we're playing and not strip."

Inside, she turned to look at him. "Yes, why?"

"Just making sure." His face was a mask, damn him. "Not that the latter might not be interesting," he allowed. "It just never occurred to me to play it before since there were only male faces around the table."

Maybe this wasn't a good idea after all. But she'd come so far and she wasn't about to let him see that she was having second thoughts. She had to see this through.

"Regular poker is all I'm here to play," she informed him crisply.

"And you intend to cheat."

Now he had her mad. Except for one algebra test back in ninth grade, she'd never cheated on anything in her life. "What?"

Still keeping her in the foyer, his gaze was unrelenting. "Lady, you came to play dressed like that hoping to distract the rest of us."

She shot him a look. "Would you like me to put on a burka?"

He considered the idea for a moment. Granted, the woman wasn't model thin, but then, women who looked as if they'd fall over at the first sign of a spring breeze had never interested him. He liked to feel something in his arms when he held a woman.

"Might not be a bad idea," he told her. "You're blonder."

"Sunshine." She caught the tip of her tongue between her teeth.

He knew better. "In a bottle?"

"Maybe."

Ryan nodded his approval. "Becoming."

The smile started inside of her before it ever reached her lips. "Thank you."

"Doesn't mean I'll let you cheat."

She met his gaze head-on. "Wasn't planning on it."

With a nod, Sutherland turned to lead the way to his game room.

CHAPTER 29

There were five players around the circular table in Sutherland's game room, all men. All, Elisha judged, around the best-selling author's age.

Looking at them, she could almost feel the brotherhood they shared. Though they varied in size and appearance, all looked fit, as if they could go on a fifty-mile forced march with sixty-pound backpacks at the drop of a poker chip. She had a feeling that love of poker was not the only thing the men shared. They probably shared a common past, as well. A past, if her limited information was correct, that no one else would ever be completely privy to. People in that world were never entirely debriefed, not even before God.

Sutherland nodded toward the only other vacant seat at the table besides his own. "You can take that chair."

She did as suggested, noting out of the corner of her eye that at least one of the men, the one with the salt-and-pepper mustache, had half risen in his chair.

Nodding at the man, she smiled, then looked back at Sutherland. "Aren't you going to introduce me, Mr. Sutherland?"

"Yes, 'Mr. Sutherland,' where are your manners?" the man closest to her left asked just before winking at her. As blond as Sutherland was dark, he had eyes so brown that they almost looked black. She wasn't sure if he was being friendly out of kindness, flirtatious out of habit, or having fun at her expense out of the perverseness that Sutherland had exhibited most of the time she'd dealt with him.

Though she kept a smile on her face, she felt every inch a fish out of water. This was *not* the kind of situation she was accustomed to.

"Same place your common sense is," Ryan retorted in response to his friend's question. With a frown, he went around the table, shooting off names as if they were rounds being fired from an automatic weapon. He didn't even bother pointing, but she assumed that he was naming them in the order they were sitting. "Murphy, Finn, Gonzales, Conway and Jovanovich."

In response, each man bobbed his head, except for the winker. Murphy just winked again.

Elisha nodded in response, trying her best to look as if she was comfortable in these surroundings. As if playing cards with a bunch of strange men was something she did all the time. Then, because Sutherland hadn't, she introduced herself to them. "I'm Elisha Reed, his editor."

Finn, a man with a ruddy complexion and hair the color of a newly harvested carrot, smirked. "She going to be editing you tonight, Sutherland?"

Slanting her eyes toward Sutherland, she noticed that the thin line that comprised his lips grew thinner still. She saved him from making a response by saying, "And I take it that you're all former Navy SEALs, or former colleagues of his?"

Gonzales seemed amused by her innocent question. The smile on his face was kindly. Sutherland could take a lesson from him, she thought.

"If we told you what we were," he confided, lowering his voice to an appropriate stage whisper, "I'm afraid we'd have to kill you."

She would have liked to think he was joking, but she wasn't

a hundred percent sure of that. Banking down her uneasiness, she looked at Sutherland again.

His frown was creating ruts on either side of his mouth. "This is poker, Max, not a game of Truth or Dare," Sutherland snapped at her. "Are you here to play, or to talk?"

No, she wasn't going to be the field mouse to his mountain lion, she told herself. Instead, she raised her chin pugnaciously, showing him, she hoped, that she wasn't about to go cowering off in some corner.

"I didn't realize they were mutually exclusive." Then, because she saw he was about to bite off another terse comment, she answered, "I'm here to play."

"Good." He picked up the first deck of cards and broke open the seal around the box. "Then let's get on with it."

He'd never been what she would have described as easygoing, but Sutherland seemed to be unusually grumpy tonight, even for him. She wondered if it had anything to do with her being here.

Too bad. A bet's a bet. And she intended on winning hers.

Sutherland's mood did not get any better as the evening unfolded. Especially when she wound up winning far more hands than she lost. At the end of a long evening of intense playing, Elisha found herself acknowledged the big winner. Not that a great deal of money had changed hands. However, most of it had wound up with Elisha.

The men took their losses graciously. She hadn't heard a single foul word from any of them, not an easy feat if their origins had been the kind she'd initially surmised. She had to admit that she was grateful not to have been submitted to an evening of mindless, aimless cursing. She prized words far too much not to take offense at what she'd always felt were only vulgar place holders.

And then finally, with the chips gone and the beer consumed, the men called it a night.

Jerez Jovanovich glanced back over his shoulder as he slipped on his jacket and prepared to take his leave. He laughed as he looked at Elisha before turning to his host. "You might have mentioned that you were bringing in a ringer."

The frown Ryan had been sporting in one form or another all evening grew more intense. "I was bringing her in to teach her a lesson."

That made it even more humorous. "And what lesson would that be, my friend? How to plan for an early retirement on someone else's money?" the man asked with a laugh.

The rest of the men gathered in the foyer, reaching into the closet to claim their outerwear.

"If anyone learned a lesson tonight, it's the rest of us," Murphy chimed in. Standing, he was shorter than the rest. But he made up for it with determination that on occasion bordered on obsession. "Bringing a woman into the mix is too distracting. Shakes things up too much." Murphy allowed his eyes to sweep over her, even though she was still sitting at the table in the other room.

Gonzales laughed. "Speak for yourself. Me, I like things shaken, not stirred."

Finn directed his words to Elisha. "Anytime you want someone to come to Atlantic City with you—" he reached for his own coat and put it on "—give me a call. I'm your man."

"I'll be first alternate," Conway volunteered with enthusiasm, raising his hand like some schoolboy.

"You'll be first jackass," Sutherland snapped, ushering the men out and closing the door on them. He could hear the hoots of laughter on the other side before the men went to their cars. Flipping the lock, he turned around to face Elisha.

The dark cloud across Sutherland's brow intensified. From where she stood, he seemed to sink deeper into the dark hole he'd occupied for most of the evening.

Why?

Drawing her courage to her, Elisha left the shelter of the game room and walked into the foyer. "Something wrong?" she asked, her expression serious as she fished her jacket out of the closet.

"What could be wrong?" he barked. "You played well."

Was that an accusation? Didn't he know that she would have never put in an appearance here if she couldn't at least play decently? She'd taken him for a fair judge of character. This couldn't have been a surprise. "Told you I did."

He'd thought that she meant she played well for an editor. For a woman. The women in his world couldn't be placed in the same class as a riverboat gambler. But Elisha could. "Where the hell did you learn how to play like that?"

She smiled. "Just natural talent, I guess." She shrugged dismissively. Then, because he was apparently waiting for more, she added, "I picked up a lot of tips watching the dealers at the casinos."

Sutherland snorted, an angry bull waiting to be led into the arena for what could, quite possibly, be his death. "Now I suppose you'll want me to incorporate your notes into my manuscript."

So, that was what was bothering him. That and he was probably one of those men who hated being shown up. She hadn't won to show him up, she'd done it to make him more accessible. To show him that she could be in his world and that when he was in hers, he was to show her a measure of respect for what she did.

"That was the agreement," she said lightly.

His eyes were steely daggers as he looked at her. She could almost feel the sharp points. "What if I don't want to honor it?"

"You will," she told him confidently. "Because you are all about honor, Mr. Sutherland."

"You took me for three hundred dollars, Max. You can drop the 'Mr.' part."

Her eyes held his. "I'd rather drop it because we're friends."

That was something that hadn't been in tonight's bargain.

Something else hadn't been in tonight's bargain. His reaction to her.

He didn't like it.

"I don't make friends easily."

Her mouth curved, making her look younger than he knew she was. Making her look like a girl. She probably knew that, which was why she was smiling the way she was.

"I already gathered that," she told him. "Still, you have some." Something wary entered his eyes, as if he was telling her to tread lightly. Why? What was it that he was afraid of? Even as she wondered she almost laughed. What would he say if she accused him of that, of being afraid? What would she say after he choked her for daring to say it? she wondered humorously. "Those men at the table tonight, for instance."

"Collectively, I've known them more than a hundred years."

"Tough club to get into." And then, because she'd been taught to try another door when one was locked, she said, "Had to be a first day for all of them, though. I'd like my chance at a first day."

"Why?"

She didn't let his malevolent expression get to her. Or at least not show him that it got to her. "Because, for one thing, it's easier working together if we're not adversaries."

He was quick to point out the obvious to her. "It's easier still if you just go along with everything I give you."

But she shook her head. "Then I wouldn't be doing my job

and I could be replaced by a rubber stamp." She refused to allow herself to look away. Instead, her gaze challenged him. "Is that what you want?"

He realized that he'd been watching her lips a little too intently as they formed words.

"Maxwell," Sutherland warned darkly, "I think you'd be better off if you didn't ask me what I wanted."

For most of her life, there'd always been this part that liked challenging the unknown, that liked to walk into a dark room and let her imagination run wild before she turned on the light, chasing the specters away. She also had more than her share of curiosity. She liked to think it was what made her a good editor.

"Why?"

He didn't answer her at first.

And then, instead of using words, Sutherland showed her.

CHAPTER 30

His mood had been dark from the moment the woman had walked in. From the moment he'd seen her and realized that she no longer looked like the woman he'd been dealing with over the last few months.

Granted, until tonight, Elisha Reed had been the model for the somewhat frumpy, no-nonsense and no-sense-of-humor editor he was used to. He didn't particularly like the type, but he knew how to handle that kind of editor, knew where he was in the scheme of things. Best of all, he knew that he could do what he wanted without interference. Being a bestselling author had its perks and it didn't particularly bother him that intimidation was one of them.

One way or another, he was accustomed to getting what he wanted. It had been this way ever since he'd been on his own. And now, with more money coming in than he needed, he held a trump card. He could pull up stakes and go to another publishing house if he wasn't happy.

That was supposed to keep his editor in line.

But this woman, even before her transformation, didn't seem to want to sit back and just accept the positive fallout for being considered his editor. Didn't want to ride on the end of the gravy train. She wanted to reschedule the trip.

And if that wasn't irritating enough, she'd thrown a final monkey wrench into the works. She'd come here, looking more like a woman than an editor, and then proceeded to beat not only his friends, but him at what they considered to be their own game. If that wasn't adding insult to injury, then he wasn't aware what the trite saying actually meant.

There definitely was nothing to smile about.

Less than nothing. Because he realized that he was attracted to this woman who was making too many waves in his otherwise even-keel life.

Granted, it was on a purely physical level, but he didn't want to be attracted at all, on any level. Attractions meant nothing but trouble. They tended to cloud issues, to complicate life, and his life had always been streamlined. His missions might have been complex, but his life now was simple and he wanted to keep it that way.

He'd been married once, briefly, when he was in his early twenties. It hadn't worked out, as he'd sensed even at the outset that it wouldn't, but stubbornly, he'd wanted to give it a try. He and his ex, whom he no longer thought of by any other name than that abbreviated label, were so far from compatible outside of the bedroom that it was utterly mind-boggling. His ex was everything he didn't want to be.

And vice versa, he surmised.

But that was years behind him. Now, if he had a need for female companionship, he found it easily. And it lasted no longer than a few nights, with women who understood those limits. Women who wanted a little excitement for the evening and nothing more, because he damn well wasn't the kind of man any woman with a yen for stability wanted in her life.

God knew, Elisha Reed wasn't his type. Wasn't the kind of woman he normally tangled sheets with. She represented home, hearth, responsibilities, mom, apple pie and baseball. Everything that had nothing even remotely to do with him. Some men belonged in that setting. He didn't.

The woman was terminally optimistic, for God's sake.

But he still wanted to kiss her.

If nothing else, to prove to himself that this attraction was just the result of an off day.

Off like the hands of poker he'd played tonight. He'd been far from his best. So much so that during the course of the evening, he'd briefly entertained the notion of cheating. He could. He was good at it. Good at sleight of hand and substitution. He'd used that skill to his advantage in several tight spots he'd been in.

But sitting at a poker table in his own house couldn't have been considered to be a tight spot. Lives hadn't been riding on the outcome of the game.

Only pride had.

So he'd banked down his urge to win by any means and wound up losing more than he'd won. But at least he'd played fair and square. As had his friends.

And she had won.

As if to balance the score, he took her face in his hands and kissed her. Hard.

Anger, annoyance, bewilderment and a host of other things jockeyed through him, elbowing for position upfront. He wasn't even sure why he kissed her, only that he did. A gut instinct made him do it. Gut instinct had seen him through most of his life, kept him alive when the odds for living out the night were all against him. He'd simply followed another one.

And was glad as hell that he had.

His hands slipped from her face to her back. He pulled her to him and kissed her again. And again.

His lips tasted of dark promises and were as intoxicating as an entire bottle of wine consumed over the course of a short evening on an empty stomach. There was no other explanation for how she felt. Her head began to spin at the same time that her kneecaps deserted her.

None of it made any sense to her. This was the kind of reaction women fantasized about when they were penning romances. This kind of thing didn't actually happen. At least, it had never happened to her, even when she thought herself in love. Garry had never torched her world. The closest he'd come was in lighting a single match.

Everything now felt hot, very hot. She was afraid to take inventory, certain that she was incinerating along with the rest of the room. Shaking inside, Elisha put her hands on Ryan's shoulders. It was either that, or find herself sliding bonelessly down to the floor and making a complete fool of herself.

Finally, because survival was something that had been ingrained in her from a very young age, Elisha drew back. To catch her breath. To catch her perspective. And to keep from dissolving completely like a mound of sugar left out in the rain.

You're not behaving professionally. Unless you've suddenly decided to switch over to the oldest profession.

She stared at the man who had quite literally, and for no apparent reason that she could think of, rocked her world.

"Is that your way of trying to get out of reading my editorial notes?" She just managed to finish the sentence before she ran out of oxygen. Any second, she was going to start gasping for air like a deep-sea diver who'd been brought up too soon.

"I read them." His voice was surly, his breath warm as it traveled along her face.

Right. She knew that. But he'd made her forget everything, including how to breathe. She tried very hard not to shiver, not to react. Somewhere inside her a hunger materialized, demanding satisfaction.

It scared the hell out of her.

"You read them?"

"I said I did, didn't I?"

The fog about her brain began to lift. She found her tongue. It was wedged against the roof of her mouth.

"Yes, you did. Now you need to follow those notes. At least some," she qualified.

It took effort to talk, to sound as if nothing had been thrown out of sync. It was hard not to gasp, not to suck in air at the end of each statement. Elisha felt as if her lungs had just left town. Taking her sanity with them. What was left of it.

His eyes delved into hers. Seeing into the very center of her. *Not possible. Only superheroes have X-ray vision.*

She tried again. Tried to make sense. Tried to sound like what she knew she was. An editor. His editor. "We can discuss it."

He didn't look like a man who wanted to talk about books, even his own. His next question proved it. "Do you want to stay the night?"

Her pulse kicked into high gear, dragging her heart along with it. It raced up into her throat and threatened to remain there. She did her best to sound blasé instead of like some addle-brained teenager who hadn't been with a man since the Great Flood.

"That wasn't the discussion I had in mind."

"Do you want to stay the night?" he repeated, his eyes holding her prisoner.

Sex with this man would be exciting. Elisha knew that as certainly as she knew that the sun was going to be coming up again tomorrow. Very possibly it would be the singularly most exciting thing she would ever experience in her life.

But she wasn't a thrill seeker. She'd made peace with the fact that things like teeth-rattling, mind-boggling lovemaking was never going to happen to her.

It would throw everything off in her life.

"Yes," she breathed.

Ryan began to slip his hands underneath her sweater. A squeal of pleasure vibrated in her throat as she felt his fingers touch her skin. Every fiber of her being wanted to do this.

It made breaking away even harder.

She clamped her hands down on each of his, holding them in place. He looked at her quizzically.

"But I'm not going to. I told Andrea I'd be home by eleven."

The puzzled look on Sutherland's face didn't recede. "Andrea?"

Her mouth felt horribly dry, as if she'd been eating sand all day. "My niece. She's babysitting my other niece, Beth. Henry's daughters," she added needlessly. "I made a deal and said I'd be home by eleven."

He let his hands fall to his sides. When it came to women, he'd never been one to push. If the sex wasn't consensual, it didn't happen.

"You lied," he told her quietly. "It's almost midnight."

Her eyes widened. "Midnight?" How had that happened? "Oh, God, I've got to go."

Grabbing the jacket that had slid from her shoulders to the floor around the same time that her body composition had changed from solid to liquid, Elisha scooped up her purse and hurried out the front door to the vehicle she'd used to drive over here. Henry's navy-blue sedan.

Ryan didn't stop her.

He glanced at his watch again. Midnight. And the princess was running toward her coach. Too bad she hadn't left a glass slipper behind.

CHAPTER 31

Elisha hurried into Henry's house some fifteen minutes later. Added to the shaky feeling inside was the fact that she absolutely hated being late, hated breaking her word, and she'd just managed to do both.

This being part of an active family unit, of worrying about more than just herself, was going to take getting used to, she thought even as she wondered if she would ever get the knack.

"Andrea?" she called out as she locked the door behind her. Hanging her purse on one of the coat-tree hooks, she began shrugging out of her jacket. "I'm sorry. I know I said eleven, but I lost track of time and—"

Turning around, she entered the living room and stopped dead. Instead of Andrea, Anne Nguyen was sitting on the sofa. A soft blue light was coming from the TV set as someone in a purple T-shirt whose hue matched her hair was telling a sympathetic Jay Leno that she really didn't like signing autographs.

All systems went on alert. "Anne?" Elisha crossed the threshold quickly, glancing around for some signs of telltale chaos. "Is something wrong?"

"Not on my end." The petite woman rose to her feet. Her dark eyes took quick inventory. "But you seem a little flustered. Everything okay?"

No, everything was not okay. Her insides were utterly scrambled, as if she were some young woman in her late teens or early twenties instead of someone who'd resigned herself to being done with romance.

But that was beside the point right now. She wasn't the person she'd been a few months ago or even a few weeks ago. Her sphere had widened and she was responsible for more than just her own very mixed-up feelings. And *that*, not her emotional state of being, was what took precedence now.

She glanced toward the stairs. "Where are Beth and Andrea?"

Anne appeared very composed and at ease. Maybe everything was all right. "Beth's upstairs in bed and Andrea's at the party," she answered serenely.

"Party?" Elisha repeated. "What party?" She went over everything that had been said between her and her oldest niece. But there'd been no request to attend any party. There hadn't even been anything mentioned about a party. She would have remembered.

"The one she told me you said she could go to." And then a look of dismay, coupled with embarrassment, washed over Anne's porcelain-perfect features. "I've been taken, haven't I?" Anne closed her eyes, shaking her head. "I just didn't see it coming. Andrea's always been such a good girl…"

I don't need this.

Elisha dragged her hand through her hair, desperately trying to organize her thoughts. Pushing thoughts of Ryan away.

"Not your fault. It's mine. I guess Andrea and I still aren't on the same wavelength yet. But I do know that I never told her she could go to any party." Maybe the girl had said something before Elisha had left the house. She thought of waking Beth. But then, if Andrea hadn't said anything, Beth might get agitated that her sister had suddenly taken off. She looked at Anne. "Do you have any idea where she went?"

It was obvious that Anne was upbraiding herself as she shook her head.

"No. She just said a party and assured me you were all right with it." Then, because it seemed necessary to explain her lapse in judgment, the woman added, "She said that you had gotten a call and had to deal with one of your writers, so you'd asked her to ask me to sit with Beth. The story seemed plausible at the time."

"Right. Maybe I can get her under contract to write fiction for my house."

An oldies tune began to float through the air. It took her a second to realize that her cell phone, still in her purse, was ringing. She grabbed it from the coatrack and began to rummage around until she located the small silver oblong.

Elisha cried, "Andrea?" before she even had the phone to her ear.

There was a pregnant pause on the other end of the line. And then a deep male voice was rumbling words against her ear. "No. Sutherland. I thought you went home *to* Andrea."

Elisha blocked the impulse to snap the phone shut. That reaction was triggered merely by her colossal confusion, fueled by a host of other emotions that were rampaging through her, emotions she had no idea were still alive. She had even less of an idea what to do with them.

This isn't about you, remember?

Elisha blew out a breath, shook her head no to Anne, who was looking at her with a hopeful expression, then said, "I did. But she's not here."

Ryan had always been able to hear what wasn't being said, could always sense when things weren't the way they should be. "Do you know where she is?"

"No." The single word rang with distress, anger, frustration. And Ryan heard it all. "I'll be right over."

The line went dead.

Looking at it, Elisha slowly shut the cell phone and this time slipped it into her pocket. She hadn't asked for Sutherland's help, not in so many words. Not in *any* words, actually, but maybe secretly, she'd sent out a different message.

Because she hadn't a clue as to what to do next. Involving the police was far too drastic a measure and besides, she knew they wouldn't come. Not for something like this. They'd tell her to sit and wait, not knowing that it wasn't in her to sit and wait.

She felt better, more in control though nothing had really changed. Except that, magically, she had her very own ex–Navy SEAL to rely on. People like Ryan Sutherland could locate a marshmallow puff in a snowdrift. A teenage girl should be a snap for him to find, right?

Elisha looked at her neighbor's concerned expression. She felt guilty that the poor woman had been pulled into this mess. Guiltier still that she had to impose on her further. But when Sutherland went to locate Andrea, there was no way she was going to stay behind.

"Anne, I hate to ask, but could you stay with Beth a little longer? I've got someone coming over to help me find Andrea, and—"

Anne cut her off. "No problem. Do you think your friend can find Andrea?"

Her friend. Wouldn't Sutherland just light up if he'd heard that reference? Despite the fact that he'd burned off the tips of her shoes a little more than half an hour ago, she had a feeling they had a long way to go before the man would think of them as friends.

"I think he could find the Holy Grail if he put his mind to it." And she meant that.

Sutherland was there before she had a chance to go upstairs and change into something more suited to searching for an errant teenager. Opening the door to admit him, she couldn't help commenting, "You got here fast."

"All the lights were green," he said.

She had her doubts but didn't press. It was oddly comforting, seeing him here. She didn't bother asking him how he'd initially gotten the address. Despite the fact that he'd supposedly been out of black ops for over ten years now, she had a feeling the man was still privy to all kinds of information.

Which was why she was so hopeful about his help in locating Andrea. Not that she thought the girl wasn't coming back. There was every reason in the world to believe that she would. But she had an uneasy feeling about Andrea being out tonight that she just couldn't ignore. Besides, this was an obvious defiance of her authority and she had to put a stop to that right now.

Before she could introduce the author to her neighbor, Sutherland asked her for a photograph of Andrea. There was one on the mantel of the girl with her sister and she brought it over to him.

Studying it, Sutherland nodded. "Does she have a cell phone?"

"Yes."

"Give me her number," he instructed.

She shook her head, knowing what he intended to do. "I've already tried it." She'd called while she was waiting for Sutherland to arrive. Three times. All with no results. "She's not answering."

The clear water-blue eyes were expressionless as they looked at her. "I don't want the number to talk to her."

"Then why—?" she began, then stopped. She wasn't going to get anywhere by asking him questions. Quickly, she recited the number.

With a nod, Sutherland turned away from her and the other woman in the room as he took out his own phone. His voice became a low murmur, like thunder rumbling a great distance away.

Anne came up close to her, dropping her voice to a whisper as she watched the author's back. "That's Ryan Sutherland, isn't it?"

"That it is," Elisha answered, never taking her eyes off the man's back. She hadn't realized how wide his shoulders were until just now. "He's one of my authors."

Anne was clearly impressed. "I recognize him from the back of the book jacket. Jack loves his books," she explained. "He's even better looking in the flesh. Ryan, not my husband." She laughed and it occurred to Elisha that her neighbor was just the slightest bit awestruck. "Most of the time, the picture looks a great deal better than the actual person." She looked at Elisha. "He's quite a hunk, really."

Elisha shrugged. "I hadn't noticed."

Which was a lie, but that was something she wasn't prepared to deal with at the moment. That came under a completely different heading and right now, she was focused on just one thing. Getting Andrea home and reading her the riot act.

Impatient, she raised her voice. "Who are you calling?"

At first, she didn't think he heard her, but then he raised his hand and waved it at her dismissively, as if commanding her silence. He didn't bother looking her way. He brooked no distractions.

It wasn't until several minutes later that he turned around. Closing his phone, he seemed to notice Anne for the first time. Elisha knew better. She was beginning to believe that nothing got by the man.

His eyes now intent on Anne, he asked, "What time did Andrea leave here?"

Anne didn't even have to pause to think. "About nine."

He nodded, as if the information dovetailed with what he'd

expected. His pale-blue eyes shifted over to Elisha. "The name Alex Taylor familiar to you?"

Elisha came up empty. All she knew was that it wasn't any of the people she had notified about Henry's passing. "No. Why?"

"That's the last phone call your niece made before nine." He pocketed his phone. "Let's go, I have an address."

Of course he did. "How? And how did you find out what calls she made?" Wasn't that kind of thing supposed to take a while, its path littered with a lot of legal paperwork?

"It helps to have friends," he said as he led the way out the door and to his car. He was driving a black Hummer. Now, *there* was a car that could blend in well, she thought.

"Apparently," she murmured, hurrying to keep up. He had already rounded the hood and was getting in on his side. She quickly got into the front passenger seat. "Why did you call me?" The question had suddenly occurred to her.

Key in the ignition, he answered as if it was the most common thing in the world. "To see if you'd gotten home all right. You seemed pretty shaken when you left."

The protest came too quickly and was voiced too adamantly to be true. "Not shaken."

Ryan slanted a look at her before training his eyes on the rearview mirror. They left the driveway quickly. She doubted if the vehicle did anything slowly.

"Stirred, then?"

She pressed her lips together. There was no comeback for that. Besides, it was the truth. "Maybe."

Ryan's mouth curved just the slightest bit. He'd take that as a yes.

The notion was oddly pleasing.

CHAPTER 32

As it turned out, the house where the party was being held was only two developments over. It could have been in another world.

Unlike her brother's development, none of the houses here were duplicates of one another. These were the estate homes. Each had been built by a different designer and declared its sisterhood with the neighboring homes by virtue of its tennis courts and pool houses.

Elisha knew these were not million-dollar homes. They were houses whose price tags ran in the multiples of millions.

The idea tended to boggle the mind.

Elisha sat as far on the edge of her seat as her seat belt would allow. After a while, financial figures ceased to lose their meaning. So did the need for hard work. She didn't like thinking about Andrea being involved with kids who had never had to save to buy anything in their lives. Their sense of values was not the kind she knew Henry would have wanted for his daughter.

I'm not up to this, Henry.

But at least she had a commando at her side. Driving the closest thing to a civilized tank. She smiled ever so slightly.

"Something funny?" Ryan asked.

She had no idea that he'd even looked in her direction. Maybe he didn't have to. Maybe Navy SEALs were given extra sets of eyes upon graduating from their training course alive.

"Just my life," she answered.

There were no less than fifteen cars scattered about or parked in the wide, winding driveway. Many of the vehicles would have cost her a year's salary, if not more.

"This must be the place," Elisha murmured. She'd been running on adrenaline when she'd discovered that Andrea had taken it upon herself to leave. Now that the moment of reckoning was almost here, she wasn't sure what she was going to say.

She was just going to have to wing it.

Sutherland was out of the Hummer ahead of her, striding toward the front door as if this was another commando mission rather than just the act of reclaiming authority over one headstrong teenager. The look on his face was dark and forbidding. Made her glad she'd never been the enemy he'd faced down.

Maybe she should have told him she'd take it from here, Elisha thought as she hurried out of the vehicle. Better still, maybe she should have asked him to stay with Beth and brought Anne instead. God knew, the woman had to be better suited for this kind of thing than G.I. Joe.

Making up her mind, she called out, "Listen, I'll take it from here," as she hurried to catch up to Sutherland.

He glanced at her over his shoulder, his look unexpectedly tolerant. But he never broke stride and didn't bother commenting on what he obviously took to be a suggestion rather than a course of action.

Sutherland pressed his finger against the doorbell once, then twice. There was no response either time. The music coming from inside the house was just too loud.

Frowning, Elisha shook her head. "His parents must be deaf."

Sutherland gave her a knowing look. "His parents must be gone."

He tried the doorknob, ready to do what he had to in order to get in. He didn't need to do anything. The door was unlocked.

"Well, that was convenient," Elisha said. She scanned the place. With its marble floors, two-story vaulted ceiling and wide, spiral staircase, the house bore a cold resemblance to a museum. She shivered without realizing it. "Cold?" he asked, raising his voice.

She shook her head. "This isn't a house filled with love."

"Now you're a clairvoyant?"

"Just instinct," she replied. She doubted he heard. Someone had turned up the music even higher. Whoever was at the party was going to wind up deaf by evening's end, she thought. The noise was all but rattling her teeth.

"How can they stand to have the music up so loud?" she shouted to Sutherland as they picked their way through the house, moving toward the source. The bones in her face were beginning to hurt.

Sutherland seemed unaffected. Underscoring her theory that maybe the man was more bionic than real. "It's just background noise," was his answer.

Background, foreground, the music was throbbing everywhere. If she wasn't so intent on getting Andrea home, she knew that the throbbing sensation more than the actual music would have spoken to something very basic, very primitive within her.

Something that unexpected kiss at Sutherland's house had awoken.

What if it was doing the same with Andrea? Panic coupled up with anger. She had to find the girl and get her out of here.

Following the music to its source, Sutherland led the way into the center of the house. From the looks of it, no one under twenty was anywhere around. The path to the media-entertainment room, from which the music was emanating, was littered with teenage couples, engaged either in kissing or communing with a separate deity in the form of white powder lightly dusted over small surfaces.

Elisha saw the veins in Sutherland's neck become prominent. He said things, most likely to himself, that she had no way of hearing. What she managed to lip-read would have been censored by all but the freest of thinkers.

As he passed, Sutherland knocked over any and all flat surfaces containing even a trace of white powder. Angry young men struggled to their feet, enraged, only to melt back once they looked Sutherland in the eye and saw their own demise mirrored there.

Elisha covered her mouth as she saw a girl sitting in an armchair, very obviously nodding out, a stupid smile on her face. "Oh, God, this is worse than I thought."

Sutherland heard her, his sharp eyes resting on her face for a moment as he turned to look at her. "Not worse than I thought."

It was why he'd come. Why he'd offered to locate her niece. Because he'd seen this happen more than once, to good people. He hated waste of any kind, most of all the waste of a life that had potential.

And then they saw Andrea sitting on the floor before a coffee table. There was a young man sitting beside her who could have very easily posed as the poster boy for upstanding, clean suburban living.

Elisha wanted to punch him out the moment she saw the white substance before them on the glass table.

His arm around her in an intimate, coaxing fashion, the thin, blond young man with the preppy look was making his pitch to Andrea.

"C'mon, Andie, there's nothing to it. You don't want to be left out." His body seemed to be sealed against Andrea's as if they were drawn with the same brushstroke, his details not quite ending before hers began. "You know you want to. It'll make you feel like you can fly."

Elisha was close enough to hear. Close enough to read lips. Close enough to become enraged. Before Sutherland could say anything, Elisha pushed forward, grabbing Andrea by the arm and pulling her away from the table and any temptation she might have been entertaining.

"You're going to fly in about two seconds if you don't back away from her," Elisha shouted at the young man.

Sutherland looked at her, admiration mingling with surprise in his eyes. It was obvious by his expression that he hadn't thought her capable of standing up to undesirable types. Even undesirables in expensive designer clothes.

Scrambling to his feet, the young man's perfect features contorted into an angry mask at the intrusion into his privacy. Especially since the woman grabbing up his entertainment for the evening had also swept her hand through his lines of cocaine, scattering the powder into the fabric of the sofa.

Sutherland placed one hand against the teenager's chest. Fear entered the latter's eyes when he looked at who had formed the barrier holding him in place.

"I'd listen to the lady if I were you," Sutherland advised in a low, powerful voice.

"Aunt Elisha." Relief, surprise and embarrassment throbbed in Andrea's voice. "What are you doing here?" she cried.

Behind her, Alex, the teenager who'd been so intent on leading her into her virgin journey into the world of drugs, couldn't make himself scarce enough. He was already backing away by the time she glanced in his direction.

"Looking for you," Elisha answered. She felt torn between throwing her arms around the girl in a fierce hug and grabbing her by the shoulders to shake her. "You were supposed to watch Beth."

Despite her obvious relief at having the decision before her taken out of her hands, Andrea raised her chin defiantly. "Something came up."

Sutherland gave Alex a withering look. "It better not have." His eyes pinned Alex to the opposite wall. The teenager raised his hands in surrender.

"Hey, I hardly know her," Alex protested.

"Good," Elisha retorted. "Keep it that way." Her hand still firmly around Andrea's arm, she hustled the girl out of the room.

They garnered looks from the other people at the party as they made their way to the front door. Elisha could see that her niece had begun to seethe.

Once outside, she wrenched her arm free of Elisha's grasp. "How *could* you?"

"How could *you?*" Elisha fired back, opening the passenger side of Sutherland's vehicle and pushing Andrea inside. She was quick to get into her own seat and then twisted around to look at her niece. "I trusted you. You had a responsibility and you neglected it."

"You make it sound as if I abandoned Beth to the wolves." Fuming, she put her seat belt on. "I asked Mrs. Nguyen to come stay with her."

"You should have discussed it with me first," Elisha reminded her. "You didn't ask my permission to go to the party. Not that I would have let you," she interjected before Andrea could point out the obvious. "Not without parental supervision."

"You're not my mother," Andrea shot back. "Or my father."

Elisha strove for patience. Why did this have to be an argument? Why couldn't Andrea just see how worthless those people back at the house were? Why couldn't she see what a mistake she would have made, listening to that preppy? God only knew what that little bastard would have done to Andrea once she was high.

"No," Elisha said evenly, trying her best not to lose her temper, "I'm your guardian and, like it or not, we're going to have to find a way to make this work."

Frustrated, Andrea turned her ire on Sutherland. Or tried to. "Who's the muscle you brought with you?"

He looked up into the rearview mirror, his eyes capturing Andrea's. "Ryan Sutherland."

"How did you find me, anyway?" she demanded angrily.

"My 'muscle' tracked you down. Mr. Sutherland is a former Navy SEAL—" she glanced at his profile "—among other things."

"Terrific," Andrea fumed, crossing her arms before her.

Yes, Elisha thought, *actually*, it is.

CHAPTER 33

As she roamed around the kitchen, trying to get things in motion that would ultimately yield a decent cup of coffee and kick-start her morning, Elisha felt drained. Her brain and body were operating in slow motion, a result of a night that had had very little sleep in it.

Last night, after Sutherland had left her and Andrea at their door and Anne Nguyen had gone home, she'd tried her level best to get through to her niece. Had tried to make the girl see that she only had her best interests at heart. Contrary to what Andrea had accused her of, she was not out to totally "humiliate her forever."

Putting herself into Andrea's shoes as best she could, Elisha tried to make her understand that she wasn't just looking at the evening but at the bigger picture. A picture that had Andrea turning out to be a decent human being.

For the most part, negotiations had been loud, at one point waking up Beth who then had to be ushered back into bed. Eventually, she and her older niece had reached a tentative truce, with Andrea admitting that she really hadn't wanted to try any drugs, but hadn't had the nerve to say no because she didn't want to look like a dork. At that point, Elisha could have cried with relief.

She knew that by no means were things going to be smooth sailing from here on in. If anything, all this pointed to the fact that she needed to be more alert. But at least Andrea had no actual desire to experiment with drugs. That was a step in the right direction.

The coffeemaker began to sputter, announcing loudly that it was going about its business. For a moment, Elisha just stood and stared at the dark object, not really seeing it at all.

How the hell did parents do it? she wondered, completely mystified. How did they go about the job of parenting? How was *she* expected to do it? How could she possibly manage to raise not just one but two children and safely bring them to adulthood? Especially since there'd been no training period for her. She'd been thrown headfirst, with lead weights fastened to her ankles, into the deep end of the pool and told to swim like crazy. At least most parents started out with a tiny human being and slowly got accustomed to broadening their lives to include more than just themselves.

Impatient, Elisha removed the coffeepot and emptied the black liquid into her mug. There wasn't much. She shoved the pot back on the hot plate. The sputtering resumed.

Decisions that involved whether to feed the baby strained peas or carrots were a lot easier than trying to figure out how to make that "baby" understand that snorting cocaine wasn't "harmless recreational fun" the way that little bastard Alex had probably said.

With a huge sigh, Elisha lowered herself into a chair in the breakfast nook. The late-autumn sun was making everything outside appear a great deal brighter than she felt at the moment. Her hold on what Sutherland had referred to as her "terminal optimism" was slipping.

She planned to call Alex Taylor's parents to let them know what went on at their house when they weren't there. That wasn't going to make her or Andrea very popular, but it had to be done. Elisha sat there, the mug of hot coffee cradled between her hands, staring out the window and wondering how the hell her life had gone spiraling out of control like this. More important, what was she going to do to regain her grasp on the reins?

As she stared, contemplating the overwhelming situation, a movement in the garden caught her eye. Focusing, she looked harder. And then shook her head in wonder.

She must have been really sleepy, Elisha upbraided herself, not to have noticed that Beth was outside. When had the little girl slipped out the door? Her niece was still wearing her pajamas, but she had her sneakers and parka jacket on, as well. And she was on her knees, digging in the sleeping earth with a hand trowel.

Looking for buried treasure? Playing a game? Beth was an indoor child, preferring video games and reading to outdoor activities. What was up?

Only one way to find out, Elisha decided.

She took one more long sip of coffee to warm her, then went to get her coat. This needed looking into. She was fairly certain that while most children liked to play in the dirt, they usually did it when the dirt wasn't close to freezing. Doing her best to appear nonchalant, Elisha strolled over to where Beth was digging. The little girl glanced in her direction, nodded a greeting and continued to remove dirt from the ground as best as she could.

Elisha squatted beside her. In a voice she hoped sounded sufficiently upbeat, she asked, "What are you doing?"

Beth paused only for a moment as she lifted her eyes to her aunt's face. "I'm burying a feather."

Did kids do this kind of thing? Was this part of pretend or something serious? Should she be concerned? Tons of questions, she thought, no answers. "Why, honey?"

"I'm trying to grow a bird," was Beth's simple answer. "A special bird."

Her first inclination was to laugh. The idea was really darling and childlike. But she had a feeling that Beth would take it the wrong way if she laughed. Elisha caught her lower lip between her teeth to still the sound within.

"Why do you want to grow a bird?"

She was about to offer to go to the pet store and buy her any bird she wanted, when Beth repeated, "A special bird."

"All right, why do you want to grow a special bird?"

Tucking the feather in the hole she'd dug, Beth pushed the dirt back on top of it and patted it into place. Done, she sat back on her heels and looked at her aunt. "So it can fly to heaven and tell Daddy that I miss him. That I want him to come back."

Elisha could almost feel her heart twisting in her chest. She took the little girl into her arms, holding her close as she caressed her hair. "Oh, honey, so do I."

That afternoon, after a great deal of soul-searching and conscience-wrestling, Elisha made a decision. It wasn't one that she was overly thrilled with, but it was one that she knew she needed to make. She'd given her word, now she needed to do things in order to keep her word.

Walking into the den where Henry had given her the awful news about his condition a lifetime ago, Elisha shut the door behind her. Despite the fact that it was Saturday, there was no point in putting off calling Rocky. He had to be told as soon as possible so that he could make his own arrangements.

She called him at home. Though she usually welcomed his conversation, she cut through it this time like a surgeon wielding a scalpel. "Rocky, I want a leave of absence."

There was silence on the other end. As if the mild snowstorm that had accosted the city had frozen his phone lines, as well. And then he asked in a voice that was higher than normal, "You want what?"

"A leave of absence."

There was another pause. "For how long?"

How long did it take to make sure two kids would turn out all right? "I don't know." She moved around the room restlessly, the cordless receiver against her ear. "A month, two, six."

"Lise, I can't—"

"I know, you can't hold my position open for that long. I understand. I don't expect you to. You have a publishing house to run. But I can't just leave these girls like this right now."

"Like what?" he cried. "I'm not sending you to Tibet. You wouldn't be leaving them. You'd be coming home to them every night—"

"They need more than that." Although she had no idea at this point if she could give it to them. If she was even capable of giving it to them. But she knew she had to do something.

"We have a day-care center on the premises."

"They're not babies, Rocky."

"Then don't treat them like babies," he insisted. She could picture him running his thin hand along his forehead, massaging it because a migraine was forming. When he spoke, his voice was a little calmer, although the underlying desperation was still there. "Didn't you just hire Mrs. Doubtfire?"

"Mrs. Wentworth," she corrected. Sutherland had gotten back to her quicker than she'd imagined. Samantha Wentworth was worth her weight in gold. She'd hired the woman just before she'd had her "makeover" from Andrea. But gold or not, Samantha was a nanny and the girls needed something more than a well-paid stranger, no matter how kindly, tending to them. They needed someone who loved them even when they weren't lovable. Especially when they weren't lovable. "She's still going to stay on, but the girls need more."

"I need more," Rocky responded, a note of pleading in his voice.

Don't do this to me, Rocky. The last thing I need is more guilt.

"You have more. You have an entire staff of people to help you. Andrea and Beth don't." Blowing out a breath, Elisha tried again. "Rocky, I can't just walk away and go back to my comfortable little world, much as I want to, when all this is going on."

He clearly didn't follow her. "All what? I thought you had everything all straightened out."

It took her a second to realize what he was talking about. "I got the legal things all straightened out. The trust funds, transferring the deed to the house. Deciding what to do with my apartment in the city." She'd opted to keep that, at least for the time being. It made her feel as if she was bridging her old life with her new. "But there's so much more."

"Like what?" he cried.

"Andrea's tottering on the brink of being drawn into a world that has horrible consequences to it. She went to a party last night without telling me and there were drugs and alcohol. Rocky, she's fifteen. And Beth, Beth is planting feathers in the ground and hoping they'll turn into birds so they can fly up to where her father is."

"The kid needs counseling."

"The kid needs *me*. They both do."

The sigh she heard on the other end of the line was one of resignation. "And what about you, Lise? What do you need?"

I need to work, but I can't right now. "I need to keep my word to Henry."

"I know you, Andrea. Some women are born to be hausfraus. They take utter joy in making gourmet meals out of two peas and a carrot, but that's not you. You're a career woman, a dynamo. Now, maybe you can find a way to combine home and career and make it work, but I guarantee you, if all you have to look forward to is bargain shopping at the local grocery store and sewing costumes out of peacock feathers for some school play, you'll go out of your mind inside of a month. Less maybe."

He was right and she knew it, but she had no choice in the matter. Not if she wanted to help the girls. "I don't know what else to do, Rocky. If I go back when things are like this, and somewhere down the line I lose one or both of the girls, I'll never forgive myself."

Elisha sighed, hating being put in this position. She wanted her old life back. She'd spent a long time getting to where she was. Long hours of dedication had been involved. But in the end, what she had to show for it were books. Books that didn't even bear her name on them. The decision she'd made was for the best. Because it involved not someone else's books but Henry's daughters. Two human beings.

Two human beings who only had her to turn to.

"Can't I change your mind?" Rocky asked.

"I need you to be a friend right now, Rocky."

She heard him sigh again. "I hate it when you use that tone with me. Oh, all right," he surrendered. "I'll tell your authors they're being reassigned to someone else—temporarily," he emphasized. "And I'll see what I can do about holding a spot open for you." He tried one last time, playing his trump card. "You realize that means Carole Chambers will take over in your absence."

If you're watching, Henry, I hope you appreciate this. "Yes, I realize," she said quietly. "It doesn't change anything."

Rocky obviously knew when to accept defeat.

CHAPTER 34

A month went by.

She did the best that she could, laying the groundwork for the new parameters in which she and the girls found themselves. Going to PTA meetings and even attending a football game at Andrea's school. She learned the names of all of Beth's friends and did her best to coax the names of Andrea's friends out of her.

As far as her relationship with Andrea went, there were good days and there were bad days. But she gave herself points for trying and she suspected Andrea did, too.

Elisha even tried her hand at cooking and decided that some things weren't meant to be conquered by her. She left that to Mrs. Wentworth. On the woman's days off, they ordered out. She did everything she could to live up to her promise to Henry, taking on both roles of mother and father the way he had done after Rachel died. And every day, amid the tiny triumphs and small battles that were won, she died a little more.

She missed her old life. Missed the excitement of working on a new project with an author. Missed brainstorming to come up with a new idea for a new book. As much as she loved the girls and, surprisingly, loved being there for them, she still couldn't help feeling that there was a hole in her life.

She'd made a dreadful miscalculation, Elisha thought sadly one late-Saturday afternoon. She'd discovered that, at bottom, she just wasn't the homemaker type. At least, not on a 24/7 basis. It wasn't that she couldn't handle her new role. She just didn't derive the same sort of satisfaction as when she made Ryan Sutherland see her validity as an editor.

Did that make her a bad person? A selfish person? She didn't have an answer for that.

There were a lot of things she didn't have the answer for these days, but then, she'd come to accept that life was a continuous learning process. Maybe the final exam came at the end. She didn't know. What she did know was that she missed going into the office. Missed the meetings. Even missed the all-hands-on-deck crises.

She tried very hard not to.

There'd been calls. From Rocky, from some of her authors, like Sinclair. But there hadn't been one from Sutherland, and the absence of his calls bothered her more than the presence of the others. In an effort to wean herself from her former life, she'd tried to cut her ties for the time being and let her answering machine take the calls that had come in.

She'd done too good a job. Without her other world, she felt as if she was dying on the vine.

"I'm going out, Aunt Elisha," Andrea announced as she sailed through the living room when the doorbell rang. She appeared to be trying to get to the front door before another round of interrogations could get under way.

She wasn't fast enough.

Pulling herself out of the mental tailspin, Elisha beat her niece to the front door. Hours on the treadmill at night to rid herself of her excess energy were not for nothing, she thought proudly. She'd managed to build up her stamina.

"Okay, stop," she ordered her niece. "What, where, who, when?"

Andrea rolled her eyes. But her manner was far less defiant

than it had originally been. She'd grudgingly allowed that her aunt did care about her and that as the resident adult, that gave her the right to know some things.

Andrea rattled off the answers. "Movie, at the Cineplex, James, Maggi and Adam. Now—until one."

Elisha shook her head. "Twelve," she corrected. "Your curfew's for twelve o'clock, remember?"

Andrea groaned, then immediately resorted to begging. "Please? It's not a school night and the movie gets out at ten-fifty. James's father is driving us there."

She was prepared for this. It made her nostalgic for negotiations over book content. "Eleven-thirty and I get to meet this James, Maggi and Adam."

Andrea sighed as she shifted from foot to foot. "This isn't fair, you know."

In the beginning, Andrea had managed to pull the wool over her eyes a lot. But Beth turned out to be a faithful ally and could be counted on to give her sister up in the name of truth and justice. And chocolate ice cream.

"It's the way your dad did things," Elisha pointed out.

"Yeah, it is," Andrea admitted grudgingly. "Okay. I'll tell them to come in." But as she began to open the front door to call her friends in, she stopped for a second and looked over toward her aunt. "You need a life, you know."

Elisha laughed. "I have one."

Andrea looked at her seriously. "No, you've got Dad's life and even Dad didn't look a hundred-percent happy with it." She paused, her sharp eyes analyzing her aunt. "You're pretty miserable."

Elisha felt uncomfortable. Andrea was hitting too close to the truth and she didn't want it to show. "No, I'm not."

But Andrea wasn't about to be dissuaded. "You're not the Aunt Elisha I knew."

I'm not the Elisha I knew, either.

Elisha shrugged casually, dismissing the observation. "Things change."

Andrea frowned. It was clear that as far as excuses went, she considered this one lame. "They don't always have to change drastically." And then a light entered her eyes as her young mouth curved. "What about that muscle you brought to drag me out of Alex Taylor's house last month. Ronald? Roger?"

"Ryan," Elisha corrected. "Ryan Sutherland." She said the name as if he hadn't been on her mind, off and on, mostly on, for the last few weeks. "What about him?"

"Why don't you go see him? Or have him come over?"

Elisha stared at her. "You mean like a date?" she asked incredulously. Quickly, she squelched the idea before she could begin entertaining it. "I'm past dating men, Andrea."

A patient look came over the girl's face. She placed a hand on her shoulder. "I know you're old, Aunt Elisha, but you're not *that* old," she teased, and then grew serious again. "At least go back to work. You're not going to be happy until you do. And if you're not happy…" She let her voice trail off.

Out of the mouths of babes, Elisha thought as Andrea went to bring her friends back inside to be introduced.

Elisha turned around to see that Beth had been standing behind them, listening to everything. Elisha had come to learn this was how the little girl became such a clearinghouse of information.

Now that the subject was on the table, Elisha decided she had nothing to lose by asking. "Okay, how do you feel about me going back to work?"

Beth cocked her head, thinking. "Will you still be able to read me bedtime stories?"

She laughed. "Absolutely."

Beth raised and lowered her small shoulders. "Then sure, it's okay."

Elisha looked at her. Was it really this simple? Had she been agonizing over nothing? "You don't mind?"

Beth shook her head, her chocolate-brown hair swishing back and forth along her cheeks. "You like working. I heard you tell Mrs. Wentworth." She looked up at her intently with Henry's eyes. She almost sounded like Henry when she said, "I want you to be happy."

Impulsively dropping to one knee, Elisha hugged the little girl to her. "Anyone ever tell you what a wonderful kid you are?"

A muffled little voice protested, "Aunt Lise, you're squishing me," just as the front door opened again and Andrea returned with her friends.

With a laugh, Elisha released her. "Sorry," she apologized as she rose to her feet. She felt lighter than air.

"Rocky?"

Rocky's voice immediately perked up. "Lise, is that you?"

She wasn't sure how he would react. Granted that he'd made her feel that she was valuable at the house, but she had gone on leave with no notice whatsoever. He could hold that against her. Or very possibly, the house might have already moved on. Carole Chambers might have wound up doing a bang-up job. Like Anne Baxter in the movie. Just her luck.

"Yes. Look, I'm not going to beat around the bush. I don't know exactly how to put this, but—"

Rocky cut her off with a groan that seemed to come from his very toes. "You're never coming back," he guessed morosely.

"No, I want to come back." She heard him make a strange, gurgling noise. "Rocky, are you all right?"

"All right? I'm terrific." His voice fairly trembled with relief. "After all these years, I just realized that there really is a God."

She released the breath she'd been holding. "You mean it's all right? I can come back?"

"All right?" he hooted. "You always did have a flair for understatement. The *Mona Lisa* was 'all right.' This is fabulous. How soon can you start? Can I Express Mail something to you? Better yet, I can drive up tonight and—"

He sounded much too eager. She knew Rocky, he probably thought she was in the depths of despair, the way he'd predicated, and was saying this to make her feel better. "Rocky, I appreciate you trying to make me feel as if I've been missed, but it couldn't have been that bad."

"Not that bad? If you want to know the truth, I was going to call you Monday and beg. Offer you my firstborn if you came back."

She smiled to herself. She'd missed talking to Rocky. Missed being part of the literary world that had been her life for close to a quarter of a century. "You don't have a firstborn."

"I could. Someday. Single people can adopt. Until then, I'd give you an IOU." He grew serious. "I know you wanted to do the right thing by your nieces, but maybe we can work out some kind of compromise. It's been hell around here without you. Sinclair's falling to pieces, swearing he can't write a single word. Nothing the editor I assigned to him says helps. And Sutherland just called this morning to tell me that if I didn't give him someone with a brain to work with, he was going to leave."

Sutherland wasn't given to empty threats. "But you have him working with Carole, right?"

There was a very long sigh accompanying his response. "Right."

"I'd imagine that, aside from being easy on the eye, Carole would go along with anything he had to say."

"Seems he got accustomed to working harder. He doesn't like 'yes women' as he put it. I don't know how serious he was about leaving, but—"

"You don't have to worry. He won't leave." The first thing she was going to do was call Sinclair and get him back on track. Then she'd tackle Sutherland. Elisha could feel her juices flowing just at the thought of jumping back into the fray.

"Then you're serious? You'll come back and take him on?"

Take him on. That was the way to put it, she thought. "Consider it done."

"Elisha, I think I seriously love you."

"Funny, I was just about to say the same thing to you." She owed him the truth. If that involved an "I told you so," he'd earned it. "I was going crazy out here."

"Knew you would. Being noble can only go so far. Besides, if anyone can juggle house and work, you can. How are the girls?"

"Doing well." *Now.* She thought of the conversation she'd had the other evening with Andrea, and then Beth. "Seems they really don't need 24/7 care. I have a feeling I was stifling them, hovering the way I was."

"You always were a control freak." He laughed. "So, you'll start Monday?"

"Monday."

Being Rocky, he had to ask, "You're not just toying with me now, are you? I won't get a call Monday morning saying you changed your mind again, will I? Because my heart couldn't take another reversal."

It was her turn to laugh. She decided to call Sinclair tonight with the news. Dealing with Sutherland was going to require more than a phone call. Maybe she'd go see him in person. "Tell your heart not to worry. There'll be no phone calls on Monday, at least, not with excuses. I'll be coming in."

"If you don't," he warned, "I'll come and get you."

"Duly noted. By the way, let me tell Sutherland about the switch back."

"Hey, be my guest. The man's way too macho for me to deal with. He makes me nervous."

Yeah, me, too. But maybe in a good way.

She thought about how good it was going to be, coming back. Getting into what she loved doing again. "I've missed you, Rocky."

"Same here."

She was smiling when she hung up. It looked as if her life wasn't quite set yet. And that was a good thing.

CHAPTER 35

The feeling of surprise and pleasure melted the moment Ryan became aware of displaying it. Very possibly, it was one of the few times in his adult life that he'd relaxed his guard enough to allow his thoughts to register on his face. He realized the last time had involved Elisha Reed, as well.

The evening air chilled him despite the heavy fishnet sweater he wore. With his arm stretched across the doorjamb, he stood barring the entrance into his house like an overqualified bodyguard rather than the master of his domain.

She saw his eyes sweep over her. No doubt meant to intimidate her. But she'd been to hell and back, tangled with a teenager and survived, and in the process, been torn apart and rebuilt. She'd learned, in the last couple of months, that despite everything, she could survive and keep on surviving. Well.

She'd also learned that, good intentions to the contrary, she wasn't a hausfrau, as Rocky had pointed out. But she'd discovered to her surprise she wasn't a hundred-percent career woman, either

At least, not anymore. There was room in her life for both. As well as for expansion. Her life was not set in stone the way she'd once believed. More like Jell-O, always in flux as long as she remembered to jiggle the plate every so often.

She viewed Ryan Sutherland through the eyes of a woman who had gone through all that and decided that she wasn't "done" with men yet. That maybe Andrea's comment about her still being able to venture out into the social world of men and women had some validity to it.

At least it was worth a try.

And she knew just who she wanted to try it with. Someone who presented "no strings."

What was she doing here? Ryan wondered. She wasn't his editor anymore, bringing to mind that old saying, *Careful what you wish for.* He'd made no secret of the fact that he didn't want to be edited, and suddenly, he wasn't, not really. *You never know what you have until it's gone.*

He made no effort to move back, gave no sign that he wanted her in his house. As far as he was concerned, she'd bailed on him. He had no patience with people who viewed commitment so lightly. She could have found a way, despite her obligations. People did it every day.

"If he sent you here to talk me out of it, you can forget it. I'm leaving Randolph & Sons. I've made up my mind."

So it shall be written, so it shall be done. Maybe he fancied himself an Egyptian pharaoh, Elisha thought. She managed to suppress her smile only marginally.

"And we all know what a bastion of immobility that is." The wind was sharp and she was getting cold. Elisha nodded toward the interior of his house. "May I come in?"

He wondered what she'd do if he said no and closed the door in her face. After a moment, he stepped aside, allowing her admittance.

Without waiting for an invitation to stay, she shrugged out of her coat and casually placed it over the back of the gray leather sofa. There was just the faintest aroma of chili in the air. Did he cook, too? Of course he did. The man did everything. Except remember his manners, she mused.

She turned to face him. "If by 'he' you mean Rocky, he didn't send me."

The look on Sutherland's face told her that he didn't believe her. But for the moment, he didn't press the issue. Instead, he asked, "So you've suddenly had this yen to turn up on my doorstep because…?"

It suddenly occurred to her that her absence might not be the motivating factor for his leaving. *This isn't the time for self-doubt, Lise. Besides, working with Carole would drive God away.*

"Because I wanted to be the one to tell you."

One dark, expressive eyebrow rose, foreshadowing his query. "Tell me what? I've never cared for games, Max. Spit it out."

She spread her hands out on either side of her. All she needed was a drumroll. "I'm no longer on a leave of absence."

His look cut her dead. "Good for you."

This wasn't what she'd expected. Could she have been so wrong about his reaction? She tried again. "I'm back at Randolph & Sons."

As far as he was concerned, it was a matter of too little too late. She should have never left in the first place. And that vapid, golden-haired Barbie doll she'd left to fill in for her was an unpardonable sin.

Sutherland crossed his arms before his chest and gave her a steely look. "Means nothing to me."

She'd dealt with temperamental authors throughout most of her career. He wanted his ego stroked. But he was in for a surprise. "It should. I'm going to be your editor again." She smiled. "I hear you and Carole Chambers didn't quite hit it off."

His look became a glare. One that was as hard as nails. If she hadn't been privy to the nicer side of him that time he'd come to help her find Andrea, she might have been intimidated. But she'd seen the man beneath the mask and that gave her leverage.

"Chambers." He sneered, dismissing the woman with a wave of his hand. "Now, there's a waste of skin if there ever was any."

Because it cost her nothing, Elisha pretended she didn't wholeheartedly agree with him. "She seemed to be a really big fan of yours."

Sutherland snorted. He refused to believe that the savvy woman before him actually thought there was merit to her replacement. "The only one Carole Chambers is a fan of is herself. She'd work with the devil if it was to her advantage."

Elisha looked up into his eyes, her own brimming with humor. "I kind of have the feeling that she probably did."

"Now, there you're wrong. Chambers didn't work, she pandered. She simpered. She spent so damn much time flattering me, all I could think of was getting my hands on a glue gun and firing it across her lips."

"Ouch." Elisha winced, even though his words brought her immense pleasure. She pretended to look surprised. "I thought you liked having people agree with you."

"Intelligently," he pointed out. "I don't need them to stand around mouthing platitudes they think I want to hear." He looked disgusted by the very thought. "Most of all, I like being left alone."

She wondered if he was trying to give her a message, or just playing according to type. In either case, she wasn't about to change her mind about this latest decision she'd made. "Sorry about that. Not going to happen."

The disgruntled look didn't quite come off. His eyes weren't shooting lightning bolts. In fact, he looked just a shade pleased by this new turn of events. Which in turn pleased her no end.

"Then you're still going to insist on sticking your nose into my writing." It was more of a statement than a question on his part.

She inclined her head, indicating that he was right. "That's what they pay me for."

He took a step closer. She could feel her heart begin beating just a hair faster. "It's also a good way to get that pretty little nose of yours hurt."

She grinned, taking a step closer of her own. Their breaths began to mingle. "Oh, I think I'll take my chances."

After a moment, he stepped back, but only to get a better perspective. It didn't help answer his question. "There's something different about you."

"That's what you said the last time." She watched his eyebrow rise again. "When I came over to play poker," she added.

He shrugged, pretending not to remember. Pretending that it wasn't his way to remember everything about everything. "Then it was your clothes and your hair. Now it's…" His voice trailed off. "I'm not sure."

"My aura?" she supplied with a grin that could have only been described as impish. For some reason, the word fit her. She seemed a lot younger now than when he'd first met her. Weren't kids supposed to age you?

"I don't use words like that," he fairly growled, dismissing the term as pretentious. Sutherland circled her slowly, like a soldier trying to take every possible avenue of attack into consideration. "Just something," he murmured.

"That doesn't sound very descriptive. And you call yourself a writer," she scoffed with a laugh that settled in her eyes as she turned to look at him.

He was a very virile, very masculine man. He radiated manliness from every pore. Not to mention that he was attractive as hell to boot. Even when she'd felt dead sexually, convinced that part of her life was over, there'd been this "something" going on inside her whenever she was around the man. Maybe it was attraction, maybe something else. She wasn't sure. All she knew was that whatever that "something" was, it had grown to adult-size proportions and she was suddenly aware of it. Very aware of it.

"I call myself a man first," he replied to her gibe.

His eyes were so intense, she thought her knees were going to buckle again, the way they almost had when he'd kissed her.

Nope, definitely not dead yet, she thought.

The words left her lips slowly, each measured before its release. "Funny, that was the term that came to mind for me, too."

His eyes on hers, he toyed with a strand of her hair. Things began to liquefy in her body.

"What else came to mind?"

As liquid as the rest of her had suddenly become, her mouth felt dry. Breathing became something she had to prompt herself to do. "I'm not sure I follow."

"You don't follow, Max, you lead," he told her. And she was very good at it, too. She'd gotten him to revise some of his manuscript, hadn't she? No one had ever done that before. "But you're not going to lead me," he warned, moving back as if to get a better view of the woman who was invading his territory. "Not around by the nose. I want to get that out in the open right now."

"It's out." Her mouth curved. She was beginning to feel warm, really warm. So warm that she was surprised her clothes weren't melting off her body.

"Good. Now come here."

Like someone who was hypnotized, she took a step, then abruptly stopped. It wasn't going to go this way. However brief this encounter, it was going to be memorable. For him as well as for her. "Now you."

His eyes narrowed. "What?"

She held her ground. Because she had to. "Step for step. Equal."

One corner of his mouth rose just a little. "You going to edit everything?"

She was moving blindly into uncharted territory but the steps felt right. Very right. Her eyes crinkled into another smile. It matched the one that she felt blossoming inside. "Only if I absolutely need to."

"I've never had any complaints."

She felt herself getting lost in his ice-blue eyes. It took effort to anchor herself in place. "You never had an editor before."

The list of women that had passed through his life was extensive. There might have been an editor in the lot, but he didn't know that for a fact. The exchange of information hadn't seemed very important at the time. "Not that I'm aware of."

"You'll be aware, Ryan, you'll be very aware." She had no idea where this sexual bravado was coming from, only that she meant the promise she'd just made him.

His arm around her waist, Ryan pulled her to him. His mouth came down on hers as a rarefied excitement began to throb through his veins.

CHAPTER 36

The heat flared instantly.

And with it came the realization that maybe, just maybe, she wasn't in control of anything. Not the way she'd wanted to be.

From the moment she'd seen Ryan standing in her doorway she'd known the visit could only end one way. Maybe she'd even known it before she'd gotten into Henry's car and driven over here.

Even when she'd disassociated herself from Randolph & Sons and concentrated only on her responsibilities as Andrea and Beth's sole guardian, miscellaneous thoughts about Sutherland had cropped up in her head. Thoughts that had nothing to do with their former relationship as author and editor.

Thoughts that dwelled on the man's masculinity.

As he kissed her now, she felt more alive than she had in years, except for that one aberration the night of the poker game. He'd almost succeeded in making her forget herself, forget her obligations. Forget everything except the rush inside her.

Just like the one she was feeling right now.

Even when she and Garry had lived together, she'd never experienced this sort of an unbridled thrill rampaging through her. The very tips of her fingers were tingling in anticipation of what was to come.

Fingers, hell, her whole body was tingling. Tingling, priming. Waiting.

The air left her lungs, taking along what little there was left of her sanity. She didn't care. Her arms went around his neck as she clung to the moment, to the sensation. To the man.

Ryan deepened the kiss, drawing her out of her skin and into a place that was hot and tumultuous and exciting as hell. Her body throbbing, she pressed it against his. And felt the hard outline of his anticipation. Hot spots began popping up all over her, feeding a growing frenzy that had leaped out of left field and held her in its grip, making her into a willing prisoner.

It took effort to curtail the moan that almost escaped her lips. She felt his arms tighten around her. Her core moistened. Preparing.

This was a surprise. At his age, given the kind of life he'd led, he hadn't thought there were any of those left for him, but he'd obviously been wrong. Elisha Reed was a surprise. He had no idea that there was this wild creature beneath the tailored designer suits.

Oh, he'd felt a degree of attraction to her, but that was because of the way she's stood up to him, the way she held her own when he'd tried to browbeat her. None of his previous editors had had the nerve to make corrections. And she was good at what she did, which made the "suggestions" hard to ignore. But it wasn't until she'd showed up at his place the last time that he'd noticed she was pretty. More than just mildly so.

And it wasn't until he'd heard that lost note in her voice when he'd called to see if she was all right following the poker game that he'd found himself feeling protective toward her. To his recollection, he'd never experienced that feeling before. It just didn't happen and it had given him an uneasy pause. So much so that when Randolph had told him she was taking a leave of absence, he'd figured it was the perfect time to reestablish his boundaries.

Those boundaries had definitely been breached tonight. With his help.

But even so, by no stretch of the imagination had he thought that beneath her polished exterior and intellect beat the heart of a woman who was hot, raw and sexy. Or that she would inflame him the way she did.

He was no stranger to women who exuded sex. But this was a particular mixture of intelligence and sensuality that ignited him as if he were a length of rope leading up to a lethal charge of dynamite.

He couldn't seem to get enough of her. He wanted to experience her to the ultimate degree. But that could carry consequences. And he wanted her in his life in her original capacity, as his editor.

Never in his wildest dreams did he think that work could be a deterrent to having sex. At least, not these days. But if this night could somehow jeopardize their working relationship, he would have to find a way to cope with pulling back. And if he was to pull back, he'd have to do it now. Before he couldn't.

Cupping her face in his hands, Ryan drew back. His eyes searched her face. If she lied, he'd know. "You sure about this?"

Her heart was pounding so hard, she wasn't entirely certain she could speak. Especially when her lungs were so low on air.

"Not the time to have me fill out a form in triplicate, Sutherland." Elisha ran the tip of her tongue along her lower lip, tasting him. Wanting him.

All hormones alive and well.

It was a very pleasant shock. But then, from the way the man kissed, Sutherland could have gotten a reaction from an Egyptian mummy.

"If this violates some secret black-ops code, you can debrief me later," she added.

His hands rested on the swell of her hips. "I'd rather do the debriefing now."

The next thing she knew, the skirt she'd worn found itself on the floor around her feet. The thong underwear she'd bought on a whim last week was the only thing that remained between her and the last shred of modesty that still shimmered in her soul.

She didn't want modesty, she wanted him.

She grinned as her heart began to pound in double time. "Part Houdini?"

He smiled into her eyes, working the buttons of her blouse. "My hands were always my greatest asset."

Her eyes fluttered shut as he proceeded to show her just what he meant by that. Her skin heated even more beneath his touch.

"If you say so," she murmured thickly. Her blouse slid from her shoulders. He surprised her by being gentle, by kissing her slowly, languidly, moving from one bare shoulder to another. Pausing at the hollow of her throat. Making her absolutely wild.

An eternity later, she felt her bra slipping off. Felt his hands covering her instead. A fever rushed through her as she found his mouth again.

It took effort not to succumb. Not to let herself just get carried away. The hunger inside of her had gone from zero to a hundred in a matter of seconds. But as delicious as it was, she didn't want to merely be the recipient. She wanted to make Ryan feel at least half as insane, half as wild with passion as he was making her feel.

Her fingers flew over him, tugging off his sweater, working the button above the zipper free. She watched his eyes as she guided the zipper down to the base, passing over the swell of his desire. She'd never done this before, never undressed a man. Garry had always taken off his own clothes, as had the handful of lovers she'd had before him. But this was going to be different, she'd promised herself. As different as she could make it.

Ideally, they would have made it to the bedroom. But desires made too many demands for the journey to be completed.

They made love on a light gray rug in the middle of the living room.

Elisha felt as if she'd taken leave of her body, hovering over herself and watching someone she hardly knew. Someone who was filled with urges, passions, needs. She felt only part human, the rest was some sort of ethereal being. A being who only grew hotter and more insatiable with each passing second. With each pass of his hands, his mouth.

He made her feel desirable. Beautiful. Writing and black ops were apparently not his only talent. Not his only gift. Ryan set her entire being on fire and she burned gladly within his flame.

This was a hell of a surprise, he kept thinking over and over again, having trouble reconciling the image he'd had of Elisha with this wildcat who had evoked such passion from within him. His assessment of people was usually dead-on. He'd survived that way for twenty years, during the years before he became a writer. But it was obvious that he'd been off his mark here. Way off.

And he'd never enjoyed being wrong so much.

She sparked things inside of him, pleasuring him even as he strove to pleasure her. He'd never had a partner who was so single-mindedly intent on his pleasure before.

He liked the taste of her, he suddenly realized. The warm, berrylike taste of her mouth, the dark flavors of her skin. It made him want more. He'd never been in that unique position before, wanting more.

Wanting to lose himself within the taste and smell of a woman.

Never too old to learn.

His hands urgently caressing her curves, he held back for a long as he could.

But every man had his limit and he had reached his. His arms around her, Ryan positioned himself on top of her. Ordinarily, he liked to watch the woman he had sex with. He didn't like being caught unawares. His senses were keen, alert during the very act.

But not this time. This time he surrendered just a little bit of himself, sank into the sensation that welcomed him with open arms. He kissed her as he plunged in, his eyes shut.

There was a muffled cry against his mouth.

Was she trying to tell him that she'd changed her mind at the last possible moment? Was he supposed to pull away? Questions raced through his brain, but even before he could formulate another one, he felt her moving beneath him. Moving at an ever-increasing tempo. Not as if she was trying to throw off his weight, but as if she was hurrying toward something. Toward a plateau that was just out of reach.

He had no choice but to join her in her flight.

And then it came.

A climax that felt as if it jarred his very teeth down to their roots. The sensation was so overwhelming, he clutched at the only thing he could for survival.

Elisha.

He held her to him hard, absorbing every last nuance of the sensation that had shuddered through him. The sensation that was even now fading back into the recesses from which it had come.

Exhaling, Ryan rolled off her. Then, for reasons he couldn't begin to comprehend, he slipped his arm beneath her and drew her to him.

He lay there for several moments without saying a word. Staring up at the dark beams that crisscrossed his vaulted ceiling.

Finally, because this had shaken him up more than he was willing to admit to anyone, even himself, Ryan said, "This a new way to edit? Because I have to say, it has its merits."

A kind of music ran through her head. Something light and

airy that she couldn't remember the words to. Something that made her smile.

Elisha propped herself up on her elbow to look at the man who had, to use Andrea's expression, just rocked her world. What had transpired was so far beyond perfect, she wasn't sure if a word had been invented yet to describe it.

Her body continued to hum even as she tried to look unaffected. She knew he expected nothing less.

"Is that what you were after? A merit badge?" She looked down at the soft layer of downy hair along his chest and ran her hand along it. "Where would you sew it?"

"You let me worry about that." Ryan flipped her onto her back, looming over her. Wanting her again. It scared him. He didn't like being scared. "Why did you come here tonight?"

The pulse in her throat was moving visibly. "To tell you that we'd be working together. I didn't want to risk you going to another house."

"You could have told me all that on the phone."

She forced a smile to her lips. Her body was aching. Not from what had just happened, but from wanting him. Was this normal?

"I've always liked the personal touch better."

He laughed. Personal touch. She'd certainly touched him. Very personally.

"Made a believer out of me." Pulling her closer, he started to kiss her.

As his body came in contact with hers, her eyes widened, incredulous. Even at the height of Garry's feelings for her, they'd made love once a week, maybe twice. Never twice in one night. "Again?"

His eyes crinkled. The word *cute* flashed through his mind. He'd never been much of a fan of cute. And yet…

"Don't look so surprised. I'm an ex–Navy SEAL, remember?" He lowered his mouth to hers.

"That must be one hell of a training course," she managed to say just before she sank back into the flames.

CHAPTER 37

"This doesn't change anything, you know."

Elisha's soft voice broke the silence that had enveloped them for what felt like an endless amount of time. She wanted to keep things light, to let him know that there were no expectations just because their relationship had gone beyond the written word. That he had nothing to fear from her, because she wasn't the nesting kind.

Even though the thought was beginning to take on more and more appeal.

She turned to him, her body warming again from the proximity. The man was just as incredible as she knew he probably thought he was.

"I'm still your editor. I'm still going to edit your manuscripts."

His eyes held hers for a long moment. She couldn't begin to guess what was going on behind those clear blue orbs. "And I'm still going to ignore you when you're wrong."

Elisha noted with no small pleasure that the ex–Navy SEAL had qualified his statement by using the word *when* rather than simply stating that he was going to patently disregard her opinion. By his choice of words, he'd acknowledged that there were times when she *was* right. They'd come a long way.

Not to mention that *she* had come a long way. And not just as his editor.

She wet her lips, not to look alluring, but to keep them from sticking together as she spoke. "I want you to know that you're my first author."

She watched as one sexy eyebrow rose quizzically. "Are you informing me of some pecking order?"

No, oh God, no. She didn't want him thinking that she'd just rated him.

"No, I mean I've never done…this…" *Very expressive, Lise. No wonder they pay you so much to be a senior editor. Your command of the language is nonpareil.* "I've never made love—had sex," she corrected, "with one of my authors."

Just the slightest hint of amusement curved his mouth. "You might consider it. You bring a whole new meaning to stroking a man's…ego." And then he laughed because her eyes had grown so wide. "I'm not being serious, Max."

She blew out a breath—and was not unaware that he was watching the way her chest rose and fell. She felt a hint of a blush rising to her cheeks and did her best to smother it.

"I never know with you." She looked at him for a second. "And I think you kind of like it that way."

He didn't look displeased. "Guilty as charged. A certain amount of mystery makes things interesting."

Ryan knew he should be getting up, should be putting distance between them. That's what he always did after exercising his sexual muscles. But for some reason, tonight he felt like lingering. Like savoring. He didn't try to analyze it, he just did it.

His arm tucked around her, he settled back and stared again at the massive dark beams that crisscrossed his ceiling some twenty feet above them. "So, you're coming back on Monday."

"Yes." Even as she said it, a certain insecurity set it. Elisha sighed.

He eyed her. "What's the matter? Changing your mind again?"

"No," she assured him quickly. "It's just that I hope I'm doing the right thing. I mean, I'm doing the right thing for me, but as for the girls…" Was she jumping the gun? Taking too much for granted? When she'd called Rocky, it was because she felt that the girls would be all right without having her invested in every minute of their lives. But now she wasn't so sure.

She wasn't sure about anything, least of all herself.

"Do you love them?"

Elisha turned to look at him. It was the last question she'd ever expected to hear from Ryan. She didn't think the man even knew what the word meant. In any context.

"Yes."

He drew her closer, even as he continued looking at the ceiling. His mind was aeons away. "Then that's all they need. Kids can forgive a lot of transgressions, as long as they know at the end of the day that you love them and are there for them."

The man continued to be a source of endless surprises. This was actually very sensitive, especially for him. A thought suddenly occurred to her. A strange tightness in her chest accompanied it. "Do you have kids?"

"No, but I was one."

She felt guilty about the relief that shimmied through her. Guilty, too, because there was a sadness in his voice. She didn't think it had anything to do with not having children of his own. He wasn't the type. No, this was something basic.

The sadness reached out to her even if he didn't. "How was it? Being a kid, I mean."

The laugh had no humor in it. She looked at him. His expression was grim. "Lousy."

"Why?"

He wasn't in the mood to share. His life, especially his past, was his own. "Just because we tangled together on my floor a couple of times tonight doesn't mean you can dig into my life, Max."

Boundaries were for people who were afraid to venture forward. Little by little, since Henry's death, she'd found herself becoming more and more fearless.

"Why?" she repeated, her eyes intent on his. "What made it lousy?"

He had no idea why he answered. "I had no control."

"Tell me," she coaxed.

When he examined his actions later, he had no idea why he didn't just get up and leave then. Why he began to talk, to open doors that had been shut for so long. She made it easy to slip. Easy for the words that had not seen the light of day for forty years to slowly come out.

"My mother died when I was eight." Elisha made no sympathetic, almost involuntary sound at the information, but he was acutely aware that she placed her hand over his. Aware that there was sympathy in her touch. Not pity, but sympathy. Because she'd lost someone she cared about herself, he thought. "My father couldn't handle the idea of raising a kid on his own, so he gave me up."

His words refused to compute. "Gave you up?"

The words were ground out one at time, as if he was wrenching them from the grip of pain. "Handed me over to child services."

This time she did make a noise. It took everything she had not to put her arms around him. Instinct told her that was the last thing he would have accepted. It went against some manly code. But it didn't stop her from offering the sympathy she felt.

"Oh God, how awful."

"I thought so."

In his mind's eye, he could still see it. Still see the small scrawny kid he'd once been, desperately trying to hold on to the hand of the man who didn't want him enough to make an effort to give him a home. His father had pulled his hand roughly away. And the social worker had taken it. Had taken him and dragged him away.

"Especially when I begged him not to. But he said I'd be better off this way. Have a more stable home life than he could give me." He shook his head at the memory of the words. "Stable. Yeah, right. I lived in over a dozen foster homes from the time I was eight until I reached eighteen." His mouth twisted cynically. "The system turns you out when you reach eighteen. You're considered a man and on your own by then."

At eighteen he was probably more of a man than most men were at forty, Elisha thought. A man who had never been allowed to be a child.

Her heart ached for him. "Is that when you enlisted in the navy?"

It had seemed like the logical thing to do. Even if it had been a snap decision. "Wasn't much else someone like me could do. I didn't like taking orders, but I liked starving even less. Took me a while to get my bearings, to learn when to pick my fights." A few beatings from bullies had him bulking up and training almost obsessively. Until he was a force to be reckoned with. "I made some mistakes."

She couldn't believe he was admitting something like that. She felt incredibly close to him. Closer than she'd felt while they were making love.

"Such as?"

He turned his face toward her. What was there about her that made him talk like this? That made him want to share? His boundaries were being threatened and yet he couldn't seem to work himself up about that. Was he getting old?

"You're just full of questions, aren't you?" But there was no edge in his voice, only mild amusement.

She smiled, propping herself up on her elbow and looking down at him. "Thought I'd press my advantage." Elisha waited a second, then prodded. "What kind of mistakes?"

He shrugged. It seemed like a hundred years ago. When he'd still believed in things like love. "Got drunk one shore leave in San Francisco. Got married."

Her chin slipped off her upturned hand. She felt as if someone had just detonated a bomb inside of her. "Married?"

Ryan nodded. He toyed with the idea of playing this out a little longer, but that would have been cruel. He gave her the short version.

"Sweet thing. She was a barmaid and I was out of my head. I was looking for love and she was looking for a green card. Didn't last long."

"Then you're divorced?" Did that come out as if she was happy about it? She was going to have to watch her inflection, she upbraided herself.

"I'm divorced. Got the paper around here somewhere," he said vaguely.

"Is that the only time you ever got married?"

"I've been pretty sober ever since."

Did that mean he thought only people not in control of their faculties pledged to love and honor? "People get married when they're sober."

"Not me." His voice was flat. Final.

She took a stab at the reason. "Because your childhood scarred you so much?"

He looked at her sharply. Ordinarily, he put people who asked him personal questions like this in their place. Succinctly. Why he didn't now mystified him. It was like an out-of-body

MARIE FERRARELLA 263

experience and he was observing himself play the part of someone else.

"I didn't exactly get a blueprint on how to maintain the perfect home life."

"No," she agreed. "But that shouldn't have stopped you. You said it yourself earlier."

"Said what?"

"Like the Beatles sang, all you need is love."

"Some people need more." But then, who was he to judge? "Maybe drugs help some people over the rough spots."

She was trying very hard to follow his train of thought. "You have too much character for that. To do drugs."

It had never appealed to him. It meant the loss of control. And the last time he'd done that, he'd wound up with a wife. He'd learned fast. But that didn't give her the right to talk as if she knew him. "How do you know what I have?"

As she smiled at him, she trailed the tips of her fingers along his chest. Monday they'd be author and editor. Tonight belonged in a bubble all its own. A bubble that would have to break before the hour was up.

"I'm a pretty good judge of character. I know you're not as hard as nails, as you like everyone to think."

He took exception to that. "I'm exactly as hard as nails."

But she shook her head. "A man without a heart wouldn't make arrangements to have a portion of his royalties sent to a bank account for the father who abandoned him."

Anger flared in his eyes. His father had shown up five years ago, his hand out. His first impulse had been to see how far he could toss the man. His second had been to give in to the pity he felt. So he'd set his father up with a monthly allowance on the stipulation that they were to have no further contact. His father had readily agreed. So much for parental love.

"How do you know that?"

"You're not the only one with connections. Granted, mine are minor compared to yours, but then my world is a lot smaller than yours."

He could give in to his anger, but then he'd deprive himself of her company for the evening. Tomorrow there were boundaries to regain. Tonight belonged to another world. A world where the lady was full of surprises.

"You're something else, Max, you know that?" Raising her hand to his lips, he pressed a kiss to her palm.

The thrill was taking hold all over again. Showing her an Elisha she'd never been acquainted with. An Elisha she could get to like.

"No, but I'm beginning to find out."

"Let the search resume," he said, kissing her again.

CHAPTER 38

Life looked different to her now.

Every so often, she had to stop and just take stock of all the changes. Like now, in the middle of her busy day. She pulled a not-so-empty second to herself and took a long breath.

Every moment of the day was still filled, but it amazed her how much more she could cram into a day than she had before. She was a "homemaker" now, a parent. There was no time to lie awake at night, with that soft refrain echoing through her head, whispering, "Is that all there is?" in Peggy Lee's husky voice. When she went to bed at night, she was asleep before her head found the pillow, waking up only when the alarm insisted on rousing her the following morning.

Her priorities in the last few months had shifted. Her workload had not. Despite Rocky's promise to lighten her responsibilities, work continued to pile on. Elisha didn't mind. She liked what she did. Enjoyed it even when the pace threatened to destroy someone with a lesser ability to cope with stress. She'd even approached a movie icon she knew about writing a book. The man told wonderful, complex, entertaining stories and she'd suggested hooking him up with a professional ghostwriter to help him along through his first attempt. When he'd agreed, she'd turned the project over to Carole Chambers. Her former assistant had accepted the gift warily.

"Why would you give this to me?" she'd asked, smiling so wide she could have given *Alice in Wonderland*'s Cheshire cat a run for his stripes. The emotion behind the smile was just as genuine as the feline's had been. But that had no bearing on Elisha's decision. Logic had brought her to it.

"Because I think you're more suited for this project than I am. I have my mystery authors. That's my niche. This is straight fiction. More your forte," she'd added, then said with a smile, "Have fun with it."

When she had walked out of the befuddled editor's cubicle, she'd felt good about what she'd done. Not insecure, not uneasy, but content. She hadn't even gone to the ladies' room after that to check for stab wounds in her back. It didn't hurt to have Carole completely thrown off guard in the bargain.

Of course, the final decision rested with Rocky, but Elisha felt fairly confident that he wouldn't oppose it. Almost as dear to him as profit were peace and tranquillity. The project would keep Carole busy for some time. And out of everyone else's hair. Besides, Rocky trusted her judgment. If she thought Carole was suited to the endeavor, then so did he.

Moving from her chair, Elisha approached the window that had sold her on this corner office. She wrapped her arms around her waist as she stood there, looking down at the city below. It had snowed last night. More than just a fair dusting. From this height, everything appeared to look warm and cozy. The fresh blanket of white hadn't turned to slush yet, hadn't begun to turn gray from all the exhaust it continually absorbed.

It looked picturesque. Like the cover of an old-fashioned greeting card.

Christmas was coming soon, she mused. She'd already begun shopping for the girls. There were so many more details to remember this year than before. Lists littered her life now.

She'd always loved Christmas, always celebrated the holiday at Henry's place. Even when she and Garry were together, she'd always considered Henry's house home and spent both Christmas Eve and Christmas Day there.

This year, Christmas was up to her.

Turning away from the window, Elisha went back to her desk and sat down. She was going to make it the best Christmas she possibly could for the girls. It wouldn't be easy, but she was determined. She owed it to Andrea and Beth. And herself.

And Henry, she added silently with a bittersweet smile.

She wasn't going to go there yet. She missed Henry with her whole heart. The wound was still raw. She knew it would be for some time to come.

Elisha glanced at her desk calendar. There was a notation in red marked in around noon. *Lunch with Sinclair*. She grinned. Around this time of year, little children began approaching him, asking if he was Santa Claus in disguise. It never failed to tickle him.

The author was busy working away on his new book and from all indications it was going very well. There had been very few emergency phone calls from him since he'd begun. This time around, his insecurity had toned down considerably. He'd gotten it under control faster than she could ever remember. When she'd mentioned it, he'd told her that was her doing. When she'd returned to be his editor again, he'd been so relieved, he'd suddenly felt inspired.

That had been more than two months ago. Two months and he was still firing on all four burners. Obviously he'd found a way to make his inspiration last indefinitely. She hoped it remained with him until he was finished. He was far less stressed this way. And so was she.

Baby steps, she thought fondly. Sinclair was taking baby steps. They were all taking baby steps, she amended. All but Ryan.

Her mouth twisted into a smile. The man probably didn't think he needed to make any changes, but he had. Consciously or unconsciously, he'd begun to bend rather than remain inflexible. They fought passionately over her final corrections to his latest book, but even so, she won more than a handful of the skirmishes.

When the manuscript had finally gone into production, it bore more than a few of her annotations, and he had made changes in the manuscript. Most notably to his main character. The man had become not just an action figure but someone with a soul.

That was due to her, she liked to think. She wondered what Ryan would say if he knew she'd sent his book off to be reviewed by several of the more notable critics. She was fairly certain that his comments would definitely not be G-rated.

She'd half expected him to stop inviting her over for the weekly poker games now that the manuscript was no longer a bargaining chip between them, but he hadn't. She was still included. Had grown accustomed to being included. Maybe that was wrong. Maybe that was setting herself up for a fall once the invitations dried up.

But there wasn't anything she could do about that and she knew it. Somehow or other, she'd slipped into a brand-new world here, as well. And she liked it. Liked being with him.

More than liked it.

She was working without a net and she knew it.

Her natural optimism warred with reality, striking up a compromise. She didn't go as far as thinking of him as her lover, but they had gotten together a number of times since that first time. And to her astonishment, each time had been better than the last. For her.

For him as well, she would have liked to believe. But she

couldn't be sure. He never came right out and said anything. Once the moment was over, once their clothes were back on, a mask would descend over his face and a fence would go up around him. Keeping her out.

But at least it was a wooden fence, not a brick wall. Fences could be more easily breached. And she was all for breaching, Elisha thought with a smile. She'd even bring the wood chipper.

Her private line rang. The line that Rocky had agreed to have put in for her when she'd returned to Randolph & Sons full-time. The only ones who had the number were Beth and Andrea. For emergencies.

Her heart beat a little faster.

Terminal optimist my foot. You're always anticipating disasters.

Motherhood had done that to her. Having the welfare of two children exclusively in her hands had made her think differently about everything. It was both a blessing and a curse. As she picked up the receiver, Elisha struggled to keep the anxiety out of her voice. If this was Andrea, the teenager would accuse her of overreacting. And she'd be right.

"Hello?"

"Aunt Lise." It was Beth. "I need a shepherd costume," the little girl declared.

Elisha grinned as relief came flooding in. Six months ago, she would have found the request unusual. But six months ago, she wouldn't have sat up all night reacquainting herself with the sewing machine she hadn't used in years. She'd made Beth a sheep costume, a standard requirement if you were playing a sheep in the elementary school's annual Christmas pageant.

"You got a promotion?" Elisha guessed.

"Marilyn Hotchkiss is sick with the flu and Mrs. Allen said I could do her part." Beth was trying very hard not to sound joyful at someone else's misfortune, but it was fairly obvious that she was thrilled.

"Any dialogue?"

"I say, 'Hark,'" Beth told her with no small pride.

"'Hark' is good. It's a start. When do you need the costume by?" Even as she asked, she knew the answer. *Yesterday, right?*

"Tomorrow. Mrs. Allen said because you have to hurry, it didn't have to match the others, but she wants it to be dark brown. I've got a picture."

"That's good."

A pattern would have been better, but she would take what she could get. Saying goodbye to her niece, Elisha hung up the receiver. It looked as if it was going to be a long night filled with pins, pinking shears and words she didn't ordinarily say muttered under her breath.

Yes, Elisha thought as she made a note to herself to buy three yards of dark-brown fabric, her life was very full. Any fuller and it would begin to overflow. She wondered how Sinclair was going to feel about topping off their lunch date with a quick stop at the craft store for three yards of dark-brown material and matching thread.

CHAPTER 39

There was a single red rose on her desk when she walked into her office the following week. The light from the window hit the cut-glass vase at just the right angle to create rainbows along her desk. It was the first thing she noticed when she crossed the threshold.

She could use a few rainbows today, she thought.

The train into the city had been delayed because of some malfunction along the track. The trip in had taken twice as long. Consequently, she began her morning running late.

Being late never put her in a good mood.

But like a red light at an intersection, the sight of the rose stopped her dead in her tracks. And made her smile.

She'd gotten flowers before. Bouquets, carefully crafted arrangements, celebrating a book's success, an author's gratitude. The last bunch had been from Rocky, celebrating her return to the publishing world. He'd almost turned her office into a garden. And Sinclair always sent her flowers for her birthday. But she'd never received just one single, perfect red rose before.

The rose stood at attention in its tall, slender vase. It certainly had all of hers.

Elisha looked around the bottom of the vase, then lifted it to look beneath it. Nothing. There was no note.

She rang for the assistant who'd signed for the gift in her absence. When the dark-haired, lively-looking woman appeared, she asked, "Trina, where did this come from?"

Trina looked at the vase, not at her. The expression in her eyes was borderline dreamy. "The florist delivered it about half an hour ago. Pretty, isn't it?"

"Was there a note?"

Trina shook her head. Tight, black little curls bounced around her face before returning to their place. "None that I could see."

Elisha had a sneaking suspicion she knew who'd sent the rose, but she needed to be sure. That meant getting to the source. "Who was the florist?"

Trina frowned as all her features were absorbed in the act of thinking. And then her small, round face brightened.

"Capriani's," she declared as if she'd just come up with the million-dollar response in a game of Jeopardy. "It was written across the back of the guy's jacket. I noticed it because the name was Italian," she explained.

Elisha's mouth quirked in a fleeting smile. Trina was currently seeing someone who was Italian, so she was suddenly aware of everything that might have something to do with the country.

It never ceased to amaze her how things managed to arrange themselves the way she needed them to, Elisha thought.

"Thanks," she said, turning toward her computer.

Trina continued to look at the flower wistfully. "Want me to get the number for you?"

"No, I can do it myself."

With a nod, Trina slipped out again, closing the door behind her.

The search engine Elisha used had her connecting to the florist's shop in less than two minutes.

"Hello, this is Elisha Reed. I received a single rose from your shop within the last hour—"

She'd gotten the owner of the independent shop on the other end of the line. He cut in before she could get any further.

"Somethin' wrong with the flower, lady? 'Cause our flowers are perfect. I pick 'em out myself, so—"

"No, there's nothing wrong with the flower and yes, it is perfect. But there was no card."

She heard papers being shuffled. It was several minutes before the man responded, "That's 'cause he didn't want no card."

He. Okay, she had a gender. *I'll take names for two hundred, Alex.* "Did this 'he' have a name?"

The owner's tone grew sharp. "Lady, everybody's got a name."

Coffee, she thought, she needed coffee. And a boatload of patience. Obviously the florist didn't live off his charm. "And what was his?"

The huge sigh on the other end was of gale proportions. She heard more shuffling as the owner unearthed the paperwork for the order again. "Southland."

"Sutherland?" she corrected.

He made some kind of noise, as if he was considering her suggestion, then said, "Could be. Art took the order. The guy's got handwriting like a chicken dipped in ink, walkin' across a road."

"Very colorful," she said. "Thank you."

Hanging up, Elisha lost no time in dialing Ryan Sutherland's home on the island. A machine picked up and a gruff instruction from Ryan told her to leave a message. Hanging up, she tried his apartment with the same results. Frustrated, she tried his cell phone.

After five rings, someone snapped, "What?" in her ear.

Elisha smiled. The man was charming as ever. "I just got your rose."

"And I was just about to hit the showers." She thought she heard someone bang something metallic in the background. "If

I wasn't getting a fresh set of clothes out of my locker, I wouldn't have heard the phone."

His locker. That meant he was at his gym in the city, she thought. He had a full gym at his disposal at the house on the island. If he was hitting the showers, he'd just finished working out.

Leaning back in her chair, she let her mind drift, picturing Ryan wet and sweaty, his muscles pumped up and sculpted.

The smile on her lips deepened.

"I've always been lucky that way," she quipped. "By the way, it's usually customary to send a note when you send flowers."

"I'm used to not leaving behind any evidence."

You could take the man out of black ops, but you couldn't take the black ops out of the man. "What's the rose for, Ryan?"

There was a long pause on the other end. She wondered if he was debating lying to her. She imagined that he told lies and the truth with equal aplomb.

"Have you seen the review?"

She didn't have to ask what he was referring to. *Black January* was due out in two and a half weeks. Advance copies had been sent to a number of reviewers weeks ago. The first that returned with a column was the literary critic at the *New York Times*. She'd held her breath until she'd read it in its entirety.

Score one for the home team, she congratulated herself. "Roland Thomas thought this was your best book so far. Or, to put it in his words, 'the first book worth his time.'"

She heard Ryan snort. "Little snot."

That could well be true and probably was, but she focused only on the important aspect.

"He liked your book, Ryan," she pointed out. "I believe he said that 'for once, the hero had dimension and reasons for his actions.'"

"What did you do?" Ryan asked, "Memorize the damn thing?"

"No, but I always remember things that prove me right. So that's what the rose is for?" She lightly glided her finger along a velvet petal. "To say I was right and you were wrong?"

"I wasn't wrong," he informed her tersely, then his tone relented just a little. "I just wasn't as right as you were."

She laughed. Drawing the vase closer to her, she leaned over the rose and inhaled. Ryan had managed to find one of those rare roses that looked beautiful and had a fragrance, as well. He must have driven the florist crazy until he'd gotten just the right specimen.

"I'll remember that argument the next time we have a difference of opinion," she promised. And then, because she'd been waiting in vain for an opening for the last few days to ask, she forged ahead. "What are you doing for Christmas?"

"Probably playing poker with the guys. You want in?"

"No. I…"

For a second, her courage flagged. This was personal. To her. But it wasn't as if she was about to ask him to marry her, or even to move in with her. She was asking him to spend the holiday with her and the girls. The fact that it was a very special holiday to her wasn't really the point.

"Is this a hard-and-fast thing, about playing poker on Christmas?"

"No. Just something that's happened the last couple of years." She could have sworn she heard his tone hardening. "Look, Christmas is no big deal. It's just another day on the calendar."

Elisha had a feeling his philosophy, if he actually subscribed to it, had come about after years of being on the outside, of watching people in the foster homes where he'd been placed exchange gifts and affection with one another, leaving him completely in the cold.

"But it is a big deal," she insisted. Dammit, where was her way with words when she needed it most? She felt as if she had cotton in her mouth. Ryan respected the direct approach, she reminded herself. So she was direct. "Would you like to come over and spend it with the girls and me?"

He'd been over to the house several times now. The girls liked him more each time he appeared. Because he treated them the way he treated everyone else. Like responsible adults.

So when Ryan gave her his answer, it left Elisha stunned for a moment.

"No."

CHAPTER 40

"**N**o?" Elisha echoed. Just a flat no? Okay, so he was a former Navy SEAL, a macho man who took pain like an Apache warrior, with no complaint, no telltale signs of wincing. But this was a get-together they were talking about. And he'd just indicated that he had no real set plans for the day.

Ryan hated being backed into a corner. Hated having to explain himself. Yet here he was, explaining. "Look, with you it's a family thing—"

She tried to keep it light. "We could adopt you if that's the problem."

"No, thanks."

She was trying hard to understand what made him tick. Everyone was different, but some things were universal. Like spending the holidays with people who mattered.

"Ryan, no one should be alone on Christmas."

Traditional family celebrations had stopped meaning anything to him decades ago. Survival meant deliberately closing himself off from things like that. At this point, he had no interest in opening the door again. And probably couldn't even if he wanted to.

"Save it for one of your kids' books, Max. Look, I want to take that shower. Just revel in your success," he said, referring to the critic's response. "That should be enough for you. I gotta go."

And with that, the connection was broken.

Not permanently, she hoped. Hanging up the phone again, Elisha sat staring at the rose on her desk for a very long time, thinking.

And then she went into action.

The phone call came the morning of the next day. At 6:00 a.m. It jangled into her sleep. She knew who it was before she picked up the receiver. Her hand on the phone, Elisha paused and gave herself to the count of ten to fully wake up. She was going to need all her faculties for this one.

"Hello?"

"What the hell is all this?"

Ryan. Sitting up, Elisha leaned against the headboard and drew the covers closer to her. The air was crisp. The new heater she'd bought for the house last month wasn't programmed to kick in until seven.

"All what?" she asked innocently.

"I came up to the house this morning and found a fully decorated Christmas tree standing in my living room. With tinsel," he added dramatically. "Now, either the house was attacked by a band of marauding, renegade elves, or you did this."

A simple thank-you was obviously out of the question. Some people, Elisha thought, were very hard to do things for.

"No marauding, renegade elves, Ryan. Just the girls and me, bringing you Christmas. It was only a little simple redecorating, don't make it sound like a crime."

It might have been redecorating, Ryan thought, but there was nothing simple about it. Walking into his dark living room to have his vision accosted by a tree was as much a jolt to the eyes as Elisha had been to his system. To his thoughts. She'd secretly redecorated those, too, without his being fully conscious of it.

But he was conscious of it now and he had no idea how to move things back to there they'd been.

Ryan dragged his hand impatiently through his hair as he stared at the result of her physical invasion. She'd brought in a live tree. The damn thing stood at least ten feet tall. And looked oddly at home in the dark room. Like a sunbeam trying to break through a fog.

He didn't need this. Didn't need to be invaded like a Normandy beach.

"How the hell did you manage to get in here with all this, anyway?"

"I had help." She grinned, enjoying herself. "I could go into detail, but then I'd have to kill you."

He snorted, not amused. "Very funny."

"The man who runs security at Randolph & Sons is a retired cat burglar. I asked him to help."

A cat burglar. It figured. The door, when he'd gone to reexamine it, had shown no signs of forced entry, but he hadn't checked all the windows. Not after he saw the tree. "It's breaking and entering, you know."

"I'll take the fall," she responded cheerfully. "Besides, I didn't take anything out, I brought something in. A little Christmas cheer, I hope. The girls insisted on helping. They thought it was sad that you didn't have anything up."

He turned around in the room. Not only had she brought in a tree, but she and her companions in crime had put garland up along his banister and hung what he took to be either mistletoe or some not-quite-dried vegetation in his doorway. He hadn't even been upstairs and now that he thought of it, he didn't want to. No telling what she'd done there.

"Yeah, well, you can't say that anymore, now, can you?"

"Do you like it?"

Did he like it? No, he didn't. He didn't want to. And yet, somehow, it managed to speak to something inside of him. To the boy who hadn't quite died all those years ago. Hadn't died even though there'd been nothing to nurture him.

"I don't like clutter."

The man would go to the grave before admitting his feelings, she thought. Stubborn, stubborn man. "It's not clutter, it's Christmas."

Ryan said something unintelligible under his breath. She let it pass, thinking it safer that way.

Finally, he said, "Tell the girls they did a nice job."

At least he was thoughtful of their feelings. "Thank you, that'll make them happy." Since he had said something partially amiable, she thought she'd give it one more try. "So, will you come to Christmas dinner? You don't have to stay the whole day," she added quickly. "Just eat and go. Rocky's going to stop by and Sinclair always spends part of the day here. There'll be other people you know." She mentioned a few authors he'd run into at the promotion parties.

The woman was talking faster than he could process. "I'm not much for crowds and I've already told you, as far as I'm concerned, Christmas is just another day. Why are you trying to convert me?"

"I'm not," she protested, wishing that he'd stop being so perverse. He was doing it because he was afraid of something, she thought. But what that was, she wasn't completely sure. "You're free to do whatever you want."

"Thanks."

His reply was cool. She tried to regain ground. "I just wanted you to know you had options."

"Then you didn't have to go through the trouble, Max. I always know what my options are before I ever walk into a situation."

"This isn't a raid, Ryan. This is just Christmas dinner."

It was a hell of a lot more than that, he thought, and they both knew it. He was working his way across an abyss using a ladder made of paper towels. "Like you said, there'll be plenty of people around. You're not going to miss another place setting."

"You're not just another place setting." There, she'd said as much as she could. As much as she dared. But he was a smart man. He was good at deciphering code. And she had just told him that she cared for him, couching it in words that left them both safe. Mostly him. Because if she told him outright how she felt and he didn't feel anything, that would be the end of it. Words were far more lethal than any physical act they might have shared.

For all she knew, he might still regard what they'd had as sex. He might, but she didn't. As far as she was concerned, she had made love with him. Because, dammit, she loved him.

There it was again, that strange, funny little hitch in the middle of her chest, in the pit of her stomach. Like a huge bipolar reaction, happy and sad by so many turns that it made her head spin.

"Sure I am," he told her flatly.

He was telling her there was nothing between them, she thought.

Tears came, filling her eyes, filling her soul. *Agree with him, save face and be done with it. This wasn't supposed to have happened anyway.*

But it had, and she couldn't back away. "No," she said firmly, "you're not. You could be the only place setting, but you're not just 'another' one."

There was silence on the other end of the line. Silence that vibrated straight into her soul. Suppressing the sigh that rose to her lips, Elisha said quietly, "I have to go. If I don't see you before then, have a merry Christmas."

And then, when he didn't say anything to make her remain, she hung up the phone. Burying her face in her pillow, she let the pillowcase absorb her tears. And called herself a fool for feeling the way she did.

CHAPTER 41

It really was true, Elisha thought. The more things changed, the more they insisted on remaining the same. She was living proof.

In the last six months, her life had experienced nothing short of a monumental shake-up. She'd gone from being a single-minded, dedicated career woman to a woman who juggled home and family with her job. Something she'd never thought she would be able to do, even if the occasion did present itself. But she could. That was the "new" Elisha Reed.

But as far as things went on the romantic front, she was still the old Elisha. Her new evolution hadn't helped her lose her knack for being attracted to men who weren't good for her. Men who weren't going to stick around for the long haul.

It didn't matter that she'd told herself that she was past all that. That she'd made peace with never having a husband, a significant other in her life. Had convinced herself that she could just enjoy a night, an interlude of system-blowing, hot sex and be satisfied with that as long as her partner wasn't a Neanderthal. She'd thought that she'd made herself believe that the experience was an end unto itself.

It was a lie. She wanted more.

Wanted more because she'd seen that life could and often *did* offer more. Nothing was set in stone. She'd learned that. More than anything, she wanted that semi–happily ever after that she'd come to believe lucky people had in their lives.

That was the life she wanted.

Where there's life, there's hope, right? Elisha told herself as she went around the house, switching off lights. Andrea had had her friends over for a Christmas Eve party and it had been past midnight before the last guest, a boy named Adam Tomlin, had finally left.

She'd witnessed Andrea and Adam sharing a kiss beneath the mistletoe and had felt a mixture of sweet pleasure and wistful envy at the sight. Adam looked like the type of clean-cut boy parents wished for their daughters, and she was happy for Andrea.

But really sad for herself.

There'd been no call from Ryan in the last few days. No calls, no e-mails. Nothing. She had a feeling that when he'd said no to her, he was turning down more than just her invitation to Christmas dinner. He's said no to the whole idea behind it. To the whole idea of sharing himself with her beyond an interlude.

For all she knew, that part of their relationship might already be in the past.

Served her right for making a big deal out of it, she thought ruefully.

Elisha couldn't shake the sadness. All during the evening, she'd put on a front—smiling, bantering, pretending that nothing was wrong. But it was. It was very wrong. And there was nothing she could do about it.

Standing at the foot of the stairs, she paused for a moment just to look back into the living room. The house was locked up for the night. She'd done that first before playing Santa Claus and bringing out the presents she'd hidden in the storage shed behind the garage. She'd placed the lot of them underneath the tree. Just like Henry used to do.

It had been her brother's custom to wait until everyone in the house was asleep, then he'd tiptoe down and slip all the gifts beneath the tree. Like Santa Claus. The tradition had begun when Andrea was just a baby. She saw no reason to change it now.

Elisha felt her eyes growing misty and tried not to think that this was not just the girls' first Christmas without him, but hers, as well.

"This one's for you, Henry," she whispered, leaving just one light burning on the first floor.

Where there was life, there was hope, she thought again as she entered her bedroom and closed the door. But she was realistic enough to realize that as far as Ryan Sutherland went, that hope was gone. If she wanted to continue working as his editor, she was going to have to accept that. Get used to that.

She wasn't altogether sure she could.

Love sucked, Elisha thought, changing for bed. Especially the one-sided kind.

But then, she already knew that. She lifted the covers and got into the double bed that seemed so horribly empty. The sheets felt cold against her body. But then, so did her soul.

Elisha's bedroom window faced the front of the house and consequently the driveway. She'd picked it because the room received the first rays of the morning sun. She liked being woken up by sunshine when it was in the offing. But it wasn't the sun that woke her this morning. The sun hadn't even had a chance to make an appearance yet. What woke her was the noise. The noise of someone or something in the driveway.

She forced herself to focus. It felt as if she'd only just finally fallen asleep after hours of tossing around, trying to find a comfortable place on the ordinarily accommodating mattress.

Was someone trying to break into the house? On Christmas morning? She thought that seemed unbelievably crass.

Elisha sat up, listening intently.

Henry's house was close to being forty years old. When he'd first moved in, he'd done a lot of remodeling and refinishing himself. This was not a structure that groaned and creaked like some houses the same vintage. Even if it had been, these weren't the sounds of a house settling. This was the sound of a car pulling into her driveway. Of a car door being closed. And a hood being popped.

She thought about waking up the girls. Should she be calling 911?

Elisha leaned her head closer toward the window and listened harder.

Sinclair had volunteered to dress as Santa Claus for Beth's sake. The author had been almost crestfallen when she'd told him that Beth was too old to believe in that anymore.

These weren't the right kind of sounds for an invading Santa Claus.

Besides, as good as his intentions were, there was no way Sinclair would have arrived at her house at six-thirty, shrouded in the shadows of fading moonlight. He would have come to dinner, dressed in the red suit.

Her heart in her throat, Elisha got out of bed and crept toward her window. She looked out. And saw a Hummer. The black vehicle was sharply contrasted against the fresh blanket of snow that had fallen after ten last night.

Santa drove a Hummer.

She smiled ever so slightly. Opening her window, she looked out, then toward the front door. But from her angle, there was no way she could see who was standing there. The view of the front door was hidden from her.

Elisha withdrew. She closed the window and grabbed her robe as she flew out of the room. Struggling with it, she'd just managed to push her arms through the robe's sleeves when she got to the front door.

At times like this, she wished she had a dog. A big, snarling Doberman or German shepherd. Something fierce that could rear up on its hind legs while she held on tightly to its collar. Just in case the "robber" wasn't who she thought it was. But what kind of robber drove a Hummer?

The only one she knew of who had one of those overpriced vehicles was Ryan.

Taking a deep breath, she yanked open the front door. A blast of cold air rushed in, surrounding her. Elisha hardly noticed it. She was too focused on the man on her doorstep.

She was looking down at the top of his head.

Ryan was caught bending over, placing the last of the foil-wrapped packages he'd brought with him. Gifts he'd gotten up early to wrap because he'd bought them all just last night. Up until that time, he'd resisted making the purchases. Resisted giving in to what making those purchases implied. That, like it or not, he was part of something greater than himself.

He heard the door the instant she'd begun to open it. Caught, Ryan raised his eyes to hers. "Go back to bed, you're dreaming."

"No, I'm not," she replied, fighting hard to keep from laughing out loud.

"And why aren't you asleep?" he asked, snarling out the question.

There was no point in telling him he was the reason she couldn't drop off to sleep. He was here now, which was all that mattered.

"I was," she told him. "But then a noise woke me up. I decided to come down and check things out because I thought I heard Santa Claus making a last-minute run before he went back to the North Pole." She looked at the gifts on the doorstep. There were at least ten in all. All with gift tags hastily applied. One tag had fallen off. Ryan quickly picked it up and pushed it beneath the ribbon. The latter was askew.

This seemed so out of character for him, for a second she thought she *was* dreaming.

Elisha grinned, her eyes catching his. "Apparently, I did."

CHAPTER 42

He'd thought he could just leave the gifts on her doorstep and make a quick getaway. Obviously not. Why did Elisha always manage to complicate things at every turn?

Ryan began to back away. "Look, I have to leave."

She cocked her head, doing her best to look innocent. "We're not the last house on your run, Santa?"

His face clouded. He was embarrassed at being caught doing something nice. Ryan cleared his throat. "Max, I'm not—"

"Not Santa Claus? Yes, I know. But your secret's safe with me." Elisha hooked her arm through his and began to gently but firmly pull him inside. "However, I'm not above a little blackmail. Girls," she shouted over her shoulder, in case she needed reinforcements. "Company's here."

He began to tug his arm away and found that she had one hell of a grip. For a little thing, she was certainly a lot stronger than he would have thought.

"Let them sleep," he ordered gruffly.

Elisha was pretty sure she was witnessing the rise of color in his face. The man was embarrassed, she thought with a secret note of triumph.

So you are human after all. Nice to know.

"This is Christmas morning," she pointed out as she succeeded in getting him over the threshold. "Nobody really sleeps late on Christmas morning. They start waking up one minute past Christmas Eve." Her eyes swept over him as she did a quick calculation, weighing pros and cons. "If I let go of your arm, will you bolt?"

He met her gaze with an unwavering one of his own. Elisha couldn't begin to read what was going on inside his head. She only knew what she *wanted* to be going on in there.

"Can't make any promises."

Well, at least the man didn't lie. That put him way ahead of a lot of other men she knew.

"Just promise me that one," she requested. "I won't ask for anything else."

Ryan made no reply, but something in her heart told her that she could trust him to stay put. At least for now. Slowly, she released her hold. He remained where he was. She grinned at him. Inside her chest, her heart was doing somersaults.

"Good, now make yourself useful and bring in that loot you just planted on my doorstep." She stooped down beside him to help. Her robe tangled with the pile she picked up and she had to pull it out of the way. "Why would you do that anyway?" she wanted to know. "Why wouldn't you just knock and come in with your presents?"

Grudgingly, he followed her into the house, his arms laden with the gifts he'd wrapped less than twelve hours ago. "Because I didn't want this."

She set her small pile in front of the tree, gesturing for him to do the same. "This?" she repeated.

His face was as dark as thunder as he placed his armload next to hers. "A fuss."

"A fuss," she echoed. Elisha shook her head and laughed as she looked at him. "Mister, if you think this is a fuss, then you have no idea what the word really means."

Behind her, she could hear the pounding for two sets of feet as her nieces came running down the stairs. For rather petite creatures, Andrea and Beth could sound like a herd of charging elephants when bounty was involved.

"Look who's here, girls," she tossed needlessly over her shoulder.

"Mr. S.! Merry Christmas!" Beth's greeting was filled with pure joy as she rushed over and threw her arms around his waist, hugging him before he had a chance to place any gifts between himself and the little girl.

It was clear to Elisha that Beth was hungry for male influence in her life. And she had targeted Ryan to be that male. The little girl could have done a lot worse.

From where she stood, Elisha felt they both had a lot to gain from the interaction. Beth still needed a father figure and Ryan could do with the kinder, gentler influence of a family-type setting to draw on.

"Here, I'll take those," Andrea offered, making a straight line for the gifts that had just been deposited in front of the tree.

"Of course you will." Elisha could feel her eyes smiling as she watched the two girls. "Obviously, you think they're for you."

"At least some. Right?" Andrea raised her eyes in Ryan's direction.

He raised a broad shoulder beneath the pea jacket he had favored since his early days in the navy and then let it casually drop again. "There might be some with your name on them," he allowed.

Beth tugged on the bottom of his jacket. "Me, too?" she asked, her small face turned up to his. It was a long distance between faces.

The frown lines that were so much a part of Ryan's face faded as he nodded and said, "You, too."

The girls quickly divided the loot, placing their gifts on the side of the tree they had staked out the night before. Right for Beth, left for Andrea. There were several gifts in the middle. Those were intended for Elisha.

The gifts she had for the guests who were coming to dinner had been placed to the rear of the tree, out of possible harm's way until Christmas morning was officially over. She'd seen the girls' exuberance when they opened their gifts and was taking no chances.

Ryan found himself standing close to Elisha. And reluctant to draw away. The issue of his own survival, his own space, was no longer as compelling as it had been even a few minutes earlier.

In for a penny, in for a pound, Ryan thought. He looked at Elisha. "Aren't you going to ask if there's a gift for you?"

There was nothing coy or calculating in her face as she shook her head. "I don't have to. I already got my gift. You're staying for dinner."

He hadn't said so in so many words, even though he'd reversed his decision about dinner late last night. Still, he'd wanted to be the one to say as much. Ryan kept a poker face. "Don't get ahead of yourself."

"That's not negotiable," she informed him simply. Her eyes shone. "You're staying for dinner. Even if it means I have to handcuff you to the table."

There was a certain twinkle in his eye as he said, "You'd be surprised what I could do with a pair of handcuffs."

She lifted her chin, unfazed. "No, I wouldn't."

"Aunt Lise, there's one in here for you," Beth declared. From the center of the silver foil-wrapped gifts, she plucked a small square box and held it up over her head like a trophy.

"One more," Andrea added. For Elisha's benefit she held up what appeared to be a gift-wrapped index card, five by seven in length and as flat as a dime. Delicate brown eyebrows drew together over the bridge of her nose as Andrea looked first at the foil-wrapped gift, then at Ryan. "Did you flatten this by accident?"

"By design," he told her. "Always by design." He looked at Elisha. "You can open that one second."

"You're the boss," she allowed.

He laughed in response. He had no idea she could lie so smoothly. "And if I believed that, where's the bridge you want to sell me?"

"Later," she quipped. Taking Ryan's gift from Beth, she waved both girls back to their pile of presents. "Go ahead, start ripping."

Beth needed no more encouragement than that. As for Andrea, Christmas had a way of penetrating her bored-teenager-in-search-of-herself facade, turning her back into the Andrea everyone else had always known and loved. The girls went at their piles with gusto.

Turning back to Ryan, Elisha thought she detected an uneasiness in him. That was definitely a first. She'd never seen the man anything but confident before. But then, it was a morning for firsts.

"What made you buy the girls presents?" she asked.

He shrugged again. Reaching over, she began to unbutton his pea jacket. He gave her an incredulous look, then finished the job himself. "I figured I owed them something for decorating the tree."

She smiled knowingly. The man just couldn't admit to having a softer side. "I see."

He looked at the two items she was still holding in her hand. "Are you going to hang on to those indefinitely or open them?"

She looked down at the two gifts. Multicolored lights from the Christmas tree were splaying themselves across the silver foil. It looked as if she were holding fire in her hands. "I thought I'd hold on to them for a while. Savor the fact that you brought me something."

Impatience added color to his profile. "Oh, for God's sake, open the damn things."

"Said in the true spirit of Christmas," she laughed. Giving in, she began to undo the foil around the flat gift with her thumbnail.

"No." He stopped her. "I said to open that one first." Ryan nodded at the box.

"Okay." Tucking the other gift under her arm, she unwrapped the square box instead.

And found a black velvet box beneath the foil.

Her mouth grew dry as she stared at the gift. If anyone but Ryan had given it to her, she would have immediately guessed that there was a ring inside the box. But it was from Ryan, which meant that it was probably anything *but* a ring.

"Are you planning on trying to guess its weight?" he prodded.

"No." Elisha ran her tongue along her lips. It didn't help. Everything was bone dry. There wasn't enough moisture to form a dewdrop.

She held her breath. And flipped open the box.

The heart-shaped diamond caught the light coming in through the front window and changed it into a rainbow before chasing it back out onto the far wall.

She was holding a rainbow in her hand.

More than that, she was holding a promise.

Incredulous, she raised her eyes to his face. For possibly the first time in her life, she found herself completely and utterly speechless, unable to form a single word.

"Now open the other one," he prompted.

Like someone moving in a dream, Elisha did as he instructed. Her brain felt like a vast wasteland, unable to form or retain a single thought. Ripping open the second gift, she almost succeeded in ripping what was inside, as well. It *was* an index card.

And written on it was a single sentence. A single question: "Will you marry me?"

"Why…" She almost choked, her throat was so dry. Starting again, she raised her eyes to his. "Why did you write this down?"

Dammit, he couldn't read her expression. She looked shell-shocked. Was that a good thing? Or was she looking for a way to say no? Hell, he'd come this far, he had to press on. "Because I'm a better writer than a talker. And I figured you liked editing things." As if to underscore that, he handed her a pen.

There was an earthquake going on inside of her. Or at least what she would have imagined one to feel like. Everything within her body was shaking.

Willing the tremor out of her hand, Elisha took the pen and wrote something on the side of the index card.

Taking a deep breath, she gave it back to him.

Ryan realized he'd stopped breathing altogether. Stopped breathing until he read what she'd written. "'Yes.'"

He grinned as he drew air back into his lungs. He'd been in the throes of agony, sweating bullets from the moment he'd walked into the small Forty-seventh Street jewelry store. The place was run by Jacob Wolfe, a man whose life he'd once saved. Jacob sold him the best diamond he had, then proceeded to create a unique setting for it in under twelve hours.

It was a masterpiece. But it would have been nothing if she'd turned him down.

The next moment, Ryan found himself surrounded by Andrea and Beth. Surrounded, he knew, by the kind of love that had eluded him all of his life. And he was getting it on the family plan. In the depths of his soul, he had to admit that he rather liked that.

Taking the ring out of the box, he slipped it onto Elisha's finger. The fit was perfect, as he knew it would be.

Elisha's head threatened to begin spinning again. If she listened really, really hard, she could swear she heard the sound of a white charger's hoofbeats as the horse galloped up to her house, delivering the prince to her doorstep.

The sound was probably just her own heart, gone into triple time.

"Are you sure you mean this?"

His eyes met hers. She had her answer before it even left his lips. "Max, I never say anything I don't mean."

Her mouth curved. "Technically, you haven't actually 'said' anything yet."

Fully aware that women liked to hear the words, Ryan took a deep breath and forced them from his lips, one at a time like parachuted commandos, ready for action, evacuating an airplane. "Will you marry me?"

"Because?" she coaxed.

"Because?" he echoed, confused.

"Because you love me?" she supplied.

He gave a half shrug, wanting to hide at least some of his feelings until a later time. "Yeah, that."

She didn't let it die. He might have known she wouldn't. The woman was as stubborn as a mule. He supposed that was part of what he liked about her.

"Ryan, I can't edit this for you. You have to tell me why you're proposing."

He snorted. "Because if I kidnapped you and hid you in a cave, someone would come after me."

He wasn't fooling her. "And why would you kidnap me?" she persisted.

Cornered, he gave her her due. And exposed a little more of himself than he ever had. "Because I like being part of all this."

"If you liked it so much, why did you originally say no to Christmas dinner?"

"I said no to all of it because…" Oh, the hell with it, he might as well tell her everything. Wives were supposed to be privy to their husbands' feelings. "Because I thought wanting it made me weak."

"Love makes you strong, Ryan," she contradicted.

Restraint only went so far before it became counterproductive. And he wanted to leave himself open to experiencing things he'd been denied.

Ryan took her into his arms, toying with a strand of her hair. "And you'd know this firsthand?"

"I do now." She slipped her arms around his neck. Her engagement ring flashed as it caught more light. "Because right now, I could wrestle an alligator." She grinned, her eyes shining as she looked up at him. "But I'd settle for an ex-commando."

He raised an eyebrow. "Settle?"

His intimidating days were over, she thought. And he knew it. "I mean that in the best possible sense of the word."

Ryan shook his head and laughed. "You really are something else."

She tucked her body just a tad closer to his, aware that her nieces were taking this all in and almost cheering on the sidelines. As far as new lives went, this one was shaping up beautifully. "And you have an entire lifetime to find out exactly what that is."

* * * * *

MILLS & BOON
Special Edition
On sale 15th June 2007

THE WYOMING KID
by Debbie Macomber

Handsome Lonnie Ellison is used to women throwing
themselves at him. So teacher Joy Fuller's lack of interest
is infuriating…and very appealing!

THE RELUCTANT CINDERELLA
by Christine Rimmer

Megan Schumacher and Greg Banning spent *a lot* of
time together. He was handsome, she was sexy and gossip
was rife. Could this end happily?

PRINCESS IN DISGUISE
by Lilian Darcy

Princess Misha was escaping for a bit in the Australian
Outback. Brant Smith thought she had been sent to him as
a possible wife! Had fate lent love a helping hand?

0607/23a

MILLS & BOON
Special Edition

On sale 15th June 2007

EXPECTING HIS BROTHER'S BABY
by Karen Rose Smith

Brock Warner returned to find the family ranch falling to
pieces and his pregnant, widowed sister-in-law, Kylie,
in hospital. She needed help; could he keep his feelings for
her in check?

CATTLEMAN'S BRIDE-TO-BE
by Lois Faye Dyer

For four years a secret had kept Nikki Petersen and
bad-boy Cully Bowdrie apart. But when she needed his
help to save a child's life, they gave in to their primitive
hunger for each other…

FOR HIS SON'S SAKE
by Ellen Tanner Marsh

Single dad Ross Calder's young son was hostile and
unresponsive, except with Kenzie Daniels. The child was
smitten…would the father follow suit?

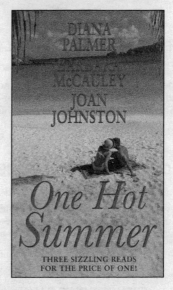